The Horse of Winter Mountain

L.J. MACDONALD LOCKHART

L.J. Macdonald Lockhart (signature)

WESTBOW
PRESS®
A DIVISION OF THOMAS NELSON
& ZONDERVAN

This is a work of fiction. All of the characters, names, incidents, organizations, and dialogue in this novel are either the products of the author's imagination or are used fictitiously.

WestBow Press books may be ordered through booksellers or by contacting:

WestBow Press
A Division of Thomas Nelson & Zondervan
1663 Liberty Drive
Bloomington, IN 47403
www.westbowpress.com
1 (866) 928-1240

Because of the dynamic nature of the Internet, any web addresses or links contained in this book may have changed since publication and may no longer be valid. The views expressed in this work are solely those of the author and do not necessarily reflect the views of the publisher, and the publisher hereby disclaims any responsibility for them.

Any people depicted in stock imagery provided by Getty Images are models, and such images are being used for illustrative purposes only. Certain stock imagery © Getty Images.

ISBN: 978-1-9736-3143-9 (sc)
ISBN: 978-1-9736-3142-2 (hc)
ISBN: 978-1-9736-3144-6 (e)

Library of Congress Control Number: 2018907139

Print information available on the last page.

WestBow Press rev. date: 09/10/2018

The summer had been hot. Acres of dried cornstalks blanketed the old hills and valleys like the patches you see sewn onto a used, dusty quilt. Waves of heat were rising off of the distant country roads, and the local farmers were ready to rest after a long season in the fields. The town carnival was now over. All of the workers were busy packing up the rides and games for the journey to the next town's summer celebration. Farmers had backed their trucks into the arena and were busy loading the animals they'd brought to compete for ribbons and prize money.

Many of the ranchers took their time loading up their animals and rather enjoyed the friendly conversation that had bonded them together as friends and family. Some animals went home with new owners. Some returned to the same barn from which they had come, and some were still waiting to be born. One special animal was doing just that—waiting to be born. In fact, it was a horse. Paint! The mare's owner, Samuel, thought the momma horse would have birthed her baby at the fair, and what a sight that would have been! But the mare showed no sign of dropping her baby. So the proud farmer took his momma-to-be home to foal.

"You take good care of that beautiful mare, Samuel," shouted a familiar voice from the arena. "Let me know when the old girl has foaled. Ya know I know a good-un when I see one!"

Samuel hollered back, saying he would tell his friend as soon as she dropped. The men waved goodbye, and Samuel headed home.

The drive was a hot one. The August sun showed no mercy as the farmer and his mare headed up the grade into the foothills of Pine Valley. Samuel heard the momma whinny. He checked his side mirrors for any other cars and pulled off the road and onto the driveway of old Mrs. Green's ranch. He turned off the engine, jumped out of the cab, and headed back to the horse trailer he was towing behind his truck. The mare was making a lot of noise, and the farmer knew what that particular kind of noise meant. The baby was coming! He looked at his watch and marked time.

"Two o'clock," he said out loud. "I'll never make it home in time for her to deliver." Samuel looked back at his watch and then decided to see if Mrs. Green might allow him to take the mare into her old barn for the delivery.

He ran to the door of the weather-beaten home and knocked loudly. In a moment, he heard the sound of old Mrs. Green shuffling her way to open the creaky white door. "What in tarnation do you want?" said the old woman with a sour, careworn look of disgust. "Git off my property, you good-fer-nothing bag of disrespectful bones!" Her face was flushed and red as if she hadn't spoken a word in years and the effort to talk had exhausted her completely.

"I am sorry to bother you," explained the frantic farmer. "But my mare is about to give birth and I need to get her out of the trailer and into a barn, *your* barn, Mrs. Green. And I have no time to waste!" He stood there, wringing his hands while beads of sweat dripped from his overheated head.

"Old barn?" she asked as if she didn't know one was even there.

"Mrs. Green!" Samuel used a stern voice as he pleaded with the cross old woman. "Please! If the mare can't lie down to deliver her baby, they could both end up hurt. Please!" His eyebrows were bunched up in a firm, bushy line of persuasion. She was still silent.

"Mrs. Green!" he said once more as his dusty boot stepped into the doorway of the house.

"Well, when you explain it like that," said the old woman, looking up at him with a sideways glare of mistrust. Samuel didn't wait for her to change her cross mind. He ran to the fenced pasture, flung open the gate, and backed his truck and trailer up to the barn doors. He jumped out from the cab, raced around to the back of the trailer, and opened its doors. Then he lifted off the wooden bar that kept the barn doors closed. With the strength of Hercules, Samuel slipped inside the barn and pushed the enormous doors open and out into the yard, taking with them all of the weeds and rocks collected from years of being closed. Birds flew out of the rafters in alarm. Motes of dust swirled up into the air as if dancing on the breath of a sudden summer wind. Things scurried in the shadows, and cats hissed in surprise. Samuel knew the moment was near. There was no time to worry about the dirty, abandoned space. He grabbed the mare's bridle and put it around her head. Making sounds with a calming tone of voice, he gently led his mare into the dusty stall. She whinnied again, only this time it was louder, and it had a different ring to it.

"Calm down, girl. Easy now," said the proud farmer. "Looks like you'll have your baby any minute." Samuel's voice was deep and kind. He stroked the mare's neck and mane with the loving touch of a man who knew his way around horses. A moment later she was lying on her side. Her large, round belly moved like a water balloon ready to burst. Samuel turned around to see. She let out one more groan, and the foal came forth in a flood of energy and relief. The farmer just stood there. With one hand, he pushed his hair away from his face. The other hand wiped his tears of joy. *The birth of life never stops being an amazing thing,* he thought. *Never!*

Before he knew it, the mare was standing. Samuel located a trough, turned on the spigot, and filled it with cool, clean water. The mare took a much-needed drink to refresh her spirit and then got busy cleaning her foal. Before too long, it was standing on wobbly legs, holding itself up for all to see. Though it was only a newborn, Samuel could see that it was a real beauty!

"A true paint if ever I saw one," said the proud father farmer. He spoke to the animal as if it could understand his words. "I must admit you are as fair as I have seen in many a year … and a little girl to boot!"

Samuel was feeling mighty lucky when he suddenly took a look down at his watch. "Oh!" he said. "I'd better go and tell Mrs. Green that we have a little girl." With that in mind, Samuel left the barn and headed over to the house. He was whistling a happy tune as he approached the unkempt yard, and he did not see that the old woman was spying on every dusty foot he placed on the ground.

"Mrs. Green!" he shouted with a smile that went from ear to ear. "Mrs. Green, we have a little filly. Would you like to come to the barn and see her?" Samuel was looking around the porch to see where she could be. "Mrs. Green—" he started but stopped in midsentence. "There you are, ma'am," he said as his smiling eyes met hers.

Her eyes weren't quite so joyful. "Git off my land!" cackled the old crone. "And you can leave that pony as payment for services rendered. The sheriff says that's a fair request, seeing that you have used my property and damaged my barn. Leave the mare too. *My* new filly needs her mother for a while anyway." Her hunched-over posture suited her witchy ways.

Samuel stood there in shock. Neither one spoke, but the air was full of naughty words.

"Services rendered?" began Samuel with an expression of confusion. "I told you it was an emergency, Mrs. Green. You have known me for years, and I didn't damage your barn either," he added as his tongue grew shorter by the minute. "The barn has been broken down for years. Everyone in these parts knows that. We see it every day." He stopped speaking, knowing that his words were falling on deaf ears.

Mrs. Green simply glared at him and replied, "See to the mare so she don't starve, and git off my property! The sheriff will be coming to see you at your house tomorrow. Now, *git!*"

Samuel didn't say another word. He turned on his heels and headed back to the barn. Luckily, he still had enough alfalfa to last a few days, so he scattered a large pile in the stall, checked the trough for water, and then lovingly patted the mare on the rump. "I'll be back tomorrow, Fiona. Mrs. Green's in a sore way, and we don't want to make her any crankier than we already have." Fiona, the mother mare, snorted and scratched the barn floor with her right front hoof as if to say she'd be fine and not to worry. The foal just lay curled up on the barn floor, enjoying its very first nap.

The night came and went as normal nights do. Samuel awoke to the crow of his prized rooster, Zeus, tidied himself up, and then poured a fresh cup of hot coffee. His wife sat and listened to him tell the story of old Mrs. Green again. She couldn't help but wonder what her husband had been thinking. Mrs. Green didn't have any friends. Mrs. Green was the town's reported witch, though everyone knew that there was no such thing as one.

"Ya couldn't find a different barn for the wee one?" asked his forgiving wife. "Everyone knows she's as cross as a one-legged rooster. Oh, Samuel! What are ya gonna do now? Lord knows she has the sheriff in her pocket."

That was the whole of it too. The sheriff was Mrs. Green's nephew. He'd do what she wanted since he was afraid of her too!

"Well, I'll speak to the sheriff when he gets here," said Samuel as he dried his hands on the soft kitchen towel. "I am sure he'll understand the situation when he hears the reason in my words." Samuel sounded confident but not quite convinced. "I am sure it will all work out fine, dear," he said to his lovely wife. "I am sure it will all go just the way the good Lord wants it to work out." He heard the sound of tires crunching on the gravel in the driveway. "That'll be the sheriff, sweetness. I'll be back in a jiffy." With those words, he excused himself to take on the first chore of the morning.

The conversation was fast, unpleasant, and in Mrs. Green's favor. According to the sheriff, Mrs. Green had every right to keep the filly since it had been born on her property. She was able to show the sheriff the damage to the barn doors and to the stall inside. The sheriff determined that the filly was as valuable as the monies needed to fix the barn, even though the barn looked as if it were going to fall down. So Samuel had no choice! The newly born filly was now the property of the wicked Mrs. Green.

That late afternoon, as the hot sun was beginning to set into the cool of the evening, Samuel and his lovely wife, Jane, stopped by Mrs. Green's with a plate of cookies and what they hoped would be an acceptable apology. They knocked at the door. Jane looked around for any sign of life. Samuel stood firm... as cool as a cucumber... They knocked again. Without warning, the door flew open, and there stood Mrs. Green with a double-barrel shotgun aimed at their noses and a stream of imaginary smoke pouring out from her ears.

"What do you want?" screamed the wicked witch herself. "I told you to stay off my property. What part of those words do you not understand?" Her eyes were steel, dark as night and just as cold. Her hair was a wiry mess of smoky-gray matted knots. Her face was dried out like the skin of a rotten apple—all pulled into tight wrinkles, hollowed and sunken and forgotten. What teeth she did have were yellow, and her breath made your eyes water before she even said a word. "We just thought ..." Innocent Jane began to speak but was struck dumb by the old woman's startling appearance.

"Mrs. Green," Samuel said, jumping into the middle of the conversation, "we just thought you might listen to reason. You are not in any position to take care of a filly. They require a great deal of work, and well, you haven't set foot in that barn for years." He was convincing to him and his wife, so he went on, "I'd be happy to pay for the damages I may have caused in your barn. In fact, I will fix them for you and then some." He was laying it on thick now. "Please, Mrs. Green, can't you see the logic in this? Your barn was so helpful to me and my family. Let me be of help to you and your farm. The filly isn't the answer to your problem. I can fix the doors and stall, and it will be just as it was before." He finished with a forced smile, and Jane held out the cookies.

"Trying to poison me, are ya? We'll just hear what the sheriff thinks of that!" Her greasy eyes darted quickly between the stunned couple. "Now, git off my land! The filly is mine rightfully!" She clicked off the safety. "The only business you have here is that dusty old mare of yours. When she is done nursing *my* filly, I'll contact you. Otherwise, stay away! Come onto my land without written permission, and the sheriff will take you both to jail on trespassing charges. *Now, git!*"

Jane was already in the truck by the time Samuel got into the cab himself. Never in their lives had they heard a person speak with such hate and bitter fury. They drove away in a hail of gravel and dust clouds and vowed to do everything they could to get their mare, Fiona, home in one piece.

A few weeks had passed when the mail carrier brought them a letter. Jane signed for the dingy envelope, and as they expected, it was a short letter from Mrs. Green. It read, "Your mare is done nursing my filly. Come and get her now! I will expect you tomorrow at noon. The sheriff will be here to keep you from causing me anymore harm! Mrs. Green."

Samuel and Jane just looked at each other. What else could be done? They didn't know. But what they could do was say their prayers and ask the Lord to bless the coming day and poor Mrs. Green.

Once again, the morning came and went. Jane tidied the kitchen as Samuel fed the livestock and tended to the garden. They'd hitched the horse trailer to the truck the night before so that they would be ready to go, and now it was just a game of waiting for the time to tick away. Nine. Ten-thirty. Eleven. At eleven forty-five, they silently walked to the truck, fired up the engine, and headed out to pick up their "dusty old mare."

Enough time had passed since they'd been out to Mrs. Green's, and the first signs of fall were beginning to appear. McGregor's apple trees had a touch of gold on the oval leaves, and the walnut orchards looked proud but tired, their harvest having been gathered a few weeks earlier. All in all, it was a glorious day, all except going to see *her*.

Samuel and Jane arrived precisely at noon. The sheriff and Mrs. Green were standing side by side on the front porch of the old home. The front gate was already swung wide open. Samuel got out of the truck and started to walk over to where the frowning couple stood.

"Good afternoon. I am here for Fiona. Where is she?" Neither one spoke a word. Mrs. Green simply lifted her left arm and pointed to the old barn. When Samuel looked over his shoulder in that general direction, he saw his mare, Fiona. She was not brushed. She was a little too thin, and she looked lonely and lost. Jane stepped out of the truck and let a piercing whistle loose. Fiona snapped her head around in joyful recognition. In a second, her mane and tail were bouncing in the dry fall air. Her whole motherly body seemed to dance around the trampled ground of the neglected round pen. She whinnied! Jane and Samuel both ran with beaming smiles of delight across their happy faces. By the time they reached the mare, it was all hands and hugs. Fiona, of course, was all wet noses and slobbery nibbles.

"Oh, Fiona!" exclaimed Samuel in a most sorrowful tone. "We are so sorry to have left you here so long." Fiona responding with a sloppy, sneezy-snort!

"We've come to take ya home, my lovely lady!" added Jane in a most tender way. "Ya won't ever come back to this horrid place again!"

It wasn't necessary to bridle her. Needless to say, Fiona was already walking herself over to the horse trailer, and she stood at the back where the doors of the trailer were open.

"I do believe our girl wants to get home as much as we do, my darling," noted Samuel. "She can't wait to leave either!"

It was at that moment they heard the pony begin to neigh. Fiona jerked her head around to the side, her ears perking up in recognition of her youngin'. Somehow, Samuel and Jane knew that Fiona instinctively felt that it was time to go! *The pony did not agree!* It sounded like it was trapped inside of the barn. She whinnied again, only this time she sounded frantic.

Samuel closed the trailer doors behind Fiona. The filly was making a terrible ruckus now that her mother was loaded up into the trailer. Samuel and Jane jumped inside the cab of the truck and began to pull out of the pasture when the filly suddenly broke through a small wooden door and galloped into the round pen. She bucked and cried, whinnied and whined. She ran in circles only to skid to a stop in mid-track and then reverse her direction. The pony was furious! Before anyone on the property could try to calm her down, she mustered up all the steam she could and jumped over the railings, landing outside of the round pen and into the full space of the wide open pasture. She didn't look back! She just ran like she had never run before. The young spirited paint became like the wind. It seemed as if the young horse's hooves had left the ground it was running so fast! She, the horse of Winter Mountain, thundered away from the house and barn and disappeared into the towering realm of pine trees where the mountains saw no man, where the peaks were unexplored, where the gray crags of granite became the desolation wilderness, and where she got her first taste of freedom.

The neighborhood kept watch for any sign of the missing horse. Samuel and Jane drove by Mrs. Green's property with their eyes to the rocky ridges of the mountains that jutted up from the valley floor of the wide-open pasture. Every now and then, the sheriff (Mrs. Green's nephew) would throw a flake of alfalfa over the fence with hopes of luring the young horse out for a snack. Unfortunately, that didn't help either.

The fall holidays came and went. Soon it was time to think about Christmas and the first snows of the long winter season. The filly was only a few months old, and Samuel couldn't help but worry about her survival.

"Maybe we should drive up into the mountains to see if she's trapped or hurt," Samuel said to his wife over a hot cup of morning coffee. "She may be trying to come home but can't find her way."

Jane knew her husband was very worried. She felt it was best to listen to his suggestions and then decide their course of action.

"Mrs. Green won't budge," added Samuel with a look of hopelessness. "She acts as if she couldn't care less about the paint. Oh, Janie. The animal is a rare beauty! Did you see her markings?" His eyes were pleading. His love for the filly was real. "All her legs are white. Snow white! Clear up to her belly and rump. She's spotted with patches of gray and brown in the sway of her back, and her mane is brindled with copper, silver, and streaks of brownish blue. Oh, her face, Jane. It's white with a solitary star of smoky blue like the color of a granite boulder." He stopped talking and pushed his coffee cup forward, taking some of the tablecloth with it. "She's spirited too," he said, looking down at his hands and then back up into the eyes of his patient wife. "In all that snow, she'll disappear, Jane. We'd walk right past her and not even notice her up against the rocks and snow on the ground. I guess my biggest fear is that she'll freeze to death. Blankets don't grow on trees!"

Jane knew Samuel was frustrated. She took him by the hand and said these words: "Trust that the good Lord will take care of our precious horse. Trust that the Lord has a special place for her to be safe in the winter months to come. Have faith that the Lord knows best, and your faith will allow you to make peace with a situation that is out of your hands." She paused, sensing that Samuel was listening with more than his ears. Jane gave him that smile he loved so much and she then added, "Trust that *the spirit* in our beautiful paint is touched by the hand of God. Set her free to discover her own faith. We are all creatures of the Lord, my dear, sweet Samuel. Pray for guidance, and she will feel your love." Jane stopped speaking but kept her warm hand tucked into his. He knew she was right. When a situation is out of your hands, the best way to cope is to have faith in a positive outcome. Pray for the right and the good. Believe.

They sat for a moment in silence. Jane stood up, grabbed the coffee pot, and refilled their cups.

"Thank you, my love," said Samuel with his heart on his sleeve. "You're right. The filly will be okay. Did you see how strong and how fast that little girl ran? Why, something so young which can run that fast and is so sure-footed must be touched by the hand of God. Thank you for reminding me." He stood up. "Now I best get to my morning chores. Those chickens do love their breakfast."

He kissed Janie on the cheek and buttoned up his warm winter coat. He opened the kitchen door and then stopped, adding, "If ya like, I'll hang those Christmas boughs you've got tucked up in the closet. Grab 'em, and we can put 'em up today." He flashed his handsome, beaming smile, and she blushed. They adored each other very much, and on this cold winter morning, their love was in the air. Christmas came and went. No horse! Mrs. Green never came to church and hardly stepped out of her house. No one paid much attention to her anyway, and that was just how she liked it. The snow fell, and the temperatures dropped. But Jane and Samuel kept the faith, warm and dry.

The New Year came in with a roar—and a snowstorm. Power went out. Roads were closed, and faith for the missing pony was a hard thing to muster. But still, they prayed. In fact, the whole town prayed. The horse had become the topic of conversation on everyone's tongue, and it was decided that they'd send out a search party as soon as the winter storm finished up.

The funny thing about abundant prayer is that it works! It happened that the pony was fine and warm and dry. She managed to find a cave. A stone cave that went back into the mountain so far that the winter winds and snow couldn't get to her. Now mind you, there wasn't a fire or talking animals or even magical gnomes, but what was in this safe, hidden cave was a trickling stream that allowed grass and onions and carrots to grow! The afternoon sun would cast just enough light so that these wonderful foods could grow. A few different animals had burrowed down for the winter too, so it was warm from the heat generated by the other hibernating creatures, especially the big black bear! Yes, an enormous black bear slept soundly in one of the many corners in the large room of the cave. The pony didn't mind being inside the place. In fact, she'd go outside in the daytime and put herself back in the evening. When the snow was too deep or the sky too angry, the growing horse would stay inside all day. The rabbits and she became snuggle buddies. Even the deer were on their best behavior.

The young horse felt safe, and as the town continued to pray, she sensed this special spiritual regard and grew into a thoughtful creature as she passed the coldest months of winter.

The search party of neighbors had no luck. Three times they went up into the mountains. Three times they came home without the horse. It dawned on Samuel that the filly had no name. He thought about asking Mrs. Green if she'd picked out a name, but on second thought, he felt it would be best if he just left her alone.

Jane served a lovely dinner that night—homemade soup, roast-beef, and mashed potatoes. Samuel asked Jane what she thought about picking out a name so that their prayers would be more complete. She thought giving the filly a name was a wonderful idea. Samuel swallowed a mouthful of potatoes and said, "Well, she was born in early August and ran away in the fall." Then he added, suddenly worried, "Goodness. She's only six months old now. How in the world ..." and his voice trailed off.

"Samuel," said Janie in a motherly way, "Have faith and remember?"

"Yes, of course you are right, dear. But she is still so young, and this winter has been harsh. I just can't ..." and his tone sounded doubtful.

Quickly, Jane changed the direction of the conversation. "What do you think of Wildfire? The way I saw that filly race away from the old barn was as if her tail had been set ablaze! She ran for her life like anything would do if it knew it was in danger."

Samuel looked up from his dinner, his eyes saying yes. "That's perfect, my love. When did that name come to you?" he asked as he shoveled in another steamy bite of roast and potato, but then he added, "You are right enough about her running as if she'd had her tail set ablaze. She raced faster than any pony I'd ever seen before." And he admitted as much with a nod of his head and a wipe of his napkin. "Wildfire it is! The town will like the ring of it too!"

Jane just smiled and took a sip of tea. She knew her husband very well—very well, indeed!

Easter was just around the corner and the trees in Pine Valley were beginning to awaken from a long winter's nap. McGregor's apple orchard was coming into its next growing season, and it had been rumored throughout town that old man McGregor had taken on a young family in trade for refurbishing the family's historic house. No one had lived in it for years, so it was in need of a few repairs, and this particular family was in need of a fresh start.

They moved into the dusty old house the Sunday before Easter. There was still a bit of snow on the ground, but that didn't stop the Fitzwilliam's. They knew how lucky they were to have a place to live, and a way to make a living during hard times. The thought of an apple orchard was pleasing in itself, but it was especially pleasing to their little girl, Molly. She was a fresh-faced six-year-old. Her hair was a long mess of lovely blonde curls. Her itsy-bitsy nose was covered with a snowstorm of freckles, each one placed precisely where it should be as if angels had blown them from the palm of their loving hands. Molly's smile could light up a room, and her general sense of happiness affected all the people who knew her. I guess you could say this little girl had a big heart and an even bigger spirit!

It took three days to move into the house. Some old furniture had been left inside of the home, so Mrs. Fitzwilliam's was eager to remove the dust sheets and explore the new treasures. When all was said and done, the home glowed from within the old-fashioned walls. You might even say that the house was glad to have been awakened by the Fitzwilliam's. The bones of a home are always happiest when the people who live inside make the house a home.

Molly's room was the smallest and closest in view to the open field of the winter woods. She had one window that overlooked this ever-stretching pasture, and she loved to look out in wonder at the mountains, allowing her imagination to carry her away. She imagined all sorts of things. Could there be bears? Could there be fairies in the burrows beneath the rocks? What else could there be? And her mind filled with possibilities until her momma finally called her to dinner.

At dinner Molly asked, "Papa, do you think we could walk up into the forest tomorrow? I think I saw a deer today, or maybe it was a bear. I don't know, Papa, but do you think we could? Huh, Papa?" She was chewing the whole time she spoke. She was rambling actually. Her father answered with a grin.

"I will think about that, Molly. Remember though, if ya saw a bear, the last thing ya wanna do is go looking for that kind of trouble." He took her gently by the hand and added, "Bears are mighty hungry after their winter sleep. The last thing your mother and I want is for that hungry bear to gobble up our curious little girl." Papa paused, looked up at Momma, and sneaked in a tiny wink. "I think a walk is a grand idea though. Why don't ya help me scout out the orchard tomorrow? The trees run right next to Mrs. Green's property and peek into the winter woods. It is the proper thing to stay on our property and not trespass on Mrs. Green's, ya know. I understand old Mrs. Green is a wee bit sour, Molly. It would be best to not get off on the wrong foot and make her angry by stepping on her land." Papa stopped to see if his words made sense to his girl, and then seeing her nod of understanding, he continued, "I need your help anyway. Momma still has some unpacking to do, and it's always better if we get out of her hair." This time he winked at Molly, and Molly knew exactly what Papa meant.

The rest of the meal was chewing, swallowing, and talking. The Fitzwilliam's were an excited, happy bunch of bananas, and none more so than Molly!

It had been a busy day, and everyone turned in early. Molly stood at her bedroom window and looked outside into the frosty darkness. The sky was clear, and the moon was full. As she brushed her long, curly hair, she could see the distant mountains shining in the silvery moonlight. A few of the trees moved in the cold, cold breeze, and she was quite sure she'd never seen anything so majestic before. Even at six, Molly knew this was a stunningly beautiful backyard, and she was blessed to know it was hers.

Something was roaming beneath the far-off branches of the trees. She wiped the condensation off her bedroom window with the sleeve of her nightgown and squinted her baby-blue eyes in an effort to see outside better. She thought it must be that scraggly old buck. She kept staring. Eager, she squished her nose up against the glass in hopes of getting a closer peek. The silhouette's head went down and then up quickly as if it had been startled by something. Momma knocked on the bedroom door at precisely the same time, and Molly jumped too!

"What are you looking at, my little one?" asked Momma in her own loving way. "Surely, there's nothing out there to see at this time of night. Now close the curtain and climb into bed. We have a busy day tomorrow, and we all need our rest."

Molly did just as she was told and pulled the curtain into place. She got between the sheets of her new bed and said aloud, "What do you think it is, Momma?"

"Well," she said with a silent laugh to herself, "let's think about that in the morning. But I bet it's a deer. They are waiting for the apples to grow." Momma laughed out loud. "I think they are a little early though. The apples haven't even set on the branches yet. Now sweetness, you get some rest, and I'll see you in the morning." She tucked her Molly in at both sides, kissed her on the forehead, and walked to her bedroom door. "God bless

Grandma and Grandpa and all of our friends. Sweet dreams, honeybun."And she went to bed too.

Molly turned over onto her side. Her sheets had finally warmed up, and she could feel the fingers of sleep passing over her dreamy eyes. She yawned once and scratched her tiny nose.

Tomorrow, she thought as she yawned again. *Tomorrow will be fun.* And then she added to her sleepy thoughts, *God bless Momma and Papa too.*

She didn't know it, but a red cardinal landed on her windowsill. It peeked into the dark room and could see the sleeping form of the little girl. With the kiss of the lifting wind, the cardinal flew away and up into the woods of Winter Mountain. It was midnight. The full moon was bouncing off the deep, red color of its wings, and all of the woodland creatures could see it flying through the night. In a language we can't understand, the cardinal announced, "She is here!" Over and over it announced as it flew, "She is here! She is here!" In another instant, all was silent again, only now the forest was alerted to the news that Molly was here—the spirited little girl who would change everything!

The smell of cinnamon rolls woke up the two sleeping Fitzwilliam's. Momma had surprised them by rising early and baking a pan of her best breakfast rolls. The aroma is better than any annoying alarm, and it always does the trick.

Papa came to the table in his work clothes with a fresh red bandana tied securely to his neck. He kissed his wife on the cheek, poured himself a fresh cup of hot coffee, and took his seat at the table. Molly came to the table with combed hair, brushed teeth, and sensible shoes. Momma and Papa both looked at each other and said nothing. Evidently, Molly was ready to get to work too, and they were glad to see her act so grown up.

Everyone ate and chatted about the morning to come. Papa reminded Molly about staying on the right side of the fence line, and Momma presented her with a scavenger list of things to find and bring home. All of the words were easy to read for Molly, so she was proud to show off by reading the list aloud. "Two pine cones, three smooth rocks, one feather, and a small bunch of flowers," she recited as she finished up her breakfast. "Is that right, Momma?"

"Yes, honeybun. You read it perfectly. Now button up tightly. Here's a snack for later." Momma handed her a brown sack for safekeeping. "Be home by three o'clock. I may need your help with dinner." She kissed her girl on the forehead and her husband on the lips. "Now be careful. Love you two." And away they went.

What a beautiful day! Papa grabbed his tool belt and a shovel out of the barn. Next the two set out into the lazy field of apple trees. Everything was alive. You could hear the croaking frogs in the creek and the morning call of the wild birds. Papa pointed out a red tail fox, and Molly spied a baby calf nursing on her mother. It was a good life living close to nature. A man couldn't help but feel like he was just as important as the forest critters. The trees were in desperate need of trimming and cleaning up. Some branches had broken and were hanging uselessly for a very long time. The weeds and berry bushes had taken over in some places, and some irrigation pipes had been kicked apart by who knows what. Papa sawed and clipped the low-hanging branches. Molly collected all of the dead wood and put it into a pile they could burn up later. As they moved higher into the mountain, Papa found a hole in the fence line. He didn't have enough barbed wire to fix it properly. But this was their home now, and Papa knew he could be back later to take care of it.

"Look here, darlin'," said Papa as he knelt down to examine the trampled path between the fence posts. "I'll bet the animals that busted the waterlines got through here." He pointed to the well-packed dirt where nothing could grow. "I best get back here this afternoon to repair this hole in the fence. Bet a few deer are sad when they realize I closed the door to apple eatin'!" He stopped a moment, wiping the back of his neck with a bandanna. "I think I saw a feather over there by the stream. In fact, I think I'll sit down and take a break. Look around and see what you can find. Ya just may complete Momma's list." Papa shooed his girl off with a hand in the right direction and sat himself down with a thump!

Molly was free to roam. She never strayed too far from the sight of her papa, but she felt the freedom nonetheless. She soared like a bird with her arms stretched out on either side of her body. She jumped from grassy clump to grassy clump, pretending she was a frog. Next, Molly became a ballerina, dancing on her toes for all the forest audience to see. Papa smiled as he watched her play and wished he had half her energy.

"How about a little lunch?" hollered Papa. "All that dancing must have made ya hungry by now."

Of course, Molly was always hungry. She was a growing girl.

The two sat side by side on the round edge of an old rock and dived into the brown bag Momma had sent along.

"School starts on Monday, Molly. The bus will pick you up down by the mailbox and bring you home too." Papa stopped to be sure she was listening. "You'll be in Mrs. Carson's first-grade class. How does that sound to you?" He didn't have to wait long for Molly to say she was happy to be going back to school. The move had kept her out of school only a couple of weeks, so catching up would be easy.

"I am ready to make new friends, Papa. I bet they are country kids like me. Do ya think they have chicken and goats, Papa? Do ya think any of my new friends can ride a horse or know how to catch a fish? Papa, Papa, Papa! I am so happy!" With those last words of excitement, Molly flung her arms around her papa's sweaty neck and hugged him tightly. Papa knew there was no doubt that when the school bus pulled up on Monday morning, Molly would be waiting with a smile from ear to ear.

They finished up their lunch, collected the scavenger items on the list, and began the long walk home. The sun was high in the sky, so off came the jackets and sweaters. Molly walked along the side of Mrs. Green's fence line wondering if she'd ever meet the old woman. Surely, she couldn't be that cranky. Besides, Molly could make her smile. She could make anyone smile.

Papa whistled to get her attention and waved her over to walk closer to his side, "Remember, darlin', that isn't our land. Stay on our side, and we won't make the old lady angry." Papa smiled that reassuring, loveable smile he always had for his girl, and Molly knew he had her best interest at heart.

The day came to a close. Momma put the wildflowers in the middle of the table. Dinner came and went as dinner does. Then prayers were said, and hugs were shared. Molly was tucked in and asleep in an instant. Tomorrow was the first day of school, and she wanted to be ready to go.

The bus was on time, and Molly waved goodbye from her window seat. The school was charming. Two large buildings painted a bright brick red and surrounded by tall pine trees. The playground had swings and slides and a baseball diamond. Molly knew she would be happy here. She'd already made three new friends by lunchtime.

Meanwhile, Wildfire stood in the spring thaw of the mountains. She had grown nicely over the winter, and she was ready to learn as well. She scampered down the rocky mountainside and cautiously walked onto the pasturelands. She could smell all sorts of new things—the sweetness of spring flowers, the blooming branches of apples and apricots. She met her first honeybee and decided to leave it alone. After awhile, Wildfire's nose caught the rich smell of alfalfa. It was irresistible. Slowly and with a sense of fear, she walked down by the fence line and into view of Mrs. Green's barn. In her heart Wildfire knew this was a dangerous place, but the smell of the alfalfa had lured her into taking a risk and going against her instincts. The front door slammed open, and there stood Mrs. Green, her beady eyes alight with an expression of disbelief. The filly took a bite of the food, looked up into the eyes of the old woman, and bolted away from the bait. Wildfire raced for her life, and she knew she had to. Mrs. Green just stood there watching the filly disappear. For a moment she even cracked a grin, knowing her horse was smarter than the average animal.

"That filly runs like no other horse I've ever seen!" The old woman thought in her lonely mind. "I must catch her!" She said out loud, snapping her two gnarled fingers. "She would bring a pretty penny at market. The little magician can't outsmart me." She almost cackled like the witch most people thought she'd become. "She can't outsmart me!" With those cruel plans in mind, Mrs. Green called the sheriff, and together they hatched a plan to catch the filly. Little did they know that Wildfire was given her name for a reason!

The bus stopped at the mailbox on time. Molly skipped up the long driveway and met her momma on the front porch,

"I had a marvelous day, Momma! I learned two new words too—marvelous and splendid. Isn't it *splendid*?" Momma hugged her honeybun and smiled on the inside. Her daughter was as cute as she could be.

They talked about the school day, the mooing cows they could hear, and the price of hay at the feed store.

"Becky, my new friend, has chickens. We need chickens too, Momma. Can we get some? *Please?*" Molly pleaded her case in a way that was irresistible. "And bunnies. We need bunnies! *Please?*"

Momma began to laugh. "I am sure we will be able to get some chickens. Papa has been working in the barn all afternoon. You should go and see what he has done."

Molly didn't say another word. She ran as fast as she could until she reached the barn. She could hear Papa working inside and whistling a happy tune.

Amazing! All raked and tidy. The chickens nesting boxes were dusted and filled with fresh straw. The stalls were cleaned out too. All of the water troughs were scrubbed and filled with fresh, clean water. There were some sacks of stuff called *scratch*, and in another corner of the barn, there were bales of alfalfa.

"I met a man in town today, Molly. He's bringing us some chickens and a cow. What do you think about that?" Papa stood there with his hand on the pitchfork and flashed a dusty, contented smile. "In fact," he said as he stopped and put a hand to his ear, "I hear his truck now."

She was gone in a flash, and Papa was close behind. The truck and trailer pulled up in front of the barn, and out stepped the kindliest man. The two men shook hands, and then the unloading began. Momma came down off of the porch, and Papa introduced her to Mr. McBride.

"This is our daughter, Molly," Papa said with his hand proudly patting the girl's shoulder.

"It's nice to meet you, young lady," said Mr. McBride as he removed his hat and bowed politely to both ladies. "I do believe you are in the first grade too. My little Becky was telling me all about you today. I think she said you wanted chickens too!" Mr. McBride paused just long enough to let Molly squeal with joy. "Well, here you go, Molly, your very own chickens!"

Mr. McBride opened the trailer doors and pulled out the loading ramp. He walked inside and then came out with a large crate of squawking birds. He set them on the ground inside of the barn and said, "Are you ready?" All the Fitzwilliam's answered yes, and they opened the crate door. A flurry of feathers flew! Molly tried to catch one and pet it, but that wasn't going to happen! Of course, the grown-ups knew that she'd never catch a bird, but it was still fun to watch her run around like a chicken herself. The milk cow was mature and calm. They decided to name her Bessy, and they walked her out into a field of fresh green grass, keeping her away from the chaos of the chickens' adjustment to their new home. After an hour Mr. McBride said goodbye. The Fitzwilliam's stood shoulder to shoulder and waved a thankful farewell as he drove down the road.

Papa explained the chores of the barn and made sure his two ladies knew how to handle a cow and chickens properly. "Don't stand behind Bessy. She may look calm and sweet, but if she's a mind to, she can hurt ya with one good kick. Okay?"

"Okay, Papa!" answered his ladies simultaneously.

"I think it is time for dinner," announced Momma. "Shall we walk to the house together?"

They closed the barn door and strolled to their house arm in arm. There was a remarkable change in the house's appearance already. The weeds were down. The windows were clean and open. The porch was now an inviting place to sit and visit, and the orchard of trees in the distant pasture looked trimmed and cared for.

The Fitzwilliam's had made a big change in a short amount of time, and their hard work showed.

Spring was in full swing. Bessy was giving milk. The chickens were laying eggs, and the apple orchard was in full blossom. Molly and Becky were best friends, and slumber parties were their favorite way to spend Friday nights.

Before saying their prayers one night, Molly showed Becky the view out of her bedroom window. The same old buck was standing at the fence line, trying to reach into the orchard and take a small blossom off of the tree. Becky pointed to the animal and explained that it wasn't a deer. It looked more like a horse.

"Look there, Molly. The head is too big and the neck too long to be a buck. Besides, I don't see any antlers." Becky shared these facts because she'd lived in Pine Valley her whole life and she'd seen many bucks before.

"If ya ask me, I think it's the filly named Wildfire. Everyone's been talking about her for almost a year, and she's been lost on Winter Mountain almost as long." Becky looked at Molly and saw that she had her full attention. "Haven't ya heard the story about Wildfire, Molls?" asked Becky. She told her the story of how the filly ran for her life and then spent the winter alone in the mountains. "Nobody saw her again, and they all figured she had died during the winter. So ya see, Molly, if that is Wildfire, you have a miracle of a horse. It won't even be a year old until August

3. My pa said that was its birthday—the day old Mrs. Green took it away from farmer Samuel and locked it up in the barn." Molly couldn't believe what she was hearing. They both looked out of the window again. It was a long distance away, but their young eyes could see very well.

"Well, that's something," said Molly quietly. "It would be a miracle if she had lived. How do you think the pony survived during the winter, Becky?"

Molly's question was a good one, but she didn't have an answer. Becky simply said, "Nobody knows."

Spring warmed and turned into summer, and with the welcome heat came the apples. The girls played and swam and fished. Becky taught Molly how to care for farm animals, and the two little girls planted special seeds of friendship.

The lovely summer nights gave Molly a clear view of the fence line where she'd seen Wildfire, and you can bet she looked out her window every night before bed. One particular night when the moon was high and bright in the dark blue night sky, she saw Wildfire again. The pony was trying to lean across the fence line and pull an apple off of a tree branch. Molly watched as the lonely horse tried and tried to get the ripening fruit, and she felt bad that it couldn't reach the yummy prize.

"Tomorrow morning, I'll ask Papa if we can check on the pony and see if we can get her some food." Her thoughts made her feel better and helped her to relax and get to sleep.

The next morning came and went as a farmer's morning does. Molly awoke to find her Papa was already up and out in the apple orchard.

"Momma, may I go and see what Papa is doing?" Molly was dressed, brushed, and wearing proper shoes.

"Yes, honeybun," said Momma with a kiss to the girl's forehead. She slipped a rolled-up pancake into her hand and reminded her to play safely.

Molly ran out of the house and followed the fence line over to where she knew she had last seen the pony trying to reach for an apple. She could hear her papa whistling a happy tune. (He whistled a lot these days.) And she got his attention with a sweet grin and a wave. As she got closer to where she had spotted the pony, she could see how the push of Wildfire's body was bending the fence line. In fact, the fence post was loose now. Molly looked around Mrs. Green's property but couldn't see any sign of a horse or year-old filly. She stopped, looked at the apple tree, and then decided to climb up into its branches. It would give her a better view of the pastures and hide her away from view. Within a minute, she'd climbed up into the arms of the old, sturdy tree and set her sights on spying the miracle pony.

It didn't take long. Ten minutes later Molly could hear the rustling of dry grass and the snapping of dead twigs. Lo and behold, Wildfire appeared. Slowly and with clever eyes looking all around the familiar pasture, the pony walked up to the fence and began to push her body weight against the barbed wire. Molly saw the scars on the breast of the pony. Evidently, Wildfire wanted the apples very badly. The pony knew Papa was working over the hill, but she wasn't alarmed. What the pony didn't know was that Molly was up in the tree, watching her. Slowly, Molly changed her footing and prepared herself to jump down out of the tree. She knew it would startle the horse, but she was willing to take the risk of scaring it off.

One. Two. Three. And then she jumped! Wildfire bucked up and ran over to the edge of the towering pine trees. Molly clicked her tongue like Becky had shown her, and then she picked an apple off of the tree. She held it up high enough for the pony to see. She clicked her tongue again and then quieted down. Molly had Wildfire's attention, and that pony was hungry. The filly seemed interested but irritated. The only human she knew was mean and frightening, but Wildfire moved closer. She wanted the apple, and Molly wanted her to have it. Wildfire moved closer. The two girls locked eyes, neither one budging. The pony snorted and stomped, and the girl was still and full of love. Wildfire moved closer. The pony could smell the apple and the child. The child could feel the heat of her body and could smell the tang of her sweat. Molly held the apple out in front of her, and Wildfire, still locked with her eyes, and gently took the apple from the small hand. The pony stood, apple in between her teeth and just looked at Molly. Neither one felt fear. You see, when one shares love for the sake of love, fear has no power. Wildfire chewed the apple with loud, crunching happiness. Molly picked three more and tossed them into the field. The pony ate them all. When she was done with her apples, Molly watched the pony trot away from her and head back up into the pine trees of Winter Mountain. Molly knew from that day forward she'd never be the same, and neither would Wildfire. They'd found each other, and together, they would show the town that the pony had lived and that little Molly had rediscovered the horse of Winter Mountain!

One thing you can count on is the passage of time. The time Molly passed with Wildfire was the very best! She became the town hero for discovering Wildfire living in Mrs. Green's pasture, and she was also considered a *horse whisperer* of sorts. Little Molly was sure to point out that a lot of her smarts came from the friendship she'd made with Miss Becky and that Becky should be given a piece of the credit too.

Samuel and Jane were relieved to know that Wildfire had lived and that cranky Mrs. Green hadn't outsmarted the year-old filly. In fact, Mrs. Green scoffed at the idea of the filly having survived the winter and proclaimed, "Molly is a strange child. She must have an imagination bigger than the great outdoors!" Now we mustn't forget that Mrs. Green and the sheriff had hatched a plan to catch the filly after the old woman had seen her nibbling the lure of alfalfa in the pasture that early spring. No one in the township knew the filly had survived the winter, no one except for Mrs. Green and her nephew. Thanks to Molly, their plans were foiled.

Wildfire remained elusive. She never came onto Mrs. Green's main pasturelands or anywhere near the old crone's house. On the contrary, Wildfire stayed nestled up in the shadows of Winter

Mountain, where she'd made a home and where she knew no one would venture up to find her.

Molly knew that Wildfire needed more than apples to eat, so with her father's permission, she began to leave piles of alfalfa along the high pasture fence line where the orchard of apples met Mrs. Green's property. Mr. Fitzwilliam's let Samuel know that his daughter was *sneaking* the filly additional food, and the three felt it was in the best interest of Wildfire not to tell Mrs. Green about their decision.

Summer came and went. The harvest in the small community of Pine Valley was abundant and all of the neighbors shared their good fortune with one another. Everyone bartered—oats for alfalfa, apricots for straw, even wheat for timber. It seemed that God had blessed everyone in the town except Mrs. Green. Occasionally, she was seen standing on her porch, looking up into the mountains. Her nephew had given her a pair of binoculars, but even they couldn't offer her a glimpse of her precious horse. It didn't seem possible to most; however, the old woman became meaner and uglier as the school year restarted, and that made her the butt of many mean jokes.

"Maybe she could be a pumpkin face for a Halloween jack-o'-lantern," said a smart-mouthed kid from the back of the bus.

"No," shouted another from a window seat, "I think she'd make a better witch. Did you see her teeth?"

The conversation was too much for Molly, and she spoke up to the loud voices with the right words. "Maybe we should be kind to the people who look unhappy, mean, and lonely." Her words hushed the noisy bus and caused the eyes of her fellow students to slowly look at her. "There isn't a person on this bus who has ever been nice to Mrs. Green." Her tone was mad, but at the same time honest and mature. "Maybe we should be kind to someone we don't know. She could look the way she does because she has been left alone too long." The bus was silent. "How would you feel if people teased and ignored you because of your face? Why, you'd stop smiling too. Your head would hang down, and you would stop caring. I bet she could use a friend with nice words and not mean ones." Molly stayed in her seat, her eyes looking out of the bus window, her thoughts on poor, poor Mrs. Green. The bus stayed quiet all the way to school. Molly had planted a seed of thought into the minds of her friends, and she prayed that it would take root and grow.

The school day came and went as most students hope they will. A few kids came up to Molly and apologized for their rude comments on the bus. Molly didn't hold any hard feeling. For some reason, she knew change was in the air. This *horse whisperer* was rescuing more than a pony on Winter Mountain. She was inspiring her friends to save themselves.

That night as she was going to bed, Molly asked her momma a very thoughtful question. She said, "Momma, would it be wrong to try and be neighborly to Mrs. Green?" A distant thought filled her soft blue eyes as she looked up into her mother's. "The Bible says to 'do unto others as you would have them do unto you.'" Molly stopped and listened to what her momma had to say,

"Well, honeybun, you must ask God about that question. You will hear his answer as long as you listen with ears of kindness." Momma stopped a moment and tucked Molly into her cozy bed, "Only you know the right path to take. Even as young as you are, Molly, you know the difference between right and wrong. 'Ask and you shall receive' is also God's Word. Think about that too." She stopped for a moment and looked out of Molly's window and in the direction of the orchard. "I remember a little girl who was so curious about an unknown animal across the pasture that she worked on the mystery until she discovered the truth. If you are concerned about Mrs. Green, sweetness, approach her in a way that won't scare her off. Let her know that you care." Her momma stood up and walked over to the bedroom door. She stopped, turned around, and finished by saying, "Take her an apple."

Wildfire was growing quickly. A little nip of fall was in the air, and you could see the evidence of the chill in the thick nap of the pony's coat. Molly was taller too. A year had passed now, and the two were good friends. Wildfire now allowed Molly to brush her, though she would allow her to do anything that involved an apple or two.

"I am going to see Mrs. Green today," Molly announced to the horse as she braided the multicolored mane. "I am going to take her a basket of apples. What do you think about that?" Of course, Molly knew Wildfire's thoughts on Mrs. Green, but she shared the news all the same.

"I am nervous, to tell the truth," she said as she leaned into the ear of the pony. "But somebody has got to try to melt her cold, cold heart. She can't be all that bad."

Wildfire snorted and scraped the ground with her foot. If only Molly could read the mind of the pony, she would have thought twice about her plan.

The sun was setting earlier now that the winter months were around the corner. Molly told her parents her plan to visit with Mrs. Green, and they both listened with cautious pride. Their daughter was going into the lion's den. Thank goodness she was taking apples as a peace offering. They watched her walk down the driveway with a small basket of apples nestled in the crook of her arm. A moment later, she was at Mrs. Green's house. Momma held her breath, and Papa stood on guard in the barn with one eye on the neighbor's front door and one hand on a pitchfork.

Molly knocked, but there was no answer. Molly knocked again, only this time she added sweetly, "Yoo-hoo. Mrs. Green?" Again, there was no answer. She stood there, rocking back and forth on the soles of her sturdy shoes and looking around the front porch. The windows blind were closed up tight, but the chairs outside were dusted and tidy. Geraniums were growing in her window boxes, and as a matter of fact, they appeared to have been watered recently.

"Mrs. Green, it is Molly, and I have a surprise for you!" she said.

Then all of a sudden, she heard, "And I have a surprise for you too, little missy!" The front door flew open wide, and there stood old Mrs. Green, gray hair standing on end and two bloodshot eyes staring down the double barrel of a loaded shotgun.

"Git off my property!" the old witch roared. "You have no business being here. What did your folks send you over here to do? Spy on me?" She stopped and snorted down the barrel of the shotgun with a flaring red temper. Molly started to stammer, but Mrs. Green spoke again, "You, little missy, are trouble. Trouble I tell ya! Luring my pony away from me with apples and food," she kept on going, the spray of foul spit flying out of her mouth with every syllable. "The sheriff knows all about you and your crooked parents. Yes, he does, and you can be sure he'll find out about this attempt to poison me!" She was getting louder. "I know what you kids say about me. Don't think I am a fool and suppose I'll take those deadly apples. I hear you call me a witch! I know you all want me dead so you can take my horse and property!" She stopped and nestled the shotgun into the crook of her shoulder blade.

Molly stayed calm. She could see Mrs. Green was shaking. She could see her hands jittering as she held up the gun. Now was Molly's chance to speak, but instead she grabbed an apple out of the basket and took a huge bite out of it. She took another bite, chewed it with the same gusto, and said, "Mrs. Green, these apples aren't full of poison." Her speech was a little slurred by the bits of fruit dribbling out from her mouth. She swallowed so she could speak more clearly. "They are full of love. I picked them for you and only you!" Molly eyes were locked and loaded with kindness and sincerity as she looked up the open end of the poised shotgun barrel. She didn't even blink. "I came here with a happy heart, and I won't let you spoil that. So here." She placed the peace offering at the woman's feet. "These are for you. Maybe you could make a pie or some apple butter." Molly turned to leave and then stopped. She turned around with a smiling face that only she could make and added, "I would never call you a witch, and I don't want you to die! I want to be your friend!" Molly paused one more time and then finished by saying, "God bless you, Mrs. Green. I hope the rest of your day is blessed." And she walked down the porch steps, out of the yard, and back toward her home.

Mrs. Green just stood there, finger on the trigger and a basket of love at her feet. They say she stood there for a full ten minutes, stunned and silent, which was an uncommon occurrence for old Mrs. Green.

Molly walked home with a special sense of accomplishment in her soul. She knew in her heart that she was doing the right thing. Mrs. Green needed friends. We all need friends. Guardian angels say, "No man is a failure who has friends." So she knew she couldn't let the old woman live without any. Friendship is the peanut butter on your toast, the salt on the garden ripe tomato. Molly knew, *but* did Mrs. Green?

They say the valley is just as beautiful now as it was when Zachary White homesteaded the land more than a hundred years ago.

Of course, no one had planted any crops, and the roads didn't exist. But Zachary could see the richness in the soil and the potential for a community of Americans, so he filed the proper papers with the state and marked the boundaries of the land he'd call home. He cleared an area for the natural creek to form a deep pond and removed the round rocks from the open space he'd use to construct a corral for livestock. His strong arms and disciplined needs motivated him to harvest a number of trees, and with those timbers, he built his home and barn. It was the first home in the meadows on the pasture, and it was that home where Mrs. Green lived today.

Her great-great-grandfather, Zachary White, was a legend in those parts of the county. His vision and faith were the driving forces behind the building of Pine Valley, and in fact, he chose the name of the township itself. Times were different then, and Zachary had the spirit needed to succeed in a world on the edge of change.

Mrs. Green was born Maggie Mae White. Her father was the grandson of the town's founder—the revered pioneer family who was proud of their roots and kept their successful accomplishments alive and well in the telling of stories and in the picturesque way the town evolved. Maggie Mae grew up in the same house she lived in today. In her lifetime she'd seen a town grow up around her. You could almost say that she and the town of Pine Valley grew up together. She saw the grocery store being built as well as the schoolhouse and its playground. When she was fifteen, she watched the construction of the wheat mill, and she witnessed the planting of the apple orchard—the very same apple orchard that Molly's family was caring for now. Anyhow, Maggie Mae had a normal life in an exceptional town. She finished her primary education at the age of seventeen, much to everyone's surprise, and she went away to college to become a teacher. Everywhere she went, people noticed her—the way she spoke and the golden color of her hair. But it was the rich shade of her moss-green eyes that caught the attention of strangers. Most people who had seen her for the first time thought she was beautiful, but she didn't know the effect of her beauty. She only knew she was happy, content, and glad to be a teacher.

When she moved back home, her parents were very joyful, and the township threw her a glorious "welcome home" party. That was a day she'd never forget because it was the day she met Johnny Green. From the moment they clapped eyes on each other, their love began to grow. He worked at the apple orchard as a farm hand, and she educated the children at the school. The two were together from that moment on. Whether fishing on the creek or caring for the trees in the orchard, they were inseparable.

Johnny was tall and lean. His hair was a dirty brown, and his smile was sincere and kind. He could speak with his eyes, and the way he looked into Maggie Mae's left no secret untold. The town knew they were in love, and it was just a matter of time before there would be a wedding.

A memorable year of courtship passed, and Johnny asked Maggie Mae's father for permission to ask for her hand in marriage. Johnny showed Mr. White his bankbook and rolled out plans for building a caretaker's house among the trees in the apple orchard. Johnny promised him that his heart was pure as well as his knowledge of love and that Mr. White need not worry about his daughter living a life that would be anything other than happy. Johnny took Maggie's father by the hand, and man to man, he pledged his undying dedication to his daughter. Mr. White said yes through tear-filled eyes. There isn't a father on this good, green earth who doesn't want to hear those precious words spoken for the sake of his daughter. That is how a father feels about his baby girl. He wants her to be safe and happy.

They married that spring among the blossoming trees in the apple orchard. The entire town attended. Maggie Mae couldn't have been more beautiful. Her dress was as simple as her bare feet and as white as the first snow of winter. The greenness of her honest eyes and golden light in her hair made her appear to be an angel. Johnny stood at the base of the tallest apple tree. He never looked more handsome. It was as though he had become the tree—strong, steadfast, and true. Pastor Smith stood humbly to his right, looking out into the crowd, and the two men waited for the wedding to begin. The people gasped when the father walked the bride down the aisle of orchard soil. Maggie Mae's mother held a hanky to her face while the tears flowed from her grateful eyes. The pastor asked Mr. White if he gave his daughter freely, and he said that he did. So the simple ceremony began. By the time Johnny was kissing his bride (now his Mrs. Green), the entire party was standing on their feet! Cheers and tears were flowing all around the orchard. Hands were clapping, and people were patting one another on the back. Pine Valley was alight in celebration for the love they could all feel, the love they had all seen grow.

It didn't take long for the orchard house to be built. The enthusiasm among their neighbors was so great that the construction only took three months, and they moved into the freshly painted home two months before the apple harvest.

All was right with the world. A barn had been built at the time the trees were planted, so there was no need to worry about finding a place to store the autumn crop.

Johnny and Maggie were as happy as two people could be until it came time for the first harvest. Winter had come on early that year. The township knew the urgent need to get the apples picked, and they all came to the rescue. The women prepared the barn, and the men picked the apples. In four days' time, the harvest was in, and it was none too soon. The big snowstorm came on the fifth day, and Johnny was crushed by a falling tree. It all happened so fast. One minute he and a friend were heading back to the barn, and the next, his friend was yelling for help. The first person to hear the screams for help was Maggie, and she was there as fast as she could be. A pine tree from what had been named "Winter Mountain" had gotten overloaded with snow and had fallen. It came down on top of Johnny, and it pinned his legs to the ground. They did the best they could to free him; however, the damage to his legs was too great, and the tree was too heavy to move. Maggie didn't have time to cry. She didn't have time to feel. She dug with her bare hands down into the frozen ground doing anything she could to free her husband's injured limbs. She felt his hand on her shoulder. She looked up, and Johnny said, "My love. I must go now. The tree is too big, and I am hurt badly. You must go on. You must live and love and be happy." He reached his icy hand up and cupped her heated face. "You are the angel I knew you always were, and I am so lucky to have loved you. Love again, Maggie Mae. Please ... love again."

He forced a grimaced smile as she saw the light go out of his eyes. She saw the strength in his body go limp. She saw her husband die by her side, and with what she saw, so did she.

She never set foot in their home again. That night as the news of the tragedy spread through Pine Valley, she walked to her great-grandfather's home and into the arms of her weeping parents. She felt alone and chilled from that devastating night. Her heart and soul were as cold as the endless storm that now lived in her broken heart.

*T*he school bus came and went. Molly took her regular seat and happily visited with the other students. It was harvest week, and the time of year when the town's history was the educational topic. All of the students were prepared to ask historical questions, especially Molly.

The playground was the outdoor classroom for the day. The town museum had set up a booth along with many of the local farmers. Animal husbandry and farming are an admired quality in Pine Valley, and the local families thoroughly enjoy the school's annual tradition.

Molly and Becky started exploring the museum's booth first. Since Becky had grown up in Pine Valley, she had already learned some of its history. Molly, on the other hand, was just beginning to learn some of the many secrets her community held.

"See? Look, Molly," said her best friend, grabbing her arm and pulling over to the photo display. "This is the house you live in now." Becky pointed to one of many pictures. "I mean when it was first built." They both leaned into the old photograph and studied its faded beauty. "My momma says it was built a long time ago but sat empty right after it was finished. Something about an accident, and the owner was killed." Becky added, "Now look at this picture. If you look way off in corner, you can see your house again, only the house in front is Mrs. Green's house." Molly recognized the two houses and the pasture that separated them. She stopped looking at the photo and gazed up at Becky, her eyes wide open, her lips zipped! "Did you know Mrs. Green's house is the oldest house in town? Her great-granddad built it." Becky seemed proud of her history lesson, so Molly continued to listen. "Momma says Mrs. Green has had a tough life. After the accident she never stepped back into her home again. She just went back to the old house she lives in today." Becky pointed to another picture that showed the bride and groom on their wedding day, and the photo stunned Molly. Becky went on, but Molly was so shocked by the old wedding picture that she didn't hear a word Becky shared.

Their names were written underneath the keepsake. The ink now faded and splotchy was still easy to read. It said, "Johnny and Maggie Mae Green."

The two young ladies looked up at each other, Becky still talking.

"That's what old Mrs. Green looked like?" said Molly in a state of surprise. "I never thought she'd have looked like that. She is so ... beautiful!"

"She truly was," chimed in the museum teacher, overhearing the two girls discussing the incident. "She was rumored to have been the loveliest young lady for many miles." The two girls hung on every word spoken, so the teacher went on, "Maggie Mae was a teacher at our school. Yes, this school, and she met Johnny shortly after coming home from college. A year later they were married." She pointed to another picture. "This photograph shows the wedding ceremony. They were married in the spring beneath the falling blossoms of the flowering apple trees. Some of the old diaries written by the local womenfolk describe what they saw that day." She pointed to another display and brought the girls' attention to copies of the old handwritten entries.

"Her hair was bathed in the light of the sunshine. It shone like the crown of almighty God himself!" one journal entry said.

35

Another said, "The day was truly blessed. I've never felt so much love before! I will pray for a husband like Johnny Green." The teacher detected a hungry curiosity and continued, "Here is a picture of the funeral wagon." Molly stopped and looked up at the lady from the museum, her eyes welling up with tears, "Oh, honey," the teacher said, sensing Molly's sadness. "It was a long, long time ago." Molly wrapped her arms around the waist of the kind woman and buried her eyes from view. "Johnny's been gone a long time. Everyone's forgotten the sadness. Please don't make yourself cry. It's history now," the teacher said.

Molly swallowed her tears and said, "Not everyone has forgotten, ma'am. Mrs. Green never forgot. She can't forget. Those sad memories are her only company. That's why she looks so ugly and mean. She has been alone too long, and she misses her husband." Molly's observation rang true in the heart of the teacher. She wiped her eyes and added, "Mrs. Green is my friend. I won't let her be lonely again!"

The two young ladies walked away from the cluster of students and sat on a bench by a large oak tree. Neither one said much. Someone rang the lunch bell, but they both stayed put. A minute later, Becky said, "Do you really think Mrs. Green wants a friend? Don't get me wrong, Molly. You are right to be friendly." Becky took her by the hand and said, "But Momma says Mrs. Green's gone 'round the bend. She's crazy and might hurt you." Becky's sincerity was genuine. Molly knew that, but what Becky didn't know was what had already happened between Molly and Mrs. Green. Molly told Becky about the basket of apples and the shotgun pointed at her very own nose. For a moment, Becky thought Molly was crazy too, but the girls knew that if you wanted to make a change, you first had to take a risk. If you didn't try, you would never know, and Molly knew. She knew down to the soles of her feet why Mrs. Green was so miserable.

The girls heard their tummies rumble, and they both giggled. "We'd better eat before lunch is over," they said. "Race ya!" Molly yelled, and they ran over to grab their lunch bags.

Molly's mind was made up! She was going to visit with Maggie Mae, Mrs. Green, again soon. When? She wasn't sure, but it would be soon, very soon, indeed.

A busy mind is a good thing to have, especially when your imagination is so vivid that you believe anything is possible. Such was the case with little Molly. By the time the school bus dropped her off at her mailbox, she had hatched a plan to visit Maggie Mae and have a tea party. Now Maggie Mae was long overdue for a tea party, and Molly convinced herself that Mrs. Green—or "Maggie Mae," as Molly preferred to say—would enjoy nothing more than a tea party with a sympathetic, chatty little girl. I mean, really. Who wouldn't want a party with someone so delightful?

Molly grabbed the mail from the box and skipped up the gravel path, practically smelling the tea brewing in her imaginary teapot. Her momma heard her coming in the front door and had to smile to herself. Molly knew how to make an entrance, and today was no exception!

"Momma, Momma! Where are you?" hollered her little girl. "Momma? Oh, there you are," she said, smiling from ear to ear. "I had the most splendid day today."She put the bundle of mail on the kitchen counter and continued, "We learned all about Pine Valley history today." She paused and kissed her momma on the cheek. "You'll never guess who Mrs. Green really is!"Molly couldn't catch her breath for a full five minutes. She just continued telling her story until she had wrapped it up with her plan to melt Maggie Mae's cold heart with a tea party. Her momma sat and listened. These two loveable ladies sat and chatted over graham crackers and milk when they heard the sound of a car door slamming shut. A moment later they heard Papa in conversation, and when they came to the front porch to see who'd arrived, they saw the sheriff's car and the town's sheriff in person. The two men were talking in a very neighborly fashion. In fact, Papa had a smile and a look of rosy embarrassment. The sheriff looked up at the porch, tipped his hat, and smiled at the two curious ladies. His face was at ease, and his manner was relaxed. All things considered, he was trying to be a good neighbor now, not there representing the law.

"Well, Mr. Fitzwilliam's, I don't know how to thank you enough. My aunt tells me, you know, Mrs. Green," he said and pointed to the old house across the pasture and on the corner of the road. "She tells me that your daughter stopped by the other day and brought her a basket of apples."

Papa looked down, took out his bandana, and wiped the sudden ball of sweat that was now running down the back of his neck. He silently hoped Molly hadn't done anything naughty. The sheriff continued, "Anyhow, my aunt asked me to apologize to Molly if she scared her any. You know how the old woman loves her shotgun," he said, trying to laugh off the overreaction of his aunt's behavior. "Well, tell Molly that Mrs. Green was touched by her kindness, and this is for her." The sheriff reached into the car and pulled out a jar of something that looked delicious.

"I am telling ya, Mr. Fitzwilliam's, whatever it was your daughter said to my aunt really rattled her. She hasn't touched an apple in years, and well, this is homemade apple butter. It's the best in the county as I recall. She hasn't whipped up a batch in many years." The sheriff stopped and looked at the porch and directly at Molly. "Thank you, Miss Fitzwilliam's. Thanks for taking the time to speak to Mrs. Green. She's hoping she didn't scare you too badly the other day. She's thinking you'll enjoy this." Then he handed the jar to her directly. "She made it just for you!" The sheriff smiled proudly. "I don't know what ya said, but I am so glad that you did. Mrs. Green said you could stop by again if ya like. She promises she'll have better manners."

The sheriff chatted only a minute longer and then excused himself. "Duty calls. Now you folks have a fine evening." Then he got into his vehicle and left.

"Well now, Molly," said Papa with an inquiring tone. "Perhaps you should tell me and Momma what you have been saying to Mrs. Green." His question was a fair one.

They sat on the front porch, basking in the last rays of the warm autumn sun. Molly told her parents exactly what she had said and also about the shotgun Mrs. Green used in her self-defense. Her parents listened intently, but they still sat shocked, thinking about an adult pulling a gun on a little girl. Molly said she wasn't scared of the gun. She was more offended by the lady's bad breath!

"She really does need to brush her teeth!" At that remark they all had a good laugh and then went back into their cozy home.

It was almost dinnertime. Papa went back to the barn to ready the animals for the night, and Molly helped her momma set the table.

"I think it is sad that Johnny died and this house sat empty and alone for all those years. Poor Maggie Mae," said Molly. "She didn't even have a baby. The museum lady said her parents didn't live much longer either, and Maggie ended up in the old house alone ever since." Her voice trailed off in a way that told her momma that she was sad.

"Sounds to me like your prayers are being answered, honeybun." Momma knew how to speak so that her girl would listen and learn. "Just the other night, when you were going to sleep, you told me about wanting to be friends with the old woman." She stopped and tipped her head to one side as she looked into her girl's sentimental eyes. "Sounds to me like God heard your prayers. Your Papa and I are very proud of you. You should be proud of yourself as well." Momma stopped again and then suggested, "We're having pork chops for dinner. I'll bet the apple butter would be a yummy treat on the side of the meat or just on your roll. What do you say? Should we give it a try?" Molly didn't say a word. She just ran to her dear momma and gave her a big hug. They placed the special jar on the dinner table and used a silver spoon to ladle the apple butter onto the plates. It was agreed. Maggie Mae's apple butter was the best they had ever tasted, and so that night they shared a dinner like none other—a dinner in a rediscovered house, a dinner at a table of love and hope, a dinner of good fortune and answered prayers. And they knew this was the beginning of many more to come.

What a glorious morning! As the sun rose, it cast a colored light into the sky that would remind one of a pink grapefruit. Ribbons of thin white clouds were braided in between layers of steel blue mist, and then there came that pink! It was a pink so vibrant that it cast its morning glow into every nook and cranny of the Fitzwilliam's home. Everyone awoke to the rosiest light and the dawning of a new day.

Molly was the first one up. She dressed properly, put a log on the coals in the fireplace, and headed out to the pasturelands. The air was damp and clean. Fall leaves dangled from the branches of the trees, and Wildfire pranced out in the field. Molly had heard her making noises as the sun was rising, so it was only natural to say good morning and toss her a juicy bunch of alfalfa. The two of them were best buddies now. Wildfire nudged and played with Molly, allowing her to hug and kiss the pony like she was a pony herself.

"The bus will be here in a little while," she said out loud to the growing horse, "so I can't stay long. Here are a few apples." She pulled three from her pocket and tossed them onto the breakfast pile. "Now you be good and stay safe. I'll be home later, and I'll give you a good brushing."

Wildfire nodded as if she understood what Molly had said and began to eat one of the apples off the top of the feast.

"Molly … breakfast," shouted her momma with a sleepy-eyed grin. She ran back to the house and walked into the warm smells of cinnamon oatmeal, her very favorite.

"Momma, I am going to write a letter to Maggie Mae and suggest that we have a tea party at her house. What do you think of that?" Molly's matter-of-fact tone was convincing as she stuffed a bite of oatmeal into her hungry mouth.

"I think that is a fine idea, honeybun." replied her momma. "When it is ready to be mailed, we can proofread it together, and I'll get you a stamp."

"Okay, Momma." answered Molly as she finished up her morning meal.

"Here is your lunch. Peanut butter and jelly! The bus will be here shortly," added Momma. "Don't forget to button your coat. It's chilly outside."

Papa was at the table too, and he said, "Pink in the morning, sailors take warning! Pink at night is a sailor's delight."

"Pink sailors? Huh?" said Molly with an eye of confusion. "Warning about what, Papa?"

"It's a saying about the weather, sweetness. It means the weather is going to change." Papa chuckled over the top of his steaming cup of coffee. "It's an old wives' tale."

"An old wife with a tail? Huh, Papa?"

"Oh, honey, I'll tell you all about it later," he added with a sleepy smile too. "You'd best get a move on. The bus will be here any minute."

With that good advice in mind, Molly buttoned her coat, grabbed her lunch and school folder, and headed down the driveway to the bus stop. Her parents stood on the porch and waved goodbye as she stepped into the orange bus, and they, too, agreed it was very chilly this morning.

"Looks like there is going to be a change in the weather, dear." observed Papa as he held his coat closed with one hand and opened the door for Momma with the other.

"Well, my jolly sailor-boy, why don't you come in out of the cold and help me wash these dishes." She said with a smile on her lips and wink in her eye.

Molly worked on her letter during her free time at school. She asked if she could go to the library and look up some historical facts, and her teacher allowed her to go.

The library was a fun place to learn and explore. The librarian, Miss Getchell, had grown up in Pine Valley, so she was a treasure trove of knowledge.

"What else do you know about Mrs. Green, Miss Getchell?" asked Molly as she sat down at a table. She hung on every word the librarian had to offer.

"Well," she began, "Maggie Mae is one of the last living pioneers of our community. She had a tragic past, as far as her marriage went, but before that, she had a good life. She was blessed with a solid family tree and born a true beauty. It wasn't until the tragedy that her life became difficult. She was talented in many ways." Miss Getchell went over to a large book and opened it up to a chapter dedicated to the White family tree.

"See here, Molly," she said and pointed to pictures of the entire family. "Maggie Mae had it all. This is her in a school play." The picture showed an old-fashioned wig and Victorian dress on Maggie. Below it was the caption "Fancy Day.""She starred in the school production of a Thomas Hardy novel titled *Under the Greenwood Tree*. The local paper reviewed the play and said she was brilliant!" The librarian turned the page and pointed to another article. "This says she could ride a horse like no other young lady in the county. It says she rode with one leg on each side of the horse *and* without a saddle!" She stopped to check Molly's reactions. "They also recall her being a bit of a tomboy in her early years. It says she could out fish anyone and was good at pitching a baseball. So you see, Molly, Maggie Mae had a good life until she lost her husband in the orchard accident."

Miss Getchell stopped, closed the large volume, and turned to look Molly in the eyes. "Why are you so interested in her life, dear? She is an old woman now, and she keeps to herself. She stays away from everyone and everything in town. It is almost like she never existed. Maybe that is what she wants. Sometimes that much sadness and loss changes a person, Molly. There's not much that can be done anymore." She stopped speaking and put a gentle hand on her shoulder.

"Thank you for sharing this book with me, Miss Getchell." Molly pushed herself away from the table and stood up to leave. "Maggie Mae may have had many years of sadness, but I am her personal friend now, and I am going to see to it that she has sunshine in everyday. We're having a tea party, ya know!" And with that statement, Molly marched out of the library and back to her classroom. After she left the library, Miss Getchell just stood there, shocked and corrected in her hopeless opinion by the faith of a hopeful child.

Wildfire loved her good brushing after school. Molly and she spent a lazy afternoon playing and exploring the open pasture Molly still minded the rules and stayed off of Mrs. Green's land. As dark approached, Wildfire said goodnight by the way he ran off beyond the reach of Molly's fence line. When the pony reached the crest of the mountain ridge, she whinnied with all her might, rearing up into the darkness when her silhouette simply disappeared into the cold of the night.

The house felt inviting and warm. After dinner Molly sat down with her mother and showed her the letter she'd written to Maggie Mae.

Deer Mrs. Green:

Thank you for the delishus apple buter. We had it four diner and it was veri yummy!!! If you are not to buzy, I wood like to visit on Saturday and hav a tea party with you. I will bring the tea and sum cookiez. Wood1 o-clok in the afternon bee ok? Pleeze rite me back and let me no. Have a happy day! Your friend, Molly

P.s. I thnk you hav a pretty name. Can I call you Maggie Mae?

Mrs. Fitzwilliam's was very pleased with the first letter Molly had ever written. She wouldn't dream of making any corrections

43

to the misspelled words, and instinctively, she felt Mrs. Green would love the thoughts behind the words and not the lack of proper grammar. They sealed the envelope with a prayer and stamped it with the correct postage. Molly slipped on her coat and ran it down to their mailbox. She pulled open the small wooden door and placed the special letter inside. She wondered how long it would be until she received a letter back from Maggie Mae, and she hoped that she would say yes to her idea. All in all, Molly's heart was in the right place. Now all she had to do was be patient and let her hopeful prayers unfold.

By the time she reached the front door of the house, it had started to rain. The barn was closed and secure for the night, so the Fitzwilliam's planned on spending the evening inside. Checkers, books and dinner would be the evening's entertainment along with warm baths and a little tickle time.

Bedtime always arrives sooner than Molly hoped. Yawning, she knew it was almost time to turn in, but sharing special fire time with her parents was better than bed. Papa picked up his big girl and commented on her not-so-little size. "My goodness, Molly, you are quite the big kid now. Why, you must weigh a full fifty pounds and not an ounce less!" He weighed her as though he was appraising a lamb at market, but he could see with his own eyes just how big his little girl was becoming.

Papa continued "It seems that you are quite a grown-up young lady these days. I understand you and Mrs. Green are becoming friends." He stopped and looked at Molly, who had open eyes of interest. "The whole town is talking about it, darling. First, you befriend Wildfire, and now Mrs. Green." He paused and brought Momma into the conversation. "Momma said you even included Mrs. Green in your prayers." Momma nodded yes, and Molly beamed.

"Do unto others as you would have them do unto you, Papa." Molly's words were spoken softly and humbly, and from the look in her eyes, they had clearly come from the heart as well. "It's that simple, Papa." Her tone was matter-of-fact.

Papa didn't move a muscle. He took a deep breath, swallowed back a few prideful tears, and smiled. "Yes, my darling, it *is* that simple."

Papa tucked Molly in that evening, and before he turned out the light, he said, "I am mighty proud of you!" Then he changed the subject. "We'll be picking the apples this week, and the harvest looks very good. Mr. McGregor said he would share the profits with us. You'll be needin' a bridle for that pony ya call Wildfire." He stopped and looked directly into her eyes. "If Mrs. Green says it's okay, she just might let ya tame her pony. Sleep on that one, Molly. Sleep on the thought of *riding Wildfire!*" And he turned out the light.

"Sleep on that one!" Papa said as he left Molly's room. Well, those words didn't allow Molly to fall asleep quickly, but when she did finally drift off to sleep her dreams were filled with adventures on Winter Mountain. She saw bright red birds darting to and fro, and of course, she could feel herself riding Wildfire bareback through the trees. Her hair felt longer, and it flew and whipped in the wind of her imagination. Even her legs seemed longer, perhaps because she seemed older in her dreams. When she awoke the next morning, she told Momma all about them.

"My goodness, Molly. Those are great dreams! Write them down in your journal. You will want to remember them always."

The rain was still falling as Molly headed down to the bus stop. Momma buttoned her coat tightly and cinched her rain hat snugly.

"We will be in the orchard today. The apples need to be harvested, rain or shine," Momma said as she stood at the door, holding her sweater closed with one hand and waving with the other. "We will be working all day so we will have pie for dessert tonight!"

Molly smiled and waved goodbye as she stepped into the bus. Everyone aboard was a bit drippy but happy nonetheless.

The Fitzwilliam's had their work cut out for them. The rain hadn't stopped all night, and it was rumored throughout town that an early snowstorm was around the corner. These apple farmers knew they had to get the harvest in now, or they'd run the risk of losing them all to the freeze just like what had almost happened to Johnny and Maggie Mae Green so many years ago.

As luck would have it, the town knew of the urgency as well. Ten men showed up soon after Molly left for school, and they stayed the day to help the Fitzwilliam's harvest the crop. They worked very hard! They labored through lunch, and they picked until dusk. They managed to get every apple off of every tree and just in time too!

When they were done, Mr. Fitzwilliam's counted 125 bushels! Tired as they were, the men let out a shout old Mrs. Green should have heard! It was a blessed day, to say the least.

The Fitzwilliam's thanked everyone for coming to the rescue, shared a bag of freshly picked fruit, and promised a get-together when the weather permitted. They all shook hands and exchanged apple recipes. They were a vibrant part of their community now, and the teamwork they witnessed made them feel loved.

Mr. McGregor came by the next afternoon and was more than happy with the abundant harvest.

"Why, young man," he said with a fatherly hand on William's shoulder, "you should be very proud." He paused and looked him in the eye and said, "Yes, very proud, indeed! I admit I was worried about the weather, but you just jumped in there and got it done. I heard the town's men showed up and gave you and the Mrs. a hand." He leaned back, thumbs tucked into the corners of his front pockets, his eyes examining William's filthy apron. He kept chatting on as proud as any landowner could be. "They are a fine community, ya know. I grew up here as a lad myself." He stopped in a regretful sort of way and then continued, "My wife lived in the neighboring town, and well, you know …"He pointed up and toward the east. "Listen to me ramble. Forgive me, son. I do get a bit misty sometimes. Now where were we? Ah, yes …" McGregor dominated the conversation, but William didn't mind. "My wife and I have decided to let ya keep the entire harvest. We have all that we need, and since you have done such a remarkable job restoring the house, barn, and orchard, we want you to sell 'em and keep the money." He stopped and held out his adamant hand. "What do ya say, Mr. Fitzwilliam's? Do we have an accord?" McGregor's eyes were squinted up in a grin that would accept no refusal.

Mr. Fitzwilliam's didn't know what to say other than, "Oh, thank you, sir. Thank you! We love it here and well ... Thank you, sir. We won't let you down!"

"I thought as much, Mr. Fitzwilliam's, "said his fatherly landlord in a most calming tone."I thought as much."

The two men parted ways that day with hearts as full as the bushels of apples in the barn. Of course, Mary presented Mr. McGregor with a homemade apple pie. His eyes burst with anticipation,

"Oh, the little wife will love this!" he added with a twinkle and a wink. "It's her favorite!"

They shook hand and wished one another God's blessings. As Mr. McGregor drove down the old gravel drive, Mary took her husband by the hand and pulled him in close to her."Thank you, my love. It truly is a wonderful life!"

Molly stopped at the mailbox on her way home from school. She grabbed the rubber-banded bundle and headed up the drive. Momma saw her coming and met her on the front porch. She told her the good news about the harvest being theirs to keep. Momma also told Molly that they would even have a little money to buy ornaments for the Christmas tree this year and that Molly would finally be getting a new winter coat! Papa came in a moment later, and you would have thought he'd burst with happiness. He picked up his little girl and danced around the living room as if an orchestra was playing a tune that only he could hear. From the outside looking in, anyone could see their joy. Anyone could hear their cries of laughter, and everyone knew how much they deserved a break from the hardships of life.

The house smelled of apple everything! Momma had been cooking most of the day, and it was decided they'd eat pie for dinner. "It was Momma's idea, ya know, and who are we to say no to *pie for dinner!*"

It was the happiest day they'd known for a while, and then Momma opened the mail. Molly had a letter! Not just any letter. A letter from Mrs. Green!

The envelope was the quality of fine linen. The corners of the unique stationery were folded as if they'd been ironed, crisp and tight. The pristine penmanship was artistically scribed in the fashion of calligraphy, and as a fancy hand couldn't resist, the person had embellished the letters with swirls and flourishes to complement its recipient's personal value.

Molly just looked at it, committing every swish and swoosh to memory. When she turned it over and looked on the backside, she discovered it was sealed with a waxy blob, and impressed in the wax was the crest of the Green family tree.

Now the letter had the whole family's attention! Papa asked Molly if he could hold it too. He had never seen anything like it before, and if he was correct, you could still smell the odor in the ink.

They sat there for a full ten minutes until Momma finally suggested they open the heavenly letter and see what was written inside. Papa found a knife in the kitchen and gently pried the paper away from itself, not wishing to tear a single fiber of the fine parchment. As he handed it back to Molly, he said, "Good deeds bring good deeds back to you, Molly. I believe good things are coming to you, my Molly Joy. Good things are God's way, God's way, to be sure."

The paper inside was the same quality, only a thicker stock and cut to resemble a formal invitation rather than a casual letter. The lettering was on one side only and written by the same impeccable hand. Papa looked closer and noticed the ink was a deep purple and had the faint smell of blackberry. He pulled back from his discovery and said with a scratch to his curious head,

"I'll be. Well, I'll just be."And he wandered across the living room, his posture shrugged in all-out surprise.

"What does it say, Molly?" Momma finally asked. "Do you need me to read it for you?"

"No, Momma," replied their big girl. "I can read every word. See." Molly held the card up, and it was true. All of the words were not touching, so it was easy to read. Molly began,

> *Good day to you, Miss Molly. A tea party would be lovely! Please visit me this Saturday at noon. Bring more apples, and I will teach you how to make my apple butter. Please give your parents my kindest regards and congratulate them on the harvest.*

Sincerely,
Mrs. Green

P.S. Yes, Molly, you may call me Maggie Mae!

Molly only had to ask Momma to pronounce three or four words, and the rest she could sound out on her own.

She read her special treasure over and over again until she knew it by heart. Momma asked her to put it down for dinner, and she had to eventually take it away and display it on the fireplace mantle.

They had pie for dinner, and everyone ate their fill. Momma said Papa had three pieces. But that was okay. Tonight they celebrated, for the Fitzwilliam's were pleased to know their family had made such a big impact on such a small community. William would be able to sell their apples at market, and Molly was the reason the town's precious Wildfire had been rediscovered. The known but neglected Mrs. Green had also been stirred back into the community's prayers. And like the words that make them up, they are capable of bringing a needed change into one's life!

Saturday quickly came, and so did the snowstorm. Molly arrived at Maggie Mae's on time. Wind, storm, or sleet could not get in her way. With a large basket of apples in one hand and a harvest wreath over the inside crook of the other arm, the freshly snowed-on Molly knocked, and Maggie Mae answered her door right away, "Oh, dear Molly," began the kind, elderly lady, "I am so glad you are here, and I am so glad you chose to forgive me for being so naughty with my shotgun." She paused for a second then added with a soft giggle, "It's not loaded, you know. It *never* is. But nobody knows that." She laughed a little louder. "Sure does frighten the looky-loos though."She stopped and grabbed the apples and the wreath, freeing Molly hands completely. "Come in, lass. Please make yourself at home."

"Good afternoon, Maggie Mae," said Molly with an exaggerated flair to the woman's proper first name. "I am very happy to be here. Thank you for the splendid letter. I love it!" Molly stopped speaking, walked inside the house, and closed the door. What a surprise! She thought the inside of the home would be dirty and sad. But instead it was clean, tidy, and decorated like an old museum. There were antique rugs on the wooden floors. The hanging lamps were jeweled and polished. Every facet of glass cut perfectly. The furnishings were dark and oversized. There were armoires and bookshelves, plant stands and hat stands. A Victorian pattern of classic floral elegance graced the sofa and winged-back chairs. Molly knew she was visiting the fanciest room she'd ever been invited into.

"What a pretty room," said Molly, looking around at the surroundings. "I think it's the prettiest room I have ever seen."

"Yes, dear, I agree. It is lovely, and most of it was my grandfather's. My family and I have lived our entire lives within these walls, and we have collected many beautiful things." Maggie Mae walked over to the young admirer and wrapped her arm around hers. Slowly and with great respect, she walked Molly through her home and explained some of the things on display. "This portrait is of my grandparents, and this one is of my parents. There isn't one of me and John ..." She caught herself midsentence, stammering only for a moment, and then she changed the subject. "And these, of course, are paintings of my grandfather's prized horses. I grew up hearing about the horses he raised in the very barn you see out in the pasture." Her boasting was filled with pride, and her story was a clue into the reasons behind her selfish actions regarding the pony known as Wildfire. Molly listened like she listened in school, and Mrs. Green spilled the beans.

"Great-grandpapa was a horse man. He picked these lands to settle because he claimed the area was keen to a strong horse's way of life." She went on talking as she patted the back of Molly's hand. "He always said," she said and then suddenly switched to talking in a Scottish accent, "soft horses are raised in the flatlands. Real horses, powerful horses, have the mountains in their blood. Breed your horses in the majesty of the crags that touch the sky and you forge an equestrian line of legend." Molly laughed at the silly accent but thought it made the story heartfelt and believable.

Maggie Mae drifted off a bit, but she came back around at Molly's suggestion to brew a pot of tea. "That is a capital idea, Molly. Capital, indeed."

They headed off to the kitchen with the basket of apples in hand. Maggie pulled out her kitchen utensils and bowls and made a spot ready on the large wooden worktable. Molly slid her admiring hand across the smooth surface of the old wood planks. She could she scorch marks and knife cuts. Her imagination was full of delicious memories for Maggie Mae. The table had been in the family for more than one hundred years, and all of the scars told a story.

"Oh! I see you've noticed some of the wear and tear, Molly," Maggie said when she noticed her young chef fingering the outline of the large round burn on the surface. "I am afraid that was my fault. We were making candy many years ago, and I didn't realize the sugar pan was so hot." Maggie walked over and ran her aged finger around the edge of her accident. "Momma was mad at me! She said, 'If ya can't listen to me when I am a tellin' ya how to make candy, well then, go outside and tend to the chickens. Now look what you've done!'" Maggie laughed to herself and added, "So, I went and played with the chickens and the sheep. They could hear my momma yellin' too." She wiped off the surface of the table with a soft cloth and then instructed Molly on the proper way to make apple butter. The two were busy bees! Maggie stepped back into being a teacher, and Molly listened with her classroom ears. Once all of the apples were peeled, cored and simmering away on the stovetop, Molly asked Maggie Mae a very personal question.

"Why don't you have any friends?" She asked the question in a way that was kind and tender. "Miss Getchell showed me your pictures in the library, and you are so beautiful." Molly continued, "You were the star of many plays and a true country girl at heart. Everyone knows about the accident that took Johnny. But why are you so alone, Maggie?"

Her question stopped Maggie in her tracks. She'd forgotten how honest and candid children could be. After a moment of searching thought, she gathered up her courage and answered Molly with some private truths. "When Johnny died, I didn't know what to do, dear." She walked over to the kitchen window and looked out onto the pasture. "I thought my life was perfect, and up till the accident, it had been wonderful. But when he ... died," she said, hesitating, her words hung up in the pain of her broken heart. "I guess I thought it was my fault he died, Molly. I knew he was tired, but one bushel of apples had been left in the field. I insisted he go and get it so that it didn't freeze overnight. The snow was already falling, but I never knew ..." And old Mrs. Green's voice choked up completely. Molly walked over to the window and took her lovingly by the hand.

"Maggie Mae," said the wise woman of seven years, "it wasn't your fault, and everyone knew that. It was an accident, plain and simple. It wasn't fair either." Molly stopped and looked out onto the snowy pasturelands. "Look, Maggie!"She pointed finger, changing the conversation. "I can see *our* house!"

Her eyes lit up by the discovery. Maggie looked down into her innocent expression and shared another tender bit of history. "Yes, that is your house. A long time ago it was Johnny and my house. The town helped us build it shortly after our wedding." Molly knew all of these details, but she wanted Maggie to share her story. After all, that's what friends were for! "We only lived there a few months, and then the accident happened. I came back to this house the night he died, Molly, and I've never been back to our home. I mean … your home." Her eyes glassed with tears. "Every night when I lived over there, Momma and I would use an old candlelit lantern to signal good night to each other. She stood at this very window." Her hand brushed the windowsill. "And me from the small side room that overlooks the field and toward this house. I know it sound silly," said Maggie, dabbing her tears with the dish towel, "but that's what we did."Maggie turned around and walked to the stovetop. "It looks like our butter is done, dear. We best git to putting it up in the jars." She managed a pink-eyed smile at dear Molly. She hadn't talked about Johnny in a very long time, but it was okay.

She turned the heat up under the large metal canning pot. They filled twenty-five jars with apple butter and submerged them into the hot water. It was just a matter of time until the seals popped on the jars and they were ready to be cooled and stored in the pantry.

There was a knock at the door. Maggie Mae spun around like a cat caught with a mouse.

"Who's that?" she said in a different tone of voice altogether, "Are you expecting anyone, Molly?" Mrs. Green was on edge.

"No, my parents know I am here. Maybe it's the sheriff?" replied Molly with a smile.

"Well, let's go and see." Maggie grabbed an old, ratty shawl and wrapped it around her shoulders. Before she opened the door, she slumped over a little bit, giving her the look of a very old woman. Molly was stumped. She opened the door slowly, her eyes pinched up into a look of wicked defense.

"Well, hello, Mrs. Green, I am Molly's father. I am sorry to break up your tea party, but the snow is beginning to fall very hard now. I thought it best to get Molly home before it got too deep."

Mr. Fitzwilliam's stood before the two ladies with a sincere smile.

"Yes, of course, Mr. Fitzwilliam's." Maggie shook off her act. "Please come in out of the cold. Let me grab you a jar of our apple butter." She was all kindness and grace. Maggie tossed the old shawl on a chair and returned promptly from the kitchen with Molly's basket in her hand. "Your daughter is a delightful child. I have enjoyed her company very much, and well, I don't have much company these days, so I thank you, sir." Maggie also thanked Molly for the apples and returned the empty basket with more than a jar of butter. "The tea towels were my momma's. I know she'd want you to have them. Please come and see me again, dear. I have many stories, you know, and I can teach you how to knit!" she said as she smiled a toothless smile. "Now, git along like a good little girl." She was patting her on the back of her tiny hand as she approached the old door. "My best to your wife." said the old woman as she opened the door. "Be careful! It can git mighty slippery when it snows." The two walked away from the house, waving goodbye, and then they happily strolled down the empty white road.

"Did ya have a nice visit, Molly?" asked Papa, his breath frosted and hanging in the chilly air.

"Yes, we did, Papa." Her breath looked like the steam escaping from the hot stack on a locomotive. "Maggie Mae is a splendid lady. Her house is like a museum. She is also a very good teacher. One thing was funny though," Molly said as she stopped her father in a drift of snow. "Her breath never smelled bad. She actually smelled of rosewater, and her hair was tidy. She looked ... pretty." Molly summed up her assessment with a sense of self-accomplishment in her tone. "I guess she was excited to have company, and she dressed for our tea party. I can't wait to see her again." Molly took her papa by the hand and smiled up at him. With a feeling of joy, they resumed their walk home.

The snow was beginning to pile up on the sides of the farmhouse. Marbled gray clouds hung in the sky as if they were beginning to bear down and deliver a good wallop. The two got home in time to take off their coats and kiss Momma hello right before the snowstorm delivered! It was silent. The wind had calmed, and the orchard had become a lonely, wicked mess of snow-kissed, arm like branches.

Molly remembered what Maggie Mae had said about the lantern and how she and her momma would signal each other at the end of every day. She told her parents about the old tradition and asked their permission to rekindle the kind gesture. There was no reason not to, and in fact, the same old lantern was still in Molly's room hanging from an old iron stake that had been hammered into the wooden wall long ago. Papa went into the room and took the antique down from its long-forgotten perch.

Momma wiped it down with a damp cloth and handed it to Molly. There was still a stub of a candle inside of the holder. For a moment they all stopped and lovingly looked at each other. So many miracles had been blessing their lives recently that the moment felt almost too good to be true. Papa pulled some stick matches from his pocket and handed them to Molly. He glanced at Momma to make sure she was okay with their girl touching them. That knowing look crossed between them, and they decided she would be safe from harm.

Molly pulled the sheer curtain aside and peered out of the frosted window. The pasture was covered with snow, but as luck would have it, only a small flurry now fell down from the wintery twilight sky. The sun hadn't quite set yet, so the softness of the light backlit the hanging clouds and rendered them angelic.

Molly took a closer look at the lantern and could see how the young Maggie Mae cast her signal. The lantern was made from hammered tin and was framed in by four small panes of glass. In front of one pane, a wooden door was hanging from tin hinges. When she closed the little door, it blocked the light from the burning candle inside the lantern. When she reopened the door, it allowed the light to shine out. It was really quite simple, and Molly was ready to give it a try. (Maggie Mae had no idea what Molly was up to, but Molly believed it was certainly worth a try to end Maggie's day on a memorable and magical note.)

Molly scratched the wooden match briskly against the sandpaper on the side of the matchbox. It lit! She held the tip of the match up to the neglected wick in the faded candle. It flickered and sputtered as if the candle was apprehensive about lighting. At last it caught, and the flame shone brightly from within the tiny space. Molly handed the matches back to Papa and walked over to the window. She set it down for a moment and then turned to her patient parents and said, "Let's say a prayer in hopes that Maggie Mae will see the light." Of course they agreed. The three held hands around the glowing candle, and Molly started, "God, please bless Maggie Mae on this cold winter's night. Help her to know that we are her friends and help her eyes to see the candlelight. Thank you, God." And they finished their prayer by all saying, "Amen."

"Look outside," said Papa with a sound of surprise in his voice. "The snow... it's stopped! Well, I'll be."

"That'll make it easier for Mrs. Green to see the candlelight, right?" added Momma, her hand resting gently on Molly's shoulder.

"Let's find out," said Molly, and she held the lantern up in front of the window. They could see the far-off light in Mrs. Green's house, and Molly knew it was the kitchen window that faced them. She closed the small door on the lantern, counted to three, and opened it. She did it again and waited to see if they'd get a reaction from across the snowy field. Mrs. Green's light went out. For a moment Molly felt a hollow pang in the pit of her stomach. She followed the same routine again and waited... nothing.

While standing at the sink and doing her dinner dishes, the random light caught Maggie Mae's eye! She put down the dishrag and slowly turned her head to look out of the steamed-up window. She blinked in disbelief. Slowly, she walked up to the window as she dried her soapy hands on her apron. Maggie strained her eyes to see across the field. There it was again! She flushed pink and remembered her and her mother's tradition. The lantern was right where her mother had left it. She grabbed it, rifled through the top drawer of the buffet, and found a box of matches and the nib of an old candle. She quickly trimmed the wick and placed it into the heart of the antique. Her stomach was filling with butterflies! Next she turned out the kitchen light and began to smile to herself. Her thoughts lightened, and her mind rejoiced. *That Molly*, she thought to herself. *What a blessing!*

She went to the window and pulled the lace panels apart. There was another flash of light from her dear Molly. She took a breath, struck the match, and lit the candle. As she held her mother's lantern up to the windowpane, she, too, said a prayer under her breath. "Heavenly Father, thank you for this special day. Thank you for Molly and her genuine kindness. Thank you, Father. Amen."

Molly saw the light!

Maggie Mae saw the light!

They stood at their windows for only a moment longer, casting the sacred beacons of light between them, when once again, the snow began to fall. Molly was tickled to know that Maggie Mae was her friend. Maggie Mae was humbled to know that she was still capable of making a friend even after all the years she'd spent being angry and bitter. It was enough to know that these two families slept with the grace of God in their dreams that night. It was also by the grace of God that Wildfire was stowed into the warm cavern on Winter Mountain, her collection of familiar friends tucked in as well. All was right in the world of Pine Valley that winter night. All was right and good.

Molly and Maggie spent two days a week getting to know each other better, and they discussed all sorts of different topics, including the best way to help Wildfire become more comfortable with Maggie and her farm. One afternoon Molly noticed a set of dentures in a dish on the bathroom counter and asked Maggie why she didn't wear her teeth. She felt comfortable with asking her friend such a personal question, and the answer surprised her.

"Well," responded Maggie, taken aback by the precocious child, "nobody sees me, so why bother?" Maggie looked down at her hands, obviously hoping to change the subject, but our dear Molly was relentless.

"Let me see what they look like when they're in." Maggie looked at her with startled eyes. "I'll bet you look very nice," she said, smiling coyly. Maggie couldn't resist the innocent question and agreed. Next thing they knew they were laughing and grinning in the bathroom mirror together. Maggie had the pearly whites in place, and Molly was smearing on a thick coat of the prettiest pink lipstick she'd ever seen.

"My dear," advised Maggie Mae, "not so much!" She was giggling under her breath as she took a tissue and cleaned up the corners of Molly's mouth. "A little goes a long way, dear. Here ..." She took the tube of lipstick and demonstrated on herself, which was exactly what Molly was hoping she'd do. "Now if you start at the top of the lip, you'll find the peak of little mountains." Maggie knew her lipstick technique. "Now ... down from the top peak of the lip to the corner of the mouth and then to the other side and down to the corner of the mouth." She was being so dainty and careful that Molly was sure she'd worn lipstick before. "A good swipe across the bottom lip and then press your lips together. See how that works?" Maggie turned to face Molly so she could see the result. Maggie smiled, and Molly sat with a look of disbelief, "What's the matter, dear?" Maggie said instantly, concerned by Molly's face. "You look like you've seen a ghost!"

"Oh, I am okay, Maggie. It's just that you look like your pictures." She stopped and then caught herself staring. "I've seen your pictures in the library, and it wasn't until this minute that I recognized *you*, Maggie Mae!" The little girl began to tear up. "You are beautiful!" Molly held up her arms, encouraging Maggie to hug her, and she did!

"Oh, Molly..." said the old woman, blushing with embarrassment. "That was a very long time ago." While they hugged, Molly noticed something strange about Maggie Mae's hair. The hair she could see wasn't her hair at all. It was a wig! Suddenly, Maggie knew her secret wasn't a secret anymore. As she stepped back from the hug, Maggie saw Molly's face again and knew that she had seen her camouflage! "Yes, Molly, it's a wig," admitted Maggie, walking out of the bathroom toward the living room. Without warning, she burst into tears. As young as she was, Molly was confused by Maggie's reaction. Many questions were going through her young mind, but the one thought that stuck was the question *why*. She followed Maggie into the living room and sat down by her side. Molly took Maggie's hand and said with the greatest tenderness, "Why are you covering up your head, Maggie Mae? The pictures I remember show that you have beautiful hair." She just sat quietly and waited for an answer. Maggie dried her tears and turned to face Molly.

"Well," she said in a tearful, croaky voice, "after Johnny died, I just quit." Maggie let go of Molly's hand, stood up, and walked into the middle of the room. "After the accident I didn't come out of my room for a week. I could barely eat. My mother and father did their best to care for me, but I just climbed into my sad, broken heart, and I never left." She stopped a moment and looked to see if Molly understood what she was saying. "The years flew by, and when my parents passed, I just stayed tucked away and out of people's view." Maggie walked to the window and looked outside as if she was trying to see a glimpse of yesterday. She turned and faced Molly, forcing a slight grin, her eyes still puffy from crying. "My neighbors tried to comfort me, but I rejected them all. And one by one, they stopped coming over. They forgot me, and I chose to ignore and dismiss them. I stopped caring, Molly. That's why I chose to look so wicked." Maggie caught Molly's eyes, which were filled with surprise. "Nobody bothers a hermit, and an ugly hermit works best!" They said nothing for a while. Molly stayed seated, and Maggie kept looking out of the window.

When enough time had passed, Molly asked a simple question. "May I see your real hair, Maggie?"

Maggie knew that question was coming and didn't hesitate to remove the wiry gray mess. The first thought that crossed little Molly's mind was, *all come tumbling down*, and that was what the old woman's hair did. It all came tumbling down! Her lovely locks were still there. Only now the long silky golden hair was as white as the field of snow that lay between their houses. Molly stood up and walked over to Maggie so that she could admire her exposed secret up close. "Oh, my goodness, Maggie Mae, you have beautiful hair. In fact, it looks like moonbeams. Why do you hide it?" Molly reached up to stroke the strands of light as if they were a rediscovered treasure.

Maggie looked down at her feet as if at a loss for words and took the compliment with a grain of salt. "Oh, I don't know, dear," she replied, sounding discouraged. "Every time I look in the mirror, I see what was taken away from me. You see, Johnny loved my hair. When we were first married, it was very long, and he'd brush it for me." She had a distant look in her eyes and a soft volume to her voice. "Johnny said my hair was like the sunshine had been trapped inside of each strand, and when he brushed it, the glow from the sun would shine through. My goodness!" She stopped, her eyes again exploring the carpet from side to side. She laid a finger to the side of her mouth. "I haven't thought about that tenderness in years. Anyhow, that's why I keep it covered, Molly. I want to forget. I need to forget." Maggie stopped and looked at Molly in a way that told Molly that she had revealed enough. The two smiled demurely at each other. "How about a snack, Molly?" Mrs. Green suggested. "We have plenty of apple butter!" The two laughed and walked into the kitchen. Molly was pleased to see Maggie Mae toss the old wig on a chair, and as they dined on biscuits and apple butter, she couldn't help but notice how Maggie Mae enjoyed running her fingers though her hair. Molly felt she was right to ask all of those personal questions. After all, genuine friendship grows in the heart of honesty.

The two said their farewells with a hug and a kiss to the cheek. Molly asked Maggie Mae to throw that old wig away, and she promised to think about it. As she walked out of the house and toward the path home, she stopped and turned back to see old Mrs. Green standing on the porch, waving goodbye. The sun was shining down upon her in all her radiant glory with her pink lips and long, bright white hair. *She looks younger!* Molly thought to herself. "I love you Maggie Mae!" she hollered with all her might.

"I ..." the old woman said and stuttered, "I ... love you too!" And the old, wicked Mrs. Green had uttered three words she hadn't spoken in forty years!

She continued waving goodbye in the clear afternoon sunshine until she could no longer she Molly strolling home. She ran her fingers through her sun-warmed hair and looked around. The air was clean and refreshing. The snow lay in frosted drifts, reminding her of the old sleigh, forgotten long ago and still hidden in the decaying barn. Her leafless, snow-laced trees now seemed enchanted with unseen potential. At this moment Maggie Mae knew in her heart of hearts that this was the end of a day that promised new beginnings. As she walked into her home, she looked around and counted her blessings. The family's treasures looked back at her and nodded with understanding. Her tummy stirred with eager anticipation. Acceptance filled her soul, and her aching, lonely heart pained no more. She smiled in the mirror and again ran her fingers through her lovely hair. Then she pulled the veil off of Johnny's portrait and let his likeness fill the room. She stood back and looked at his face as if she hadn't seen him in a very long time. She blew him a kiss and dropped her head in prayer. At last she chose to move on from the tragic past and into the promising future. What was it that Molly had done to awaken old Mrs. Green's desire to live again? What was it that had happened to her that freed her soul from the tragic pain that had haunted her for so many decades? Maggie didn't over think the feelings she was experiencing. She simply basked in the lightness—the lightness of mind; the lightness of being, the light in the lantern, and the light that had always shone from the eternal brightness of God. Maggie Mae finally knew the truth. The sacred room needed a fire, so she built one. A pot of tea was called for, so she brewed one. And as the sun set onto the mountains outside of her kitchen window, she and Molly lit their lanterns and signaled goodnight to each other. Then she threw the old wig into the fire.

*T*he next morning was beautiful. Some of the newly fallen snow had begun to melt into slippery puddles of autumn mud, creating a messy challenge for the Fitzwilliam's doing their morning chores.

Molly knew that Wildfire would be heading out of the mountains and on to the pasture because of the warmer temperatures and she made a point of tossing him a healthy flake of alfalfa. "Maggie Mae said it would be a good idea to build Wildfire another place to sleep, Papa." Since he was helping her toss the bulky feed over the fence line, Molly felt this was the best time to tell him about the decision she and Mrs. Green had come up with.

"Oh, that's a great idea, Molly. But lumber is mighty expensive, and I don't know if we can afford to build a proper stable," Papa said, knowing how important the pony was to Molly and Mrs. Green. He hated the idea of disappointing them.

"Oh, that's okay, Papa. Maggie Mae said she would pay for the wood and nails if you could do the work. She feels that since Wildfire spends so much time at our end of the pasture, she will take to a stable where she feels the safest." She was irresistibly beaming again, and Papa knew in an instant that he now had another project on his to-do list. Later that day the hardware store contacted William and informed him that Mrs. Green had given him permission to charge what he needed to build a stable for Wildfire. The owner of the hardware store had to admit to him that he'd never heard Mrs. Green sound so happy and youthful. In fact, he said she even laughed out loud and made a point of wishing him a blessed day! Both men smiled and acknowledged that Molly's hand of friendship had made quite a change in Old Mrs. Green, and it seemed to them that the tables of sadness had turned for the lonely old woman.

Over the course of the next week, Mrs. Green was the talk of the town. It seemed someone with bright white hair had been seen outside of her home, working on the flower beds and scraping the flaked paint off the neglected house. Some of the locals decided it must be a cousin or niece doing all of the work because no one knew of any other family members besides the sheriff. Anyhow, it didn't matter much. It was comforting to know that the historic home was getting a much-needed face-lift.

"We don't know who is working on the old place," was one comment Mr. Fitzwilliam's overheard while buying lumber at the hardware store. He minded his own business, but he smiled on the inside. He hadn't been authorized by Mrs. Green to share her new outlook on life, and he certainly didn't want to speak without her blessings.

The hanging bell jingled as the front door of the hardware store opened. An older lady walked inside of the well-stocked room and up to the customer counter. She wasn't from around town, and her appearance got some stares. Her hair was white and flowed to the middle of her back. She had on a navy blue wool skirt and black polished boots. The coat she wore was colorful tweed, and the scarf around her neck was a lovely shade of burgundy. Her face was familiar, and when she smiled, her dimples looked youthful; however, her voice was the real give away. It was Mrs. Green!

"Oh, Mr. Fitzwilliam's," she said, standing by his side. "I am so glad to see you here this morning." Her tone was soft and kind. She took him by the inside of the arm and walked with him as he selected some small items for Wildfire's shelter. One could have heard a nail drop everyone was so quiet! The gawking customers who were in the store stood in shock as they witnessed Mrs. Green escort Mr. Fitzwilliam's through the paint and nail sections. Some people even followed them through the aisles as they picked out their wares, staying far enough back so they wouldn't get caught spying.

"Thank you for helping us with Wildfire's shelter. Molly had a very good idea suggesting that it should be built." She had a genuine sound of love in her voice for Molly, and Mr. Fitzwilliam's could not have been prouder of the effect his little one had had on the lonely woman.

"Yes, ma'am, we are very proud of her too. The move to Pine Valley has been a good one for us all." He spoke in a way that was humble if not downright grateful. He changed the subject. "I'll be getting started on the stable today, Mrs. Green."

And she stopped him midsentence with a tender correction to his address and a raised finger to his face. "That's Maggie from now on." He smiled and agreed, but only if she'd call him William and his wife Mary. The two laughed at their formality, shook hands, and finished their shopping. A small collection of customers had collected at the cash register and stood there as if waiting to see a movie star. As Maggie turned around to leave, she stopped suddenly and turned back around to catch everyone moving as if to follow her out of the store. "It is a pleasure to see everyone here today," Maggie Mae said with a bit of emotional croak to her voice. "I am sorry for all of the years I stayed locked up in that old house. I simply forgot how nice it is to have friendship." She looked around, catching each one's eyes for a brief second. "You'll be seeing a lot more of me from now on. I hope you can forgive an old woman for being so sad that she forgot to live."

She left it at that and smiled affectionately to the room of people. She waved goodbye to William and walked out of the store. Everyone stood quietly, stunned for a moment, and then they scrambled to the front window to watch her walk down the busy street. Many other people stopped too and watched the strange woman move about the shops. Some elbowed each other in recognition of Mrs. Green, and the others just stared.

All in all, it was a memorable morning on main-street, and then Mrs. Green walked to the elementary school and introduced herself to the principal. She explained how Molly had motivated a change in her life, and now that she was feeling so much better, she wanted to volunteer in the children's library. She produced her graduate papers and a diploma as proof of her qualifications. The principal looked them over, and without any hesitation, he held out a welcoming hand of acceptance. They agreed that she should get started on Monday, so with those plans firmly in place, Mrs. Green walked out of the principal's office and headed down to the farmer's market. The fall afternoon couldn't have been more warm and welcoming. News of Mrs. Green's rebirth had spread through town like ... wildfire, so it was no surprise that she was greeted at the market with many approving eyes and the kindest of regards. She purchased a few necessities and went to walk home when she found herself walking next to Samuel and Jane. It was Samuel's craning neck that caught Mrs. Green's eye first. He looked as if he'd seen something unbelievable, and it was Janie that nudged him to turn back around and stop staring. Mrs. Green knew that they'd seen her and that she owed them an apology, so she cleared her throat and asked them if they'd mind stopping for a moment to talk.

"Please allow me to apologize for the way I treated you both when you came to my house with your plate of cookies." She paused and then added, "On second thought, I'd like to say how sorry I am for being such a horrible neighbor all these years! I treated you and your beautiful mare very badly, Samuel!" She continued in a most sincere fashion, not letting either dumbfounded person get a word in edgewise, "I'd understand if you don't wish to forgive me. I behaved in a most unforgivable manner, but I do hope we can work through my naughty actions. Wildfire has come down from the mountain, and I am having a shelter built for her on the Fitzwilliam's end of the field." She paused to collect her apologetic thoughts and then added, looking directly into Samuel's eyes, "She is *your* horse after all, and I felt it best to encourage her to feel safe on the pasturelands. Molly ... have you met her?" She looked into their faces, searching for a yes. "Well, she has made friends with Wildfire, and her parents have agreed to build a temporary shelter. You know, till she's tame enough to go back to your farm." Maggie Mae was nervously rambling on.

She began to ring her hands together as she struggled for words when Samuel cleared his throat and spoke, "Oh, Mrs. Green ..."He ran his fingers through his mane of hair. "It's mighty nice of you to apologize." He was taken aback not only by her words but by her face and clothes. She was lovely. "We all make mistakes."

He was searching for words when Janie stepped in. "Mrs. Green, how lovely to see you today, and may I add how beautiful you look?" She was all kindness and sincerity. "Thank you for your apology today. We were very concerned about your well-being the last time we saw you. I am glad you're feeling so much better." Janie stopped and then took Mrs. Green by the arm, "The shelter sounds like a good idea. Don't you think so, Samuel?" She noticed her husband's happy smile and continued talking, "There's no hurry to bring Wildfire home, Mrs. Green. I am sure she is fine where she is, and we both look forward to meeting

Molly." Janie's tone was calm and reassuring. "I understand you are working on your family's home." She completely changed the subject. "Please let me know if there is anything we can do to help. Samuel is still willing to work on your barn if ya like, and I am handy with a paintbrush!" Janie was just as pleased as Mrs. Green. "Christmas is just around the corner, and it would be the town's delight to see your home polished and decorated. What do you say, Mrs. Green. Is it a deal?" Janie already had her hand out to shake, but Mrs. Green grabbed her and hugged her instead! She insisted that Samuel and Jane promise to call her Maggie from now on, and she said she'd be honored if they'd like to help her during the remodel. In fact, Maggie admitted she'd let the family farm go and that she was ashamed to see the condition it was in today.

"I am very pleased to see you two. Neighborly angels have been fluttering all around me today, and bumping into you has been … well, let's just say, a blessing." Maggie beamed with a genuine smile. She truly was a lovely lady.

"Let's get started tomorrow," said Janie, jumping right in. "Samuel and I will be there at eight in the morning."

"Capital, Janie. I'll be looking for your smiles!" Maggie added as she vigorously shook each one's hands. "I'll have some hot coffee when you get there. Do you like scones?" Her question brought an enthusiastic yes from each nodding head. "Then I'll see you tomorrow. By the way," said Maggie with a twinkle in her clever eyes, "I have a surprise for you two. Bless your hearts!"

"Thank you, Maggie, truly." Janie held her hand up to her chest and over her heart, "Thank you!" Maggie could see a tear of appreciation in Janie's big brown eyes.

Evening was quickly approaching, and Maggie knew it was time to get going. She declined a ride home from Samuel and assured them that the walk would do her good. As she strolled down the lane, waving hello to all passersby, she acknowledged the joy welling up inside of her heart. As she came within view of her home, she caught the sight of Wildfire! She was stopped in her tracks not only by how big the filly had become but by the fact that she and Molly were playing together out in the pasture. Molly had a lead rope loosely tied around the pony's neck, and she was leading her around in circles. The pony seemed to be having a marvelous time. A moment later Molly held out her hand and Wildfire took something from her palm. Maggie decided it must be an apple.

The pony is home! Maggie thought to herself, *Molly did it! How on earth?* And she stopped in the middle of her thought when she noticed Molly waving at her from across the open field. Both gals waved with arms high up in the air. In a second Molly had sprinted over to the fence line and greeted Maggie Mae properly.

"Did you see, Maggie Mae? Did you see?" She was out of breath, but Maggie nodded yes.

"Dear child," said Maggie Mae, "I do believe you are a horse whisperer. How did you get that wild beast to calm down?" Her eyes lit up with surprise and interest.

"Love, Maggie Mae. Love and apples!" The two laughed wholeheartedly at Molly's reply, and she promised Maggie to keep up the good work.

Wildfire let out a loud whinny, and Molly knew that she wanted to play some more. They said their goodbyes, and Molly raced back to the pony as Mrs. Green finished walking home. When she got there, the sheriff was waiting. Maggie handed him her bag of groceries and invited him into the house.

"I have been told a strange woman has moved into your house, Aunt Maggie," he said as he set the bag down and looked up her. "I gotta say you don't look like the same old lady anymore." He stopped and then realized what he had said.

His expression let Maggie know that he felt bad about what and how he had just spoken to her, but she interrupted him and said, "Yes, Bobby, I know." She tipped her head to the side and looked up at him in a way that sought his forgiveness. "I chose to be the way I was. I had lost all hope. But I don't feel that way anymore." She was shaking her head from side to side. Then she waited for a reply.

"Well, Maggie, I am glad to see it!" His face was alight with joy. "That lil' Molly did the trick, I'm-a-guessin'. Well, that's something. I will have to thank her for myself," the sheriff said as though he were the mayor of Pine Valley. "Yes, ma'am!" Smiling, he stepped forward and put out his arms. Mrs. Green welcomed the warm embrace, hugging him back in a way that made up for all of the lost years of family affection.

"Wildfire is out in the pasture, Bobby. Molly tamed her, and now Samuel and Janie have a pony to work with!" Her admission that Wildfire truly belonged to Samuel cleared her conscience. "It's traditional to see a pony in the pasture, Bobby. It's just like my great-grandfather did for so many years!" Her eyes were welled up with tears, a phenomenon he hadn't seen in the whole of his life. "Molly says she tamed the pony with love, Bobby. Isn't that something!" Her grin sprung a tear loose.

Her nephew took her by the hand and said, "I think that is what she used to tame you too, Auntie." He stopped to see if he'd gone too far, and seeing that he hadn't, he added, "I think that's what she used on you."

Maggie buried her head into her nephew's chest and sobbed. He held her close and let her have a good, long cry.

Time passed, and the afternoon transformed into a fine, soft evening. Maggie waved goodbye to Bobby as he drove away, knowing good and well that he was right to say that Molly had accomplished her deeds through the act of love. Maggie felt confident that she and Molly could mend the hard feelings between her and Wildfire, and the thought of honoring her grandfather's tradition became a wish she knew they would fulfill.

Maggie sat at her desk and wrote down a list of things to accomplish when Samuel and Jane showed up in the morning. Preparation to paint topped the list along with tidying the outside of the old barn. She knew the winter snows would be upon them soon, so the barn remodel would need to wait until spring. Her mind dallied into daydreams as she remembered her childhood in the old home—the years spent exploring the woods, days working with her grandfather in the horse pasture, and of course, the friendships she'd made at school and in the community itself. She thought of old girlfriends whom she hadn't thought of in years and hoped they'd not forgotten her.

Would they forgive me for being so rude? She thought to herself. She could feel herself sticking in a web of doubt and sadness. When she looked up and out into the yard, she caught her reflection in the pane of glass. She wondered if she actually deserved to be forgiven and began to feel her confidence slipping. She looked so different these days. There was no more wig. Her hollow cheeks had filled in, and the joy of not being alone had eased the signs of age. She had to admit that it felt wonderful to look healthy again, and she had to give the credit to Molly and Samuel! Had it not been for the birth of the filly, she may never have met Molly. Funny how one miracle can bring on another. Now she caught herself smiling in the reflection she was still gazing at. The truth in her reflection overrode the sadness that was trying to creep back into her mind. "Don't over think it, Maggie Mae," she said aloud."Tomorrow is a busy day. Best git some dinner and a lantern ready for a goodnight."She put down her pen and pushed away from the desk. The sun was down now, and the night sky had become dotted with a few eager stars. The kitchen was warm, and a simple dinner hit the spot. Molly was already on her second lantern flash when Maggie lit her candle, each gal sending only three bursts of light to each other. Of course, Maggie decided the three meant "I love you," and she was right!

A rooster crowed in the morning, and there was a good hard rap on the front door. Maggie was there in a flash! When she opened it, she was greeted by not only Jane and Samuel but a large collection of other eager neighbors too. Their hands were gripping rakes and shovels and all sorts of gardening tools.

Maggie Mae gasped and welcomed them in and said, "I'd better make another pot of coffee!"

The room cheered with laughter as everyone filed into her living room, most of them stunned by the grandeur of the room itself. People shook hands and said, "Good morning," as Maggie handed a plate of scones to Janie and asked her to pass them around while a fresh kettle whistled on the stove.

The men took action and informed Maggie about their plan of raking and clearing around the base of the barn's foundation. Maggie nodded yes and checked it off the list. Another group of men and women suggested they begin gently scraping the peeling paint from all sides of the house, and Maggie agreed with another check of her list. Janie spearheaded a project to rake up the paint peelings with a small group of gals so that debris wouldn't get into the soil, and the last few volunteers suggested taping around the windows and doors in preparation for a new coat of paint.

Mrs. Green stood back and checked her list. She'd never seen so many people in her house before, let alone hear so many plans in the making, and she was unaware of her continuous smile. She was on top of the world, and her personal world was on top of the situation.

The sun was working its way up into the morning sky when the bus passed by on its way to school. The windows facing Maggie's house were all down, and the children poked their arms outside the bus, waving excitedly. Maggie saw them passing and waved back too. In fact, all of the workers waved since it was their children on the bus! The driver tooted the horn, and her passengers three times cheered, "Hip-hip-hooray!" Maggie knew she could hear Molly in the lead!

In no time the barn was tidy around the outside timbers and the stone foundation. Some loose boards were hammered back into place, and any sagging window frames or awnings were re-secured. A fire pile was started in the yard far away from the house, and all of the twigs, branches, and grasses were burned up. The house was scraped, sanded, and taped by lunchtime in addition to finishing any needed repairs. By one o'clock in the afternoon, a plan was in place to start painting in the morning, and Maggie was in agreement,

"I'll get the paint you want, Mrs. Green. What color would you like?" asked Samuel with a sudden awareness of his slip. "I mean Maggie."

He flashed that handsome smile that always melted his wife's heart and added, "Do ya want to keep it all white?"

"Well, Samuel," began Maggie, "Johnny's favorite color was green. What do you say to white sides and green trim around the windows? If that isn't too much trouble." She looked content in that moment. It was like the expression one sees when looking into understanding eyes.

"Why yes, Maggie." He was touched by her tenderness."I think that is a great idea. It will be no trouble. No trouble at all."

Janie couldn't help but overhear their conversation. She was delighted to see Maggie free from loneliness. The change in her was truly miraculous.

"I know just the color," added Maggie with a twist of her head and twinkle in her eye."A medium shade of forest green. I know Johnny would like that!"

Janie took her by the hand and said, "Yes, Maggie. He would like it very much. Now we brought some lunch. How about a sandwich?"

They all sat down around the burn pile and ate while they discussed the day's finished work and the next day's plans. Maggie was looking around her property and was amazed at how fast the house and barn had been restored. She noted how funny it was that she, too, had also been restored so quickly. In her heart she thanked God, and in her mind she thanked Molly.

As they finished up lunch and poked the burn pile, they heard a loud ruckus echoing from the distant mountainside. Everyone's attention turned when Wildfire showed up! She was moving down from the mountain like the wind barreling out of control! She came within a few feet of the house, skidding to an abrupt stop and creating quite a scene. She snorted and whinnied and reared up onto her hind legs. She bucked and pranced as if dancing for all to see. Wildfire had joined the party, permitting the rumor of her survival to become a fact. Maggie stood frozen in her steps. Wildfire let out a cry that sounded as if she, the pony, was asking Maggie to step up to the fence. Slowly and with great reverence, Maggie did just that! She walked up to the fence line and held out her hand. Wildfire calmed. They both swallowed, Maggie choking back tears, Wildfire looking for courage.

The large pony walked in closer, her head bobbing up and down as if she was nodding yes and her nose sniffing the air for any sign of danger. Maggie didn't flinch. They locked eyes, and the group of neighbors froze in place. The breeze picked up, and the world seemed transfixed in the sacred moment. Each person witnessed the reunion, and each person's heart was touched by the gift of forgiveness. Wildfire came close enough for Maggie to reach out and touch her forehead. A tear slipped from Maggie's eye, and Wildfire bowed her head in respect. They stood there for a while, simply letting the gravity of the moment sink in. Maggie gently rubbed the bridge of Wildfire's warm face. The group passed an apple up, and it found its way into Maggie's hand. She held it out, and Wildfire brought her head over the fence and took it—gently at first and then with crunchy thanks. The sound of the apple being eaten broke the intensity of the event and gave everyone a chance to softly laugh. Maggie could smell the healthy tang of the horse's sweat. Her hands were close enough to stroke down the thick, marbled mane, and she could see how carefully Molly had been brushing and braiding the long, coarse strands of hair.

In the next moment, Wildfire started back toward the middle of the pasture. Everyone watched as she instinctively began to play and frolic. Samuel and Jane walked over to where Maggie still stood, each one putting a hand her shoulder.

"Well, now," began Samuel with a large exhale of pent-up breath. "That was unexpected."

"You forgot, Samuel," advised his lovely wife, Jane, "with God, all things are possible."

"Yes," added Maggie, "all things are possible!"

Suddenly, Maggie shot up two huge eyes of surprise. "Come with me," she declared with the eagerness of Christmas morning. "Come with me!"

She walked with a fresh spring in her step and led Samuel and Jane over to the tidy barn. She asked Samuel to open the barn doors (which were now free from grass and rocks), and the three walked inside. She led them into a far corner where a large dusty canvas had been thrown over an oddly shaped, unknown form.

"Now Samuel, you grab that end, and I'll grab this one. On three, lift it up and fold it back toward the wall of the barn. Then you'll have your surprise!" He and Jane looked at each other questioningly, and Maggie began to count, "One, two, and three!"

When the fine dust settled, Samuel and Jane beheld a sleigh. A horse-drawn sleigh! The three stepped in closer as if inspecting a fine antique. "I don't ever remember seeing this in town before. Has it been in the barn all these years?" Samuel spoke slowly, his question touched with a sense of awe. "She's a real beauty, Maggie. Are you thinkin' what I'm thinkin'?" He looked up and caught Maggie's delightful expression.

Janie stood back and smiled like a parent who sees a child's reaction after un-wrapping a toy.

"I do believe that's exactly what Maggie means, Samuel. Wildfire's too young ... but not Fiona!"

They had left the barn door open, and everyone came in to see the rediscovered sleigh. Soon it was added to the clean-up list, and one local man offered to check it for any needed repairs.

Maggie sat down on a bale of straw, a bit overwhelmed, and she listened as everyone milled about. A few weeks ago, she was lost and alone, and now she was planning to go for sleigh rides! A lot had changed, and in her happy heart, she knew this was just the beginning.

The day ended with hugs and thanks all around. Maggie had only expected Samuel and Janie's help, so to have a community pitch in and work on the house reassured her that the town held no grudges and that she would be welcomed again without judgment.

Having Wildfire come down from Winter Mountain was another thing altogether. Word of the filly's surprise visit spread through town quickly, and the news had even reached Molly's ears at school. When the bus dropped her off that afternoon, Molly ran over to Maggie Mae's and gave her a big hug. The two of them were beside themselves with joy! It was all going to work out fine. The new stable was underway and would be finished in less than a week, and more importantly, Wildfire had found her courage. Molly knew that Maggie Mae was thrilled with all of the blessing of the last few weeks, so before she left to go home, Molly said, "Remember, Maggie Mae, with God ... all things are possible!"

Maggie teared up again and covered her mouth with her hand, not wishing to give away the truth that Janie has shared that same statement earlier.

They waved goodbye, and Molly raced across the open pasture toward home. Maggie stood silently at the fence and watched her friend skip and run and play.

How in the world did all of these changes happen so fast? She thought to herself. Then she bowed her head and repeated out loud, "With God ... all things are possible!"

The same crew showed up on schedule, and this time Maggie had three pots of coffee ready to go. The house painting took no time at all, and in fact, they were blessed by a warmer than usual day of autumn sunshine. The sleigh was polished and would be ready to use at the first sign of snow. Samuel decided it would be wise to ride Fiona over to Maggie's and see how she'd react to being back on Mrs. Green's property. It turned out to be a great idea. Fiona hadn't forgotten! As Samuel rounded the bend and approached the old farm, Fiona's protective instincts kicked in, and so did her desire to run! After about ten minutes of coaxing her to stop galloping, Samuel had her tamed down enough so that the two of them could approach the main gate of the property. Janie was waiting there when they arrived, and the sheer sight of her set Fiona's mind at ease, allowing horse and rider to enter into the round pen calmly.

Maggie was walking around the yard like the supervisor should, and she was relieved to see the mare's willing manner. Being the clever woman that she was, Janie pulled an apple from her pocket and handed it to Maggie. With a smile and an unspoken hint, Maggie held the apple out to Fiona. The mare is cautious at first, giving the skeptical eye of doubt to Maggie and then to Janie; however, the fruit of forgiveness overtook her memory of anger, and the apple became the bridge to friendship.

Wildfire hadn't traveled faraway overnight, so within minutes she caught wind of her mother, Fiona. Without fear, Wildfire came down to the round pen and leaned over the wooden railings, stretching her head toward her mother. A moment later Samuel dismounted and opened the side gate, allowing mother and daughter to reunite.

The work on the farm once again stopped, and all eyes were on the pair. Words are hard to find when you describe the return of a long-lost love, especially when the words are spoken in horse! They covered each other's faces with slobbery apple kisses while whipping their tails around. Fiona seemed to be admiring her filly's beauty, while Wildfire showed off her new strength and agility. They were two peas in a pod—mother and daughter created by God and brought back together by the faith of one little girl.

The day slipped by in a flash. When the bus showed up and dropped off Molly, the painting crew was gone, and only Samuel and Janie remained. Maggie took a moment to introduce them to one another, but the small-town stories of the last few weeks had already made the introductions.

"I feel like you are a daughter of our own, Molly," announced Samuel with a formal handshake and bow. "This is my wife, Jane, and may I say how glad we are to finally meet you!" He was so gracious that Molly felt a bit embarrassed.

"The work you have done with Wildfire is impressive," Jane said in a calmer tone of voice. "We weren't sure if we'd ever find the pony again, let alone see our Mrs. Green looking and feeling so well these days." Janie stopped and looked down into Molly's eyes and said, "You have stirred up the faith in Pine Valley, my dear. You have every right to be very proud of yourself." Janie's words were spoken from the heart, but they were met with an unexpected reply.

"Well," said Molly, "my prayers were simply answered. I think all of Pine Valley's prayers were heard." Humbly and with great sincerity, she added, "I just did what God wanted me to do, and the rest worked itself out. At least that's what Momma said." She was beaming with a smile.

"I look forward to meeting your parents, Molly. They must be very special people to have such a remarkable daughter like you," observed Samuel with a look of love in his eyes.

Molly paused after she gave Maggie Mae a hug and finished, "We are all what you said … *re-make-able*. We just gotta try."

Samuel and Janie stood there, silenced by Molly's use of the word *remarkable*. Maggie just looked down, her toe moving a rock around the tidy yard, and she smiled without a word. The more one got to know Molly, the more one realized the Spirit spoke louder than her words.

Much to their delight, it was Friday, and that meant Molly would be coming over tomorrow to visit. She and Maggie would be working on their projects for the autumn social, and they had it in mind to enter Maggie Mae's apple butter into competition. As far as Molly was concerned, Maggie had already won the first-place ribbon, but half the fun was making the butter and daydreaming about the victory.

Samuel and Jane mounted Fiona and waved goodbye to the two gals. Wildfire had already headed to the middle of the pasture and was trotting around like a kid in a candy store.

"I'll be here at ten o'clock tomorrow, Maggie Mae," reminded Molly."We'll need more apples, to be sure. Is there anything else I can bring with me?" Molly had a priceless expression about herself.

"No, Molly dear, I think that will do it." Maggie was scanning the air with her eyes as if checking a mental grocery list. "I have plenty of sugar and cinnamon. And the rest ... is magic!"

The two chuckled at the word *magic* and hugged goodbye for yet another day. Molly left the house and headed across the open pasture. Maggie didn't mind her doing it a bit now that the fences of friendship had been mended. Besides, it was a faster way home!

Maggie could see Mrs. Fitzwilliam's standing on the front porch, waving as Molly headed in that direction. She searched her memory for Mrs. Fitzwilliam's first name and then recalled that it was Mary, remembering her talk with William at the hardware store.

Wildfire was following at Molly's side as she crossed the pasture. As she walked up onto the porch and into the hug of her momma, Wildfire entered the newly built stall.

Maggie walked back into her cozy house unaware of the song she was humming. She stoked the fire and took her seat. Her mind wandered a little, and she dozed off. In her restfulness she saw the blossoms on the apple trees and could smell their perfume in the air. She felt the warmth of the sun on the youthful cheek of her face. The sky was so blue that she needed to squint and shield her eyes from the glare of crystalline light, and then she saw Johnny. He was right there in front of her. His hair a tousled mess and his clothes dirty from an afternoon in the orchard. As he walked closer to where she was standing, he was wiping his hands off on the handkerchief he'd always carried with him. He seemed to be smiling from within. Around his body was a glow of light, like the light one saw when he or she looked at the picture of an angel. As he moved in closer to Maggie's sun-kissed dream, she could sense his love, his strength, and his dedication. Without effort, a ribbon of opal whiteness came out from Johnny's heart and found its way into Maggie Mae's. In that instant she felt the heartbreak mend. He stood at arm's length and looked deeply into her green eyes, the gossamer link silencing their need to speak. An unknown choir of voices filled the air. A rich, musical tone lifted her spirit and cradled her damaged soul. The two stood locked in that moment; however, like all special visions, the dream faded, and Maggie was left sitting by her fire, the flames snapping and popping her back to her senses. For a second she wished she could go back into her daydream, but she knew she couldn't. The vision was a reminder that Johnny had never really left her and that he had always been right by her side.

She stirred the fire and then walked to the kitchen. Her stomach growled, which was no surprise. It was time for dinner! Out of the corner of her eye, she saw Molly flashing her goodnight. Maggie smiled and returned the favor with a full and healed heart.

She had soup, salad, and bread for dinner, and then she prepared the kitchen for the busy day to come.

"What a day!" she said aloud as she brushed her hair."Goodnight, Johnny," she added to her prayers." Thank you for the daydream." She was all tucked into bed as she said, "I should have known you would never leave my side. I should have known." She blew out the candle and was asleep in an instant.

The kitchen smelled delightful as the two busy bees ladled the apple butter into the sparking clean jars. Molly thought Maggie Mae was going a bit overboard. How many jars of butter did they really need for a competition? But Molly just smiled and kept on working by her side. Maggie thought Molly should enter her knitting project, dropped stitch and all, but Molly thought it would be better if she entered an apple pie instead."Well then," admitted Maggie with that look of cleverness, "I have the best pie crust recipe in the county. You'd best get a-crackin'."

Needless to say, the beginner baker mastered the scrumptious pie crust, and all was set for the autumn social, which was set for tomorrow after church. Maggie Mae hadn't been to church in many years or participated in any of the fall festivities, so it was with great excitement that the two friends prepared their entries.

"Momma made me a new skirt to wear tomorrow, Maggie Mae. What are you going to wear?" she asked with honest interest. "Momma sewed you a vest out of the same skirt material just in case you might wanna match." Molly was grinning all the way from her clever toes.

"Well," Maggie started, thinking about her outfit, "I hadn't thought of that. What colors are in the vest?" she asked as she dampened a towel and wiped the flour off of Molly's face.

"Look in the bottom of the apple basket, Maggie. Momma thought there was no harm in me bringing it along." Maggie put the towel down and took a closer look inside of the sturdy basket. Lo and behold, there it was. Momma had wrapped it in white tissue to protect it from a juicy apple, so the paper made a crunchy sound as Maggie took it out of the wrapping. It was lovely! Mary had picked out the prettiest fabric. It was covered with plums, pumpkins, apples, and fall leaves. Lush boughs of dark green pine needles and goldenrod were woven between the fruit, bringing your eye to the rich color of the harvest theme. Maggie gave it a good snap, and the vest unfolded,

"Oh, Molly dear, this is beautiful! Well, it's even lined." Maggie looked at the vest like a seamstress would look at an admired work of clothing. "Your momma is quite talented, Molly. How did she know I'd love forest green for the lining? Oh, this is perfect, and yes, I'll be proud to wear it tomorrow." Maggie was going on and on just the way Molly knew she would. "You know, I think this is the first gift I have received in years, Molly dear." Maggie was still holding it up to admire the craftsmanship.

"Yes, I think I am right, the first gift in many a year!" Her eyes were teared up enough for Molly to see the pools of appreciation.

"Well, Maggie," said Molly, snuggling up to her side, "let's go pick out what else you are going to wear tomorrow, and I'll know how to match you." Molly looked precious, her little face beaming with pride.

The two spent the next hour going through Maggie's forgotten wardrobe, Molly picking out this and Maggie showing her that. Before they knew it, they had opened and rifled through every drawer and cabinet. They were laughing like a couple of old school chums when they heard a knock at the front door. Molly watched Maggie. She didn't even flinch this time. They walked to the door and opened it without hesitation.

"Well, hello, ladies," announced Molly's papa with a bow of enormous swagger. "I have come to retrieve the lovely and talented Molly Fitzwilliam's and to extend an informal invitation to the Lady Green, for it is suppertime." He continued with a fancy flair, "Therefore and without further ado, I humbly request your ladies' presence at dinner."He was so silly. He even spoke with an English accent."May I tell my dear wife to expect you two lovelies in thirty minutes?" He batted his eyes as if he were a butler.

"Oh yes," replied Maggie with the same accent and exaggerated flourish. "Do let the Lady Fitzwilliam's know that we would be delighted." Molly loved the acting. "We shall be punctual, and we shall bear gifts." She grabbed the doorknob and began to close it. "Ta-ta for now, kind sir," Maggie said. "We will be there shortly." Papa bowed one more time as they began to giggle, and then she closed the door.

"Well, we'd better git going. You git one of those apple pies and put it in the apple basket. I'll put on a warmer sweater and grab my shawl." She walked toward her bedroom as she gave instructions, and then she stopped in the hallway. She turned around and looked Molly square in the eyes,

"I am going to your house for dinner?" she said with a look of sudden surprise on her entire face.

"I haven't stepped foot in that house for forty years, Molly." Molly hadn't thought of that. She just knew it as her home. Maggie stammered, "I … I … don't know if I …"

"It will be okay, Maggie Mae. Remember … you have me!"

The Lady Green patted Miss Fitzwilliam's on the cheek, reassuring her that she would be okay, and off they went. They cut across the field with an apple pie in the basket and an apple in hand for Wildfire. Molly insisted that Maggie give the apple to the pony, and of course, Wildfire took the gift with great enthusiasm. Mr. and Mrs. Fitzwilliam's were standing on the porch, waiting for the two weary travelers to arrive. As Maggie came within feet of the steps, she stopped and begged forgiveness. "I am sorry to be so silly about this, but I haven't stepped foot inside of this house for a very long time. And well …" She paused her explanation and then added, "My stomach is full of butterflies."

They all quieted down. Molly walked up to Maggie's side and said, "You do not have to do anything you do not want to do, Lady Green. We are having dinner, and you are invited … if you want to join us."

Maggie suddenly got a whiff of what Mary was cooking. "Oh, that does smell wonderful, Mary." Maggie was secretly proud that she'd remembered Mrs. Fitzwilliam's first name. "Is it roasted chicken?" Maggie asked, looking at her with hungry eyes.

"Well done, Lady Green," Mary said, playing along with the English accent game. " 'Tis a lovely table I have set in your honor tonight. Please join us," she said and then added, "'Twould be our pleasure."

Papa was laughing a bit since he knew *'twould* wasn't a word. But it sounded good, and it did the trick!

The bones of the house hadn't changed at all, but the personality of the home had changed for the better. Maggie walked up the steps and grabbed Molly's hand, and they walked through the front door together. Mary and William followed behind and quickly saw to Maggie Mae's comfort. Within a minute, she was sitting in an overstuffed chair and had an iced tea in her hand. Molly was busy showing Maggie some of her class work, and William was busy stoking the fire. The house really did smell wonderful, and the work the family had lovingly put into its restoration was well done.

"I must say you have all done a wonderful job of getting the old house in shape," Maggie said, breaking the silence with her genuine compliment. She looked up at William and went on, her nervousness making her a bit chatty. "It's been about forty years since I was in this room, and I've got to say it looks as good as the day Johnny and I finished painting it." She had a soft smile on her face as she looked around at the fixtures and furnishings. "Oh!" she said, startled. "I remember that old desk. It's funny. I'd forgotten all about it. Well, I'll be!" She then recognized another forgotten treasure. "That old clock was a gift from Mr. and Mrs. McGregor. It was a wedding ..."she started before her voice trailed off. Molly grabbed her hand and squeezed it gently.

"Dinner is ready, ladies and gentlemen." Momma was still in character. "Please follow me." She swept her hand to the side and ushered them into the dining room. Momma had outdone herself! The table look like it was set for royalty, and because of the occasion, we all became the lords and ladies we'd pretended to be.

Papa walked Maggie to the head of the table and pulled her chair out for her. As she sat, he pushed it in. He also did the same for Momma. He sat himself at the other end of the table.

"I think it only right that Maggie say our prayer tonight," Papa said to the dinner party. "Maggie, would that be okay?" He looked at her and waited.

Maggie silently nodded yes and then held out her hands so the family would hold out their hands and form a circle around the table. She cleared her throat and began, "Heavenly Father, thank you for the successful harvest season. We thank you for bringing Wildfire back into our good graces, and I, most of all, thank you for bringing Molly and her family into my life. I now know how much I have missed by staying cooped up in the old house, and I promise to never make that mistake again. Thank you for this lovely feast and table, but most of all, thank you for the life I had with Johnny." She stopped and looked around the table. Everyone was listening. "I thought I had lost him, but now I know he has been with me all along. Thank you, Father. Amen." Everyone said amen too, and Papa carved the bird.

It wasn't Thanksgiving, but it sure felt like it! Momma's potatoes were perfect. Everyone raved about her gravy and carrots! How could carrots taste so good? Without a doubt, Maggie Mae ate like she hadn't eaten in a very long time. Molly listened more than she spoke and picked up a lot of stories about Maggie Mae's youth. She told them about riding horses and winning ribbons at the fair. She recalled singing in the church choir and babysitting. She told them about her granddad giving the sleigh to her father, and she shared the story about how the apple orchard had been planted. "I must have been fifteen or so when Mr. McGregor began planting the orchard." She took another bite and added, "It was a hot summer that year, and Mac—that's what we called him—decided to git the trees in the ground a little earlier than what was advised. I'd say about six local men helped him plant those saplings, and I'll tell ya most of the town had their doubts whether they'd make it to the cooler fall months. My Pa would sit and whittle and talk behind old Mac's back, and Ma would tell him, 'Bite your tongue, ya old fool! Don't be jinxing our farm with those sharp words!'" Maggie was loading her fork with another bite as she looked down at her plate and began to laugh. "Ma ran that house with an iron fist." She took her bite. "Guess she'd have to, ornery bunch that we were." Everyone laughed with her now. You could tell Maggie had relaxed. She smiled more, and frankly, she ate like a lumberjack.

That Saturday night dinner seemed to last for hours. Before they knew it, Momma was passing out pie. The crust was the best part, Maggie said, but it was her crust recipe, so Molly shared the applause with her. As they cleared the table, Momma told Maggie she'd found some old letters in the desk when she was cleaning it out and asked her if she'd like them back. Of course she said yes, and it was with great love that Momma handed to Maggie a bundle of letters that had been tied together with a silky green ribbon. For a moment, she didn't recognize them. Then as it sunk in, Maggie remembered. She looked up at Momma with her eyes completely wide with surprise, "Where did you—"

"In the desk in a small hidden drawer. As I was dusting, I must have bumped it because it popped open and there they were just waiting to be found." Momma's explanation was simple. Then she said, "I found this too, Maggie." She handed a small green book to her. "It was in the top drawer of the dresser in our bedroom. I believe you will want to read it when you get home. It's a journal written by Johnny."

Maggie pressed the two precious items to her chest. "I remember the letters," she said as her cheeks blushed. "But I never knew about the book. You found it in the tall dresser?" Mary nodded yes, and Maggie said, "Well, that makes sense since that was his." She smiled.

Molly was sitting by her side on the rug near the fire. The quiet in the room was understandable. Momma offered them all coffee, but everyone admitted that they were full enough. After a time Papa caught Maggie looking dreamily out of the window and thought she must be ready to go home,

"Maggie," he said gently, "would ya like me to take ya home now? I'd be glad to walk ya." His face was soft and kind. Maggie nodded yes, and Molly wrapped the shawl around her shoulders. Momma kissed her on the cheek and thanked her for the pie. Everyone walked over to the pasture gate, and Molly and Mary waved goodbye. Molly clicked her tongue to get Wildfire's attention, and the pony stuck her head out of the stall window as the two entered the field and began to cross. Maggie slipped her arm through William's and leaned onto his powerful arm,

"Thank you for the exceptional evening. When I woke up this morning, I had no idea that the day would turn into a day I'd never forget." She talked. He listened, and Wildfire walked behind. The rest of the journey was silent. What else could they say? When they reached Maggie's house, William kissed her on the cheek and reminded her that they would be by at nine in the morning to pick her up for church. She reminded him about the entries for the autumn social, and he reassured her that there would be plenty of room to take them along. They waved good night one last time, and Maggie walked into her living room. The fire had coaled nicely, so one chunk of oak would spark a flame soon. She set the letters and book on the mantle below his picture and then blew him a kiss. The fire caught and lit the room with a soft, warm glow. Maggie stood back and smiled.

"I love ya, Johnny. I always will." And with those tender words spoken, she walked across the floor and into the kitchen. As William walked across the open pasture with Wildfire at his side, he witnessed the two ladies signaling each other with their lanterns. Molly was first with three bright flashes and then Maggie with three more. He scratched his head with fatherly pride. So much had changed in their lives since they'd moved to Pine Valley. They had a home, a community to grow in, and a neighbor to top all neighbors. "Thank ya, Father," he said aloud with his hand over his heart. "Thank ya very kindly."

The next day even looked like a church day! Sunshine broke through the night. Birds were on bended wings as they darted to and fro, singing their holy songs for all to hear and enjoy. Translucent ribbons of steam rose off of the old barn doors as the thin layer of frost melted with the direct rays of warm morning light. All in all, you could say it was a glorious beginning, and the excitement of the day was in the air.

The Fitzwilliam's were dressed and ready to go to church. Molly's skirt was beautiful. It came down to her ankles, and

Momma had added white cotton petticoats. When Molly spun in a circle, the skirt would dance on air. It was the prettiest skirt she'd ever had, and she knew that Becky would think it was pretty too.

They said goodbye to Wildfire and loaded up in the truck. Molly made sure there was plenty of room for their guest of honor, and off they went. By the time they got around the corner and onto Maggie Mae's drive, they saw other folks on their way to church too.

Maggie had already brought the crate of apple butters out of the house and placed it on the porch. Seeing the crate, Papa lifted it up and placed it into the back of the truck. A moment later Maggie appeared on the porch, and she was a vision of loveliness. The morning sun shone in her hair like drifts of snow. She'd pulled it back with a burgundy velvet headband, added a skirt of the same vibrant color, and applied a coat of dark red lipstick. The blouse under her vest was long-sleeved and satin gold in color, its warm and elegant sheen bringing the fall hues in the vest to life. She sparkled from head to toe, and you could see her pride in the way she smiled. She walked over to the truck and handed Momma a pie. "Now, Mary dear, hold this while I climb into the truck. Don't take a bite now. That's Molly's entry for the baking competition."She was scolding her and teasing her at the same time." Ya know, I am not as young as I used to be," she said, smiling and winking at the same time." But I think that there pie is a winner just like our girl!" She walked around and climbed into the back seat next to Molly. "Oh, Molly," exclaimed Maggie as Papa closed the truck door behind her, "you look beautiful! Why, I haven't seen petticoats in years. How charming."

For a change, Molly was speechless. She just sat and grinned, her sense of self-esteem speaking volumes.

"Well, ladies," asked Papa, securing his seat belt, "are we ready?"

The three gals answered yes, and they headed off to church.

The parking lot was beginning to fill. Papa pulled up in front and dropped his gals at the door. "I'll bring the crate and pie with me, Maggie. Go on now. I'll take care of it." He smiled, and the three ladies walked up the sidewalk and toward the doors of the church. It was almost ten o'clock, and people were everywhere. Soon Papa came up from behind. The crate and pie were taken to the hall already, and together, they all walked up the steps together. The pastor was standing to the right side of the main doors. He was greeting everyone as they entered, but he stopped when he saw Maggie Mae."Mrs. Green," he said, shocked, "is that you?" He was blocking the sun from his eyes as if it was casting an illusion. "Why, Mrs. Green! It is you!" Now he was shaking her hand and smiling, "I never thought I'd see you again. What a lovely surprise! You are looking quite well! Oh, how are you, my old friend?" Now he was rambling. In fact, he forgot the rest of the congregation and escorted Maggie into the church personally, her arm wrapped through his. The Fitzwilliam's followed silently behind, knowing in their hearts the great impact Mrs. Green's presence would have in church today.

The pastor began to lose track of time as he talked to Maggie. The choir began to sing, and the melody snapped his attention back to beginning the day's sermon. He walked up to the simple podium, dropped his head in private prayer, and then looked up and out into the eager eyes of his congregation. People could hear a subtle murmur making its way through the people who were seated. It ebbed and flowed like the salty water of the ocean waves, then finally, the pastor said, "Welcome." He stopped and smiled to the assembly." Today marks the annual celebration of our autumn social. As a community of individuals, we have many wonderful reasons to be joyful, happy, and content—the healthy birth of children and animals, the sowing and reaping of personal seeds both in kindness and deed, harvests of all types, ranging from apples and hay to walnuts and pumpkins. I stand before all of you as an honored pastor and a proud citizen. Blessings come in many different shapes and sizes, and some blessings are even concealed by time itself." He stopped, looked down at his notes, and then closed the book. He took a slow breath and then resumed the new thoughts he hadn't prepared. "Some forty years ago, a tragedy rocked the very depths of our community's soul. A young, recently married couple was separated by an accident. A snowbound tree fell on and killed the husband. Perhaps you remember Johnny and Maggie Mae Green … and the magical day I married them in McGregor's apple orchard?" He stopped once again, scanning the room for looks of recognition and nods of understanding. A stronger wave of voices flowed through the crowd. "Today, I find myself humbly pleased and profoundly touched. It has been forty years since Johnny left us and just as long since his widow came to church." Pastor Smith looked down at Maggie Mae and smiled. He held out a hand of introduction and said, "I'd like everyone to know that Mrs. Green has joined us here today for the first time in a very long time." He was nothing short of beaming from the pulpit. Without hesitation, Maggie stood up and turned around for all to see her. In that instant, a beam of morning sunshine poured through the windowpane, casting its light upon her. The timing of the ray transformed her into pure radiance! Her hair was alight. Her clothes were alight too, and her presence in the room was a spectacular sight! Tiny motes of dust caught the sunray too and danced around her like Tatiana's fairies. In that instant, the transformation of her healing was apparent for all to see, and she was pleased to share this blessing with everyone. She looked down at Molly and then over to her father, silently asking with her eyes if she could introduce his daughter. Without hesitation, he nodded yes.

Maggie held out her white gloved hand and took Molly by hers. She brought the young lady up to where she stood and wrapped a loving arm around her petite shoulder. The room was all hers, and as the miracle of the sunbeam faded, she said, "Forty years of loneliness, misery, blame, and pain are behind me now, thanks to the friendship of this little girl. She knocked on my door, these brave little lass." Maggie looked up and smiled a contrite smile to a community who knew her cantankerous ways." And she wouldn't take no for an answer. She had the faith of Midas in her golden touch. She carried the secret of Aladdin's lamp in her words. Molly believed in me in a way that I couldn't believe in myself. I saw her in her innocence hold out a hand of friendship I'd never seen before." Maggie stopped, controlled her emotions, and then continued, "Many of you tried to help me too. I am so thankful that you tried." The regret in her expression was genuine, and those who could relate took her sentiment to heart. She took a deep breath and exhaled. Looking around the room, she now saw many familiar faces. Time had ultimately changed them but hadn't rendered them any less recognizable.

Mr. and Mrs. McGregor's faces jumped out at her first, their tender and forgiving smiles. Samuel and Jane were sitting hand in hand with the smell of fresh paint still lingering in their recent memories. More and more friendly faces peeked through the crowd, and they all looked on with eyes of love and understanding.

"So," she said, "I stand before you a testimony of faith, patience, hope, and love. I've heard it said a few times in the last week that with God, all things are possible. Allow me to be the proof of those words, for without Molly's firm hand of friendship, I may have never remembered them to begin with." Maggie discretely bowed her head to the room. She and Molly took their seats and waited for Pastor Smith to resume.

He cleared his throat, a detectable tear welling in the corner of his eye, and stood silently at the podium. A few minutes later, he said, "Blessings come in many different shapes and sizes. Some blessings are even concealed by time itself. A seed is planted in the dark, damp earth. Even though you can't see it, you know it's there. Your faith is the water that stirs it to awaken. Your patience is the food that allows the seed to sprout when it is ready. Your hope is the rake that prevents the weeds from blocking out the sun a seed needs, and ... your love is the key by which all things grow because ... with God, all things are possible!"

The room sat quietly with the power of the sermon ringing profoundly in their ears. No one spoke or coughed. Silence resonated like the solid bang on a tympani drum, every soul deep in thought, every heart touched by the truth at hand.

Outside of the church, the tweeting birds got everyone's attention and broke the congregation's meditation, for off in the distance near the foot of the crags that led up into the jutting mountain range ... stood Wildfire. She, too, heard the sermon in her heart of hearts. In her experience of struggle and survival, she knew these truths to be evidence of almighty God. Wildfire knew the value of life and the value of forgiveness and courage.

She reared up and whinnied with all her might! The sound of her testimony bounced off of the mountain's jagged formations and floated on the wind down to the ears of those in church that morning. The people heard her! They all heard Wildfire's song. She whinnied one last time, and this time it went hand in hand with a flock of starlings who'd taken wing on her declaration. Their movements were in perfect syncopation with each other. No one bird in the lead. No one bird in charge. Just hundreds of starlings flying in a phenomenal pattern of unbroken harmonious rhythm. Everyone was outside of the church or standing at the window now. The show was more of a gift. It was as if God was saying, "Behold! I bring you tidings of great joy!"

Maggie and Molly stood together watching the spectacle. All you could do was just stand and commit the miracle to memory. Within the hour the birds departed, and Wildfire returned to his stable. Pastor Smith (who had also run outside the church to see the birds) ended the day's sermon with a loud thanks to all for coming and an invitation to join him for the afternoon in the great hall. Since that was the plan anyway, the townspeople all milled about, shaking Maggie Mae's hand, saying hello to Molly and her parents, and then casually strolling over to the great hall where the party awaited.

The room was large. Picture windows were built into each wall, allowing the sun to brighten the space. Historical pictures hung about and brought the spirits of the town's pioneers in for all to remember and respect. Round tables filled the main floor of the area and the competition tables were up against the walls in one long line. A sign hung down from the ceiling that said, "Start Here," and gave a starting point for the people as they walked by to see the food. It smelled like a heavenly bakery! There were pies and cakes and jams and jellies. Braided breads and sugar topped muffins were at one end of the table, and all things apple were on display in the middle.

Maggie Mae's apple butter was among the apple entries, and it had been set up in a way that even surprised her. Apparently, Molly and her papa had brought an old leather saddle and had used the saddle to display the jars. Molly had tied red-checkered ribbons here and there, and Papa had cleaned the leather until it was glossy and rich. Plus the old stirrups were holding the jars. Maggie was beside herself!

"My goodness!" declared Maggie as she twirled around to find Molly and William in the crowd.

"This is truly a surprise. Why, my grandmother would be so pleased. It is her recipe after all, and the saddle ... well, let's just say she'd be tickled. Thank you so much!" Maggie was flushed pink she was so pleased.

Pretty soon the judges came by with their spoons and clipboards. They had already judged the muffins and the breads, so they had the jams and the jellies next. Tradition insisted that the apple dishes be held for last since they were the favorite of the community.

The McGregor's came by and stopped to visit with Maggie Mae. They hadn't really seen her since the accident, and they were so pleased to finally talk with her again.

"Oh, my dear," opened Mrs. McGregor, "I can't tell you how nice it is to see you again. I don't know how you endured all those years alone." Her heart was in the right place, but even Molly knew this wasn't the right time or moment to speak about such a tender subject. "When my husband and I heard about you losing ..."

Molly saw a cloud of sadness creep into Maggie Mae's eyes and stepped into the middle of the conversation. "Mrs. McGregor, it sure is nice to meet you." She stuck out her tiny hand and shook Mrs. McGregor's with vigorous energy." Thank you for all of the wonderful apples!" (Molly may have only been seven, but she knew when to change the subject!) "Momma and Papa had enough money left to by new fabric for my skirt. And look, Momma bought me petticoats too!" Molly twirled around so that she could see her lovely new skirt." Momma even made Maggie Mae a vest to match my skirt. Isn't that wonderful? Thanks to you and your dear Mr. McGregor!" Molly was smiling and leading the old woman down a different path.

By now, Maggie was deep in conversation with another person, so Molly's plan had worked, and her friend was free from too many painful questions.

The judges took care of the job at hand, each one looking rather stuffed when the judging had finally ended. Pastor Smith took his place at the podium and began to speak, "Ladies and gentlemen." His voice was clear and joyful, "First, I'd like to thank everyone for their entries on our annual autumn social. I must say this year's participation was by far the biggest we have seen in many years." He paused a moment and looked around the hall. "Thank you all! I would like to begin with the jam and jelly division. Third place goes to ..." And so began the announcement for the awards. Maggie knew the apple awards wouldn't be announced until the end, so she took a moment to step outside to get a breath of fresh air. It was about one o'clock in the afternoon. The sun was high in the sky, and a thin wisp of clouds framed in the lovely blue vista. A few other folks had stepped outside too, and it was then that Maggie Mae felt at peace. It didn't really matter if she won a prize for her apple butter. What mattered most to her was the understanding she had come to know. She leaned forward, and her long white hair fell around the cheeks of her face. Only a short time ago it had been stuffed up in a filthy old wig and hidden from sight. She smiled and recalled how it was only a short time ago that her hollow, sunken cheeks made her look like a witch, all aged and decrepit and unusually old. She caught her reflection in one of the hall's windows and was again taken aback by her smile and the change in her appearance. She couldn't remember the last time she felt this content and happy. Well, perhaps the day she married Johnny.

"Maggie Mae?" Molly said in a soft voice. "They are announcing the apple winners now. Will you come back inside with me?"

Maggie looked down and patted her on her precious pink cheek, "Oh, of course I will, child. Of course I will."

The great hall was still bustling as the two gals strolled in through the front doors. Pastor Smith saw them enter and got straight to the awards at hand. "Now ... for the awards we've all been waiting for."

Maggie Mae grabbed Molly's hand and gave it a squeeze."Remember, if we don't win anything, Molly, we are still winners!"

Molly winked up at her and said, "Blue ribbon beauties!" Maggie grinned.

"First place for apple dumplings goes to, Ester Marie." The crowd applauded. The young lady took her ribbon with a great big thank-you and a smile.

"First place apple strudel goes to, Hans Walker." Again, the crowd clapped loudly as he walked up to the podium and accepted his blue ribbon.

"First place for apple pie goes to ..."The noise of the crowd hushed. Ten pies had been entered, so this ribbon was highly desirable. Pastor Smith checked his notes. He looked at them one more time and then looked up into the room and smiled brightly. "It seems we have a tie, folks. First place in the apple pie division goes to two lovely young ladies—Becky McBride and Molly Fitzwilliam's!"

The room came unglued! The best friends looked at each other and then raced up to the pastor, practically knocking him off of his feet. The roar of the applause was deafening! Becky and Molly accepted their ribbons and then faced the room. Each girl held her prize up high for all to see. Their parents shouted the loudest cheers in the room! Maggie placed two fingers in her mouth and let out a whistle that beat all whistles. In that instant, everyone turned to face Maggie, caught off guard by her shocking manners. Then they all burst out laughing.

The pastor stayed where he was and enjoyed the happy chaos. In a minute he used his hands to quiet down the group and regain control of their attention.

"Congratulations, girls," he said. "But there's one more. Now for the ribbon we've all been waiting for. First place in the apple butter division goes to ..." He looked up and over the top of his glasses, his gaze giving away the winner without a word. He took his spectacles off and wiped his tearing eyes with his left hand. He replaced his glasses and announced, "First place in the apple butter division goes to our very own Maggie Mae Green!" He stood back and clapped along. The room parted down the middle as if on cue, and Maggie Mae walked up to the podium with the joy of an entire community adding a lift to her step. She blushed from head to toe. Molly jumped up into the arms of her father and wrapped her arm around his neck, and he held her above the cheering crowd so she could see her friend get a ribbon too.

Samuel and Janie cheered! The McGregor's cheered! When the room finally calmed down, Maggie said, "Thank you, Mr. and Mrs. McGregor, for the apple orchard you planted so many years ago, and thank you, Molly dear, for knocking on this old lady's door. But most of all ..."She stopped and composed her thoughts. "Thank you, Pine Valley, for not losing your hope in me. I brought one hundred jars of apple butter with me. Please take one home if ya like." She held up her ribbon like a champion should and beamed a smile of victory into the assembly. As she stepped onto the floor and back into the crowd, the cheers began again!

What a day! Before they knew it, it was becoming dusk outside, and the warm temperatures of the afternoon traded places with the touch of a crisp autumn breeze. The hall was quickly tidied, and everyone shared farewells. Pastor Smith made Maggie promise to come back to church soon, and even invited her to join the ladies committee. It was a day no one would soon forget. Maggie was pleased to see that every jar of apple butter was gone. She knew that the best victory is in sharing success and passing down tradition.

"I had a splendid day, Maggie Mae," said a happy but tired Molly as they dropped Maggie off at home."We sure did a good job on our entries."

"We sure did, my darling girl." Maggie was standing outside of the truck talking to Molly through an open window. "I don't know what magic you put in that apple pie of yours, but it sure was tasty!" Now Maggie was winking and teasing. She finished by saying, "I will see ya at school tomorrow, so ya'll best get a move on." She backed up to allow the Fitzwilliam's to pull away. "Remember, I am working in the school library now." She was waving, her hair softly lit by the setting sun, her lipstick worn away by a day of kisses and treats. "Thank you, Mary and William." She was now standing on the front porch, her eyes framed with love.

"We should be seeing some snow soon. I look forward to a sleigh ride with ya'll." Her words were abundantly sincere.

Everyone waved and hollered goodnight. Maggie walked into her home and sat down in the living room. The blue ribbon was still in her hand, and it brought a smile to her lips. "What do ya know?" she said to Johnny's portrait."Did ya ever see anything so silly and yet so special? I know just where to hang it too, Johnny." She stood up and walked over to his picture."You are a first-place winner too, my love. First place to be sure." And she propped it up in front of his likeness. "Who would like a cup of tea?" she said. "Sounds like a winner."

Maggie Mae was content for the rest of the evening. Molly's goodnight lantern was on time, and so was dinner. Maggie picked out her clothes for her first day back to school and then turned in. Before retiring she said her prayers, "Heavenly Father, thank you." Her heart was full, and she knew the simple thank-you said it all, and so did God.

Maggie was early to school that Monday morning, and it was a good thing too because the entire staff was there to greet her when she arrived. The principal walked her to each classroom and introduced her to the teachers. Of course, everyone already knew Mrs. Green, but it was a professional courtesy nonetheless. The library door was already open. The heat was on, and it was clean and bright. It smelled the way a library should always smell. Towering shelves of books lined the redwood walls, and you could sense the faint, musty odor of all things old and good. A large glass vase filled with flowers sat on one corner of the librarian's desk, and propped up against it, there was an envelope with the word "Welcome" handwritten in blue ink.

"This is your key, Mrs. Green," the principal said as she handed the freshly cut key to the new librarian. "I am sure you will enjoy it here. Our students are very eager and thoughtful." She walked about with an air of authority that evoked respect. "Please don't hesitate to let me know if you need anything. Mason is the janitor, and he'll keep the room neat and tidy for you. We found a nameplate amongst some of the old items stored in the back warehouse. I am sure you'll recognize it." She held out her hand. "Welcome back to school, Mrs. Green." She took her by the hand and gave it a firm shake. "It's back to basics, and we couldn't be more pleased to have you here!" The principal gave her a nod and left her alone in her library. Maggie turned around, swallowed hard, and took it all in. She remembered her old nameplate and was shocked they'd kept it all these years. The vase of beautiful flowers lent a subtle floral fragrance to the room, and the note card was signed from the entire school staff. She walked around and sat at her desk and allowed her hands to touch the wood as if she was smoothing out the wrinkles on a clean white sheet. The corners were worn, rounded and dinged. The pulls on the drawers were also tarnished and aged—a sign that this old wooden desk was the true librarian in the room. Her supply inventory included sharpened pencils and large pink erasers. Their smell alone teased her nose and reminded her of her school days. A ruler and tape roll was tucked into the top middle drawer, and a large box of paperclips was neatly stowed beside them. A fresh, unopened ream of white paper was ready for a task along with a pot of glue. A soft bristle paintbrush sat near the glue pot, ready for someone to restore a book that had been damaged. The card catalog was to her left and made it easy for her to access the wide variety of books her library offered. She leaned back in her chair, and once again, she caught herself smiling. *Well*, she thought, *the bell will be ringing shortly. I best git ready.*

The sound of children's laughter began to fill the halls. The louder it became, the sooner school would start. Then the butterflies in Mrs. Green's tummy would take flight! The small window in the library door framed lots of tiny faces as the children got on tiptoe to peek inside. Mrs. Green tried not to pay attention, but it was hard not to join in on the fun. The bell rang, and the day began. The first visitors to the library were the third-graders. Their teacher brought them in to say hello and to talk about the proper way to check out books. When asked about her thoughts on the proper way to borrow library books, Mrs. Green answered with an eager response, "First of all, boys and girls, the library is a very special place. All of the books that you can see on these shelves should be treated with tender loving care. A good student never throws a book. A good student never leaves a book outside in the rain. A good student remembers to return the borrowed book on time because ..." She stopped to check that she had their full attention." Because someone else will want to read it too. A good student asks questions if they don't understand something in the book they're reading, and a good student never loans the book to a horse to read." Mrs. Green paused and waited to hear the reaction to her silly statement.

One student said, "Hey, wait a minute. A horse can't read!"

Everyone started to laugh, so Mrs. Green knew they were paying attention to her words.

"Are you sure?" said their new librarian with a happy smile. "Well, you are right. But my neighbor's horse, Wildfire, is pretty smart." She walked around the group with her hands behind her back. "I have an idea," she said. "If you were a horse, what book would you want to read?"

Hands went up in a hurry. One young lady said, "*Black Beauty*! Momma is reading it out loud at home."

Another said, "*Charlotte's Web*. There are lots of farm animals in that story."

"Those are wonderful stories, and we have them here for you to read too! Does everyone know how to use the card catalog?" Everyone nodded yes. "Excellent. Does anyone here have a question?" Mrs. Green looked around at all the fresh faces.

One girl replied, "What kind of stories do you like to read Mrs. Green?"

She put two fingers up to her mouth, thought about it a moment, and then said, "Well, dear, I love old English novels. Jane Austen. Elizabeth Gaskill. Stories about people and families from a long time ago."

"Yes, Mrs. Green," added their teacher, "I love Jane Austen too. The people in her books warm my heart." Then she changed the subject. "Well, class, let's thank Mrs. Green for her time this morning and get back to our classroom. We have a busy day ahead."

Everyone said their thanks, waved goodbye, and left the library.

To Mrs. Green's surprise, this was just the beginning of every class stopping in for the same introduction and lesson. She beamed with every greeting and sparkled with every answer. Mrs. Green was at her very best and couldn't have been any happier. The last class was Molly's. When she filed in and took her seat, she was grinning from ear to ear with her posture so straight and her hands folded so properly that Mrs. Green had to laugh to herself. *That Molly. I am so proud.*

She went through the same discussion, taking questions and giving answers. Molly, for the most part, sat quietly and listened. When the introduction was over, Molly walked up to Mrs. Green and said, "Momma said I may walk home with you after school today. Would that be okay?"

"Oh, yes!" responded Mrs. Green, "That would be lovely." She took Molly aside and politely whispered in her ear, "Remember to call me Mrs. Green when we are at school. Okay, dear?" Her eyes were so kind.

"Yes, Mrs. Green. Momma already reminded me." The two smiled and waved. "See ya out in front, Molly."

"Okay, Mrs. Green." And she was giggling as she walked out of the library.

Large puffy clouds filled the afternoon sky. A seasonable chill kissed the cheeks of every student as they left school for the day, and one could smell the first snow of winter in the wind. Maggie and Molly walked home together, each one carrying a book and a lunch pail. Wildfire caught sight of them as they rounded the bend and galloped over to the fence line to say hello. Molly had an extra apple, which she gave to Wildfire. They spent the afternoon doing chores. Maggie Mae now had a few chickens of her own and two goats (which she called eating machines) in the side pasture next to Wildfire's grazing field. Molly helped her in the barn for a little while; however, it was getting darker sooner nowadays, and she had chores of her own at home.

"I best get going, Maggie. Momma said it is my turn to clean out the chicken coop, and I want to get it done before it gets too cold." Molly was so matter-of-fact that it still tickled Maggie to see her act so maturely.

"That's fine, dear. Be off with yourself, and I'll see you at school tomorrow. Don't forget to do your homework and practice your spelling words." She was already sounding like a teacher. "I have a special book in the library for you, and some of this week's spelling words are in the book." Maggie had Molly hooked now!

"A new book? Tell me more."

Maggie smiled to herself, realizing how she was reviving her clever educational skills quickly.

"Well," said Maggie as she closed the barn door behind them and headed back toward the freshly painted house, "it's called *Little House in the Big Woods*, and it is written by a woman who lived during the mid-1800s. She tells the story of how she and her family traveled across the country in a covered wagon. Her name is Laura Ingalls Wilder, and the story is based on her life as a little girl. In fact, I think you are about the same age she is in the book. I think you will like it very much." Maggie stopped a moment and handed Molly her homework and lunch pail. "I have two copies on the shelf in the library. Shall I reserve a copy for you to borrow?" She looked every bit the librarian she was, even down to her formal English and her silly accent.

"Oh, yes," responded Molly with the same exaggerated flair in her voice. "That would be simply delightful!"

The two giggled as Molly entered the pasture where Wildfire stood and waited.

"See ya tomorrow, Maggie Mae," hollered Molly as she began to walk home. "Hey, Maggie, watch this!" Molly grabbed Wildfire's mane and threw her right leg up and over the back of the filly. Then she was sitting on Wildfire and was using the mane as the reigns. Molly clicked her tongue the way Becky had shown her, and the horse began to trot home.

"Oh! Be careful, Molly dear." Maggie sounded concerned. "She is still young! I think you should wait until she's a little older before you ride her, and she really should have the proper reins and a bit in her mouth." Molly couldn't hear what Maggie Mae was saying and rode the young pony all the way home.

Maggie watched and waited to be sure she got home safely, and she made a mental note about speaking to William tomorrow and getting his opinion about Molly riding a pony that wasn't yet three.

"Good idea," she said to the goats that stood chewing and staring at her. "Good idea, indeed."

The clouds were thicker now. In fact, Maggie could smell the bite of snow in the changing air. She grasped her collar and cinched it up tightly to her neck.

A truck pulled up into her driveway, and she was pleased to see Samuel step out and onto the drive.

"Howdy, Maggie. Thought I'd check in and see if ya need any help gettin' the house ready for the snow." He grabbed his collar as well and added a lil' *burrr* to his words.

"I can smell it too, Samuel, but I think everything is up for the winter." She looked around and pointed out the shelter for the goats, Abner and Daisy, and then showed him the special door that the chickens used to put themselves away at night.

"Well then," said Samuel, "you are in good shape. Once we get a few feet on the ground, I'll bring Fiona over, and we'll take a spin in the sleigh." He couldn't hide his excitement any longer and admitted that he was also looking forward to gettin' the old sleigh out of the barn.

A bigger wind caught them both off guard and sent Samuel's hat off his head and onto the ground.

"Oh, come in to the house. It's gettin' a might blustery out here." So Maggie and Samuel headed into the house at once.

"Oh, I can't say that I blame ya," said Maggie as she took off her coat and scarf. "I am excited too! In fact, I was looking through some old papers the other night, and I came across the actual bill of sale for the sleigh." She led Samuel over to the roll top desk, slid the polished top up, and handed him the receipt to read.

"See there." She was pointing to the handwriting. "That's all done in quill pen. The signature is my grandfather's. I wonder if my great-granddad went for a ride on the sleigh." She was looking up at Samuel with an expression of wonder. "Wouldn't that have been something? Look here." And she pulled out a drawer that hadn't been used much in the last sixty years." I guess they saved all their receipts, because this drawer is full of them. I am gonna put on the kettle. Would you care for a cup of tea?" She stood at the kitchen door and waited for Samuel to answer.

"Oh, yes." He was absorbed in the old paperwork." That'd be fine."

Maggie was only gone a minute, and when she returned, she saw a look of astonishment on Samuel's face that wasn't there when she left a moment before. He was sitting down and had a bill of sale in his hand dated 1908. The paper was stained a light coffee brown, and the typeset was very clear and distinctive.

"My father had a receipt like this one too," he said as he looked up at Maggie. "Do you know what this is a receipt for, Maggie?"

She walked around behind where he sat and looked over his shoulder and down at the paper in his hand. "This is an original bill of sale for a Model T. Look here." He pointed to some numbers. "This shows the number of the car and when it came off the assembly line." He pointed to the last number in the bottom right corner. "And this is how much your father paid for the Model T." Samuel was beside himself. He stood up and walked into the middle of the room. He stopped, turned back around, and said, "He paid $825.00, and the car number is ten. It also says that the automobile was delivered in a crate." Maggie listened. She'd heard of a Model T. Who hadn't? But she'd never seen her father drive one. Not that she remembered!

"So what are you sayin', Samuel?"

He looked her square in the eye and said, "That's a mighty big barn out there, Mrs. Green. I wonder if Mr. White tucked the car away in the original crate and forgot about it."

By now, both of their eyes were as large as saucers! Maggie stood up, the dawning of his suggestion tickling the fancy of her imagination. They both looked in the direction of the barn, and in a flash they were out the door and running across the yard.

Neither one heard the teakettle screaming on the stove! Neither one remembered it was time for tea. It was almost pitch black outside. They opened the barn doors, waking up a clutch of sleeping chickens, but then they figured it would be best to start in the morning. "Well," said a disappointed Maggie Mae, "I am now working in the library at school. You'll have to come and look for it yourself. But do me a favor." He looked down at her as he caught his excited breath, "If ya find a Model T in here, wait until I git home from school to move or open it. I am just as excited as you are."

He agreed without question as they closed up the barn doors. Twilight was fading fast, and looming clouds that seemed stuffed with snow hung low to the ground.

"I am gonna have to take a rain check on that tea, Maggie. Janie's gonna be wondering where I am, and it looks like I'd better get home before the storm hits!" He added, "I hear your kettle singing, Mrs. G! Sounds like it's going to be the best pot of tea you've had all day." He gave her that smile and said, "I'll stop by tomorrow afternoon, and we'll look in the barn together. Thanks again!" he said as he rolled up the truck's windows. The temperatures had gotten even colder, and Maggie knew it was time to get inside, build a fire, and savor a pot of tea.

The evening was as typical as an evening should be. Maggie and Molly signaled goodnight, and Maggie's dinner was typical too.

Her mind was preoccupied with the possibility of a Model T stowed in the barn, and so she decided to do a little further digging through the gold mine in the desk. She took her seat but stopped when she remembered the journal. The fire was roaring nicely now, and there it was below Johnny's picture, next to the stack of their love letters. She changed her mind about the desk for now, and she grabbed the green journal instead.

She was feeling weary after her busy day at school and opted to sit in her favorite chair by the fire. Once tucked and cozy in the arms of the warmed chair, Maggie opened Johnny's journal and began to read.

September 1,

> *I met the prettiest girl today. She stopped my heart. Roy said she'd just gotten back from college, and she was now a teacher at the elementary school. When she speaks, I can't. When she smiles, I look like a fool. When she walks by, I am frozen in place. This is the one! I could feel God whisper her name in my ear after I got home. This is her ... the woman of my dreams! I will see her again, I know I will. Tomorrow is church. I will be there, and so will she. Bless you, Miss White ... my, Maggie Mae. Bless you.*

Maggie closed the book and held it to her chest. She remembered meeting him too. How tall and powerful he was as he stood there. How his sky blue eyes darted away from her if she tried to catch his gaze. The crooked charm of his nervous smile and deep golden tan of his skin also lingered in the back of her mind. She remembered him watching her as she mingled about her homecoming party and how he'd pass by her, breathing deeply as if trying to catch her fragrant air. She remembered it all. How could she forget!

Maggie teared up, and knowing how special it was to read his private thoughts about her, she let her tears humbly fall.

Maggie couldn't read anymore. She closed the precious journal and set it back on the mantle. This particular day had been phenomenal, and she was ready for bed. With her clothes picked out for the next day, Maggie stopped at her bedroom window and looked out onto the pasture. Clouds finally obscured her view, and she could no longer see the Fitzwilliam's' house. One could see the distant branches of trees whipping in the wind like the naked arms of a conductor leading an orchestra through a dramatic musical score. She rubbed her eyes and yawned. "Bet there's snow on the ground by morning." She looked around her room as if she'd lost something. "I need a kitten," she said aloud. "Something to snuggle with. I'll get one tomorrow." She climbed into bed. "I think I'll name it Snowball." And after she turned out the lights, the snow began to fall.

At dawn it looked like Pine Valley had become a Christmas card. The prediction of snow had come true, so everyone in the community had to stop and rethink their plans for the day. School was canceled, and so was the postal service. In short, it was a play day, and it was shaping up to be a play day to beat them all!

Samuel and Jane saddled up Fiona and started riding over to Maggie's. Molly and William made sure that Wildfire had her wool blanket securely cinched to her warm body, and Mary started a huge pot of vegetable soup.

Molly was the first visitor of Maggie's day. "Good morning, snow bunny!" shouted Molly from the back of the house. She'd traipsed across the white pasture in snowshoes, which was a cute sight to Maggie's eyes this morning.

She had spied her as she was crossing the frosty span and couldn't help but admire her sense of adventure. By the time Molly reached Maggie's, a kettle of water was set to boil. "Git in here!" responded Maggie with a bit of motherly irritation. "It's too cold out there right now. You do not want to catch your death." By now, Maggie was standing at the back door with her arms folded, trying to keep herself from the chill of the first winter snow. "Are you an Eskimo or somethin'? Git in this house right now!"

Molly walked into the house with a frozen smile. Her nose was pink. Her cheeks were pink too, but her heart was warm. "Good morning, snow bunny!" she repeated as she walked into the mudroom at the back of the house. Together they unstrapped the old snowshoes and hung up Molly's damp coat. The cold winter air was sure to fill the toasty home, so Maggie was quick to close the old door as Molly finally got inside.

They beelined for the kitchen and poured out a piping hot pot of cinnamon tea.

"Momma said you'd be standing at the kitchen window, looking out onto our winter wonderland. Could ya see me coming, Maggie? I mean, snow bunny." Molly's face was still frosted pink. "Do you see anything different about me, Maggie Mae? Ya may have to look closer."

Maggie brought the teapot to the kitchen table and sat down. She poured Molly her cup and then took a good long look at her. "Let me see," said Maggie, pushing a warm plate of shortbread toward Molly. "You still have pink cheeks and a pink nose. Is that a new scarf?" And then she smiled. Not just any smile but a humungous smile, "Oh, my goodness, Molly dear! You have lost a tooth! Isn't that wonderful!"

The two gals laughed and giggled the morning away, Molly biting her shortbread with the side of her teeth and Maggie handing her a napkin when the nibble began to dribble.

The clock struck eight, and there was a knock at the door. "I'll be right back dear. I think it may be Samuel. Remember the sleigh in the barn?" Maggie's eyebrows were arched up, her question testing Molly's memory. "We just may be taking a sleigh ride today."

When she opened the door, she discovered Pastor Smith. He, too, was on horseback, but he was pulling a road scraper. It was old-fashioned and worn, but it worked like a champion. "Mornin', Maggie. I'll be clearing the main roads today, and I thought I'd check and see if there is anything I can clear for ya."

"Good morning, Pastor. Please come in." He walked in but stayed by the front door. He didn't want the snow to melt off of his boots and onto the hardwood floor." If you could circle around in front of the barn and push the snow toward the side of the yard, I would be much obliged. May I get ya a cup of hot cinnamon tea? I could put it in an old mug you could take along."

"I must admit that sounds mighty nice, Maggie Mae, and may I say again how wonderful you look. It's like a miracle."

"That *little miracle* is in the kitchen having tea with me." She smiled and added, "Stay right there. I'll be back in a jiffy!"

As Pastor Smith patiently waited, his eyes wandered over the walls and by the furnishings in the living room. To him, it was as if he was seeing old friends again. Maggie's parents had a picture on one wall, and of course, there was a lovely oil painting of her grandparents too. He craned his neck around the corner and over to the fireplace, and it was there that he saw Johnny's portrait. His heart lightened, and a peaceful smile spread across his lips. When Maggie reentered the living room carrying the tea and a treat, she couldn't help but notice the kind respect on the pastor's face. "Yes, Pastor. That's my Johnny." She handed him the steaming mug and a tightly wrapped package of shortbread. He took the items and looked away from the picture and down into her softly aging eyes.

"I couldn't look at it for years," she admitted. "But now …" She paused as she looked down at her slippers and said, "I realize now that with God, all things are possible!"

He smiled and took a deep breath, intending to hold back his tears. "Yes, ma'am, you are right there." He cleared his throat of humble frogs and added, "Is this your famous shortbread? Well, that'll make all this plowing worth the work. Thank ya, Maggie. I'll get the mug back to ya later today. It's mighty kind of ya." He nodded his thanks again, and Maggie held the door open as he walked back out into the cold morning. He looked at the house and the land. "The hard work paid off. The ranch looks beautiful. I'd best get to work now." He took a sip of tea and held the bread up in one last motion of gratefulness. Maggie closed out the bitter cold again and called Molly to come and join her in the living room. She stoked the fire and suggested they watch as the pastor cleared the snow.

Pastor Smith was already in his saddle by the time Molly walked in to stand by the fire. He pulled the collar of his rain slicker up tightly around his neck and set his hat on his head again. He clicked his tongue a special way, and the mare began to walk forward slowly. He pushed down a special lever and an angled piece of iron lowered down to the ground. He looked back to make sure that the scraper wasn't too close to the snow, and then he clicked his tongue again. Now the mare picked up her speed and Pastor Smith signaled her to make a wide circle in front of the barn. The snow piled up in front of the scraper, which then pushed it all off to the side by the angle of the blade. The two gals looked at each other with silent awe. Pastor Smith knew what he was doing, and by the looks of it, he was having fun too. He made one more sweep by and then cleared the snow all the way out to the main road. He let a piercing whistle loose, waved his hat up and over the top of his head, and signaled goodbye. They both waved from the comfort of the picture window and watched as he headed to town.

All in all, it only took him about ten minutes and now they could get into the barn!

Maggie was dressed in two shakes of a lamb's tail! Molly strapped on her snowshoes, buttoned her coat, and met Maggie around at the front of the house. As the two ladies walked out into the new day, Samuel and Janie showed up on cue. "Good winter's morn, ladies," said Samuel, his clothes snugly tucked around his head and shoulders.

"Good morning to you two, too!" said Molly, proud of her use of all three homophones in one sentence.

"Are ya ready to get into that barn of yours, Mrs. G? I couldn't sleep a wink last night I was so excited!" Janie sat quietly. Her assessment of his night's sleep clearly differed from his.

They walked across the yard and stopped in front of the barn doors. "The pastor did a fine job, Mrs. G. It'll be right easy to get inside with all of the snow moved."

"Did you ask him to come and plow my yard, Samuel?" Maggie—or Mrs. G—had her hands on her hips, and her face looked mighty skeptical.

"Maybe," replied Samuel with the look of a kid not wanting to get in trouble for being sneaky.

"Looks like he hasn't lost his touch. Clean as a whistle." His observation was right! It would be easy to open the barn doors, and that was just what they did. A rusty old potbelly stove stood proudly in one corner of the historic barn. Samuel, not knowing how long they'd be in the barn, walked over to it and got a fire roaring in no time. Within minutes the chickens felt the warmth and began to nest by its sides.

"Where do we begin, and what are we looking for?" asked Molly, eagerly ignorant. "It's the model of a T? I haven't ever heard of that before."

Everyone chortled at her funny question, it was a good one. "Where do we begin?"

"Honestly, Samuel," stated Maggie, "I haven't worked in this barn since 1908, and I never saw a crate in any corner, and I don't recall anything being delivered."

"Don't mind my sayin' so," spoke Janie for the first time, "but wasn't that about the time you met Johnny? Couldn't there be a chance that while you were off gallivanting, your daddy could have had a crate delivered?" Janie didn't need to say another word. The seed in her words took root and sprouted before their very eyes.

Maggie sat on a bale of straw next to the fire. "Well, I suppose so, Janie. But why wouldn't he tell me, and why wouldn't I have seen it when I came out to the barn? I should think Momma would have said somethin'?" Maggie puzzled over a logical explanation until her puzzler was tired.

"Fact is we have a bill of sale, so it must be somewhere," said Samuel with a gentle nudge of inspiration. "It's huge in here. Why don't we just start looking around. Janie, you and Molly look behind the milking stall and Maggie and I will take a peek in the grain room." He sounded like Sherlock Holmes—all logical and reasonable. "I don't think they'd store it up in the loft, but I could be wrong. You do have a pulley system and tall doors on the south wall." Samuel's eyes were looking up and toward the dark, dusty hay loft in the barn. "Your father could have had it hoisted in, making it really out of sight."

Everyone broke into their appointed team and began to search. Nesting hens flew out from hiding, and a few burrowed mice escaped too. Janie let a startled whoop out at the sign of scurrying mice, and Samuel had to laugh, but quietly. "She hates mice!" And he smiled with a finger to his snickering lips to signal they be quiet.

The newly delivered alfalfa was stacked tightly against the walls, so it would be impossible to hide a crate there, and the whole room was empty for the most part.

The search teams met back in the middle of the barn, but none of them had discovered a crate.

"What's that sound, said Molly with her ear straining to make it out. "It sounds squeaky and far away."

Everyone stopped and quieted down. The most pitiful cries faintly emanated from the loft area.

"It sounds like kittens," said Janie. "kittens in a barn. That's nothing unusual."

"Why yes," said Maggie. "I've been feeding the mother for weeks now." She stopped again, tipping her head to the side in recollection. "Now that ya mention it, I haven't seen her in days. She usually has a saucer of milk at my back door. I hope nothing has happened to her. The babies must be about six weeks now. Oh, I'd better go up there and see what's going on." She looked at Samuel with pleading eyes, "Come with me, Samuel."

The two headed up the ladder at once, and the others followed thereafter.

They followed the tiny cries into the corner of the loft. There were old saddles and bridles hanging in the rafters along with milk cans and stools. Nail barrels and dusty ropes lined one corner of the wall, and off in the distant corner by the tall delivery doors were the crying kittens. Their mother was nowhere to be found. Molly slowly walked over to the fluffy creatures and bent down to catch them. There were only two, but they were scared, and rightly so. One was an orange marmalade, and the other was pure white.

"Well, my goodness, what do we have here?" said Maggie, picking up the white kitten and bringing it up to her neck to snuggle. "Just last night I said I needed a kitty, and here you are." Her words from the night before repeated in her mind. She opened her coat and placed the precious find inside the folds to keep it warm. She walked over to the corner and sat down on an old box.

"Maggie," asked Molly, "if Papa says its okay, may I keep this kitten? Look. It likes me!" The poor, frightened thing was shaking and hiding in Molly coat pocket like a prisoner caught and jailed.

"I don't see why not," said Maggie as she sat and petted her new family member.

"Come sit down by me, Molly dear. Maybe they'll calm down a little if they are close together again." Molly sat down, and the two kitten owners spent the next five minutes discussing names and collars and all sorts of feline folly. Janie just stood there with the biggest smirk on her face, while Samuel was still milling about the loft, not wanting to waste precious time.

"Ladies," said Janie with an air of authority, "what is it that you are sitting on? If ya ask me, that's a mighty big box, or is that a crate?"

Samuel spun around and walked over to where the gals were sitting. Maggie, lost in her love for the new kittens, said, "What was that again, Janie?" Her expression was framed with doe-eyed innocence. "What?"

"Stand up," advised Samuel with loud excitement, "Mrs. G, I think you've got it!"

The four of them just stood for a minute and let the gravity of their discovery sink in. If it hadn't been for the kittens, they may not have found the crate as quickly, and this box was definitely a crate!

Samuel scanned the side and top of the old wood. There was so much dust and debris he couldn't make out anything, and a parcel like this would definitely have a shipping label as well as manufacturing information branded into the wood. "Janie, there are some old rags in a box downstairs. Would you mind grabbing a few and bringing them to me?" Samuel was cautiously running his fingers over the surface of the crate as if he were a doctor looking for the patient's complaint.

Janie returned quickly with not only the rag, but a small bucket of water as well.

Samuel dunked the rags into the cold water and gently wiped off the top of the crate. He applied a little more pressure, and the grime came off quickly. It was still too dark to really see what they were trying to read, so Samuel looked at the pulley system on the upstairs loading doors, grabbed the rope that allowed the doors to open, and gave it a hard tug. They were stuck at first, but soon they gave way and groaned like an old man being awoken from a very long nap.

Streams of light poured through the opening for the first time in decades. Dust scattered and danced in the freedom. Spiders, caught by surprise, dashed for cover between the splintered dry walls, and the clear blueness of the sun brought to light the words on the crate. In large block letters were the words, "MODEL T."

Samuel kept cleaning the surface until it was clear enough to read everything written. MODEL T 1908 ASSEMBLY NO.10 — BLACK. Deliver to Henry White, No. 3 Apple Orchard Rd., Pine Valley, South Dakota."

Maggie stood quietly and read the branded words in the wood. "I had no idea." She looked up at Samuel struggling for words. "I don't know why he'd buy something like this and then leave it in the barn forgotten and unused."

Janie walked over to where she stood and put an arm around her shoulder. Gently, she said, "Look at the delivery date, Maggie." In the upper right hand corner, Maggie read, October

14, 1908. "Wasn't that right around the time that Johnny ..." Jane stopped talking and let the date awaken Maggie's memory.

"Yes, you are right, Janie. No wonder I didn't know about the car. That's about the same time my Johnny passed." You could see the dawning in her eyes. "My father had me to take care of and all the preparations for ..." Maggie's voice trailed off. Everyone stood silently.

Molly took Maggie by the hand, the soft cries of the kittens the only sound to be heard. Samuel walked over to the open doors and looked out into the snowy world.

"Ladies," he said, "let's think about the Model T later. It's a beautiful day. What do ya'll say to hitching up the sleigh and taking it for a ride around town?" He turned around and smiled.

Molly quickly broke the melancholy mood with her enthusiasm. "Oh yes, that would be splendid! Momma and Papa would love to meet my new kitten, and we could take them for a ride too. What do you say, Maggie Mae? Would that be okay?" Molly had that convincing face again, and the idea sounded like the perfect way to spend an afternoon.

Samuel closed the large doors with one good push and escorted the ladies down to the main floor of the barn. Fiona was patiently waiting beside the warm woodstove as they began to ready the sleigh. Samuel tightened her wool blanket, connected the sleigh's harness straps to her bridal, and signaled to Janie to open the barn's large doors. A brisk wind raced into the warm room. Chickens squawked in complaint, but there was no turning back.

Samuel led Fiona out into the groomed yard. As the sleigh moved out of the barn and into the sunlight, Samuel noticed that Fiona seemed excited too. She began to snort and stomp her front hooves as if saying, "Come on. Let's go!"

"All aboard!" hollered Samuel like the conductor on a train. "First stop ... the Fitzwilliam's!"

Maggie and Molly came aboard and took their seats. Maggie found some lap blankets and tucked them in place. Janie closed up the big barn doors and took her seat by her husband. Everyone looked at one another and grinned, the cold of the afternoon coloring their cheeks pink. Samuel clicked his tongue, and Fiona was off!

Old jingle bells still hung off the back of the sleigh, so with every bump and angle, the bells would jingle and jangle. Folks could hear them coming from every direction. Before they reached Molly's front door, Momma was already waving from the porch, and Papa was walking out of the barn, wondering who was here. "Well, I'll be!" said Papa with his own pink-cheeked smile. "Aren't you all a merry sight to see!"

The sleigh was beautiful! All the wood had been polished to a mirror luster. Every brass corner piece was clean and bright. The leather reins were freshly oiled, allowing the burgundy stain in the leather's grain to glow. All in all, the old sleigh was every bit the stylish ride it ever was.

"Papa!" shouted his darlin' Molly, "I have a kitty! Maggie has its sister. We found them when we were looking in the barn. May I keep him, Papa? *Please?* You could help me name him." Molly was off the sleigh and across the snowy yard at a racing pace.

"Oh, what a precious kitty," he replied as he lifted the wee ball of orange fluff up for Momma to see, "It looks like we have a new member of the family, Momma. What do you say?"

Momma smiled yes with her eyes and her lips. "What will we name the dear lil' one?" said Mary with her heart on her sleeve.

"Tiger!" suggested Molly as she ran up to her momma to give her a hug. "It's a boy, and it is orange just like a tiger. What do you think?"

She smiled down at her daughter and said, "Perfect. Tiger it is!"

Maggie held up her kitty and introduced it. "I'd like everyone to meet Snowball." Two black eyes stuck out of the middle of what actually looked like a snowball, so her name was also perfect.

"Fiona's all warmed up if ya two would like to go for a ride," said Samuel, offering a ride to William and Mary. "The ladies could probably stand a bit of warmth right about now, and ya'll could trade places."

That'd be grand," replied William, untying his apron and putting down his tool.

"Let me turn down the soup, and I'll get my coat," answered Mary as she slipped back into the house.

"I'll keep an eye on the kitchen for ya, Mary," said Maggie as she and the gals stepped off of the sleigh and walked into the warm house. "Whatever you are cookin' sure smells good!"

"Thank you, Maggie," said Mary as she dipped her hand into the pocket of her coat and grabbed her scarf. "It's a pot of soup and homemade bread. When we get back from our ride, perhaps we could all have lunch together?"

"I wouldn't want to put you out, Mary," said Janie with the kindest eyes.

"Well," replied Mary, "that was the plan all along. Now go and give it a good stir. The bread is resting, and the honey butter is whipped. We'll be right back and have lunch. Molly, show Jane where the tea is." She kissed her on the forehead and walked out the door.

The day couldn't have been better. The sky had cleared of the ominous clouds, and now Pine Valley was as pristine as a frosted cake. Tall pine boughs hung heavy with crumbling pockets of snow. Creek beds seemed to have come to life with a small trickle of fresh water, and red barns seemed to be decorated for the holidays, their bright, cheerful color framed by the heavenly plop of white.

The trio laughed and smiled and waved as the village of residents returned their joyful greetings. Back roads became a whole new world. Familiar vistas seemed changed by the layer of fresh powder, the sun kissing each unique flake as if they were diamonds scattered by fairies. Folks seemed enchanted. The sudden change in the weather had sparked a reminiscent quality in their actions, and joy was in the air. When the sleigh-riders finally returned to the apple farm, Wildfire was prancing around in all her excited glory too. They unhitched Fiona from the sleigh and put her and Wildfire into the main barn. William stocked his potbelly stove in the barn, threw in a large flake of alfalfa and a handful of apples, and lovingly swatted them both on the rump. He closed up the barn and joined those getting the house ready for lunch.

"Oh, it smells like heaven, Mary. Did ya make that honey butter too?" William was practically drooling as he sat down to join the table.

"You've never tasted anything as good as my Mary's honey butter, Maggie Mae." He took a big dip out of the crock, plopped it onto his bread plate, and then noticed that everyone was holding hands around the table. Embarrassed by his grumbling tummy, he put his knife down and joined the prayerful circle.

"Heavenly Father," began Maggie with her head bowed in respect, "we thank you for this glorious day and this lovely meal. We appreciate all of the new wonders you have awakened our eyes to, and we are grateful for your guidance, in Jesus' name, amen." Maggie finished the prayer, and everyone else at the table echoed amen. Mary served the soup, while William passed the loaf of bread. Molly was already licking the honey butter from her fingers, but no one minded. Hot tea steamed from mugs, and the special snow day luncheon began.

The conversation never sagged. Maggie asked William if he'd seen Molly on Wildfire's back, and he admitted he had.

"She is a fearless child, William, but please remind her that the pony shouldn't be ridden until it is three years old and it is best to train the horse with a saddle and bridle before anyone rides her." She sounded firm, not angry. "I saw some old saddles in my barn, and with the way you restored the saddle you two used in my apple butter display, I am sure you'll be able to fix the old one right up!" She was smiling as she finished her speech. "Remember, we need to help Molly learn to ride the filly properly. She must never grab the mane to ride. It could hurt the young horse and cause her to go sour. Do you follow me?"

William agreed as he stuffed another bite of honey-buttered bread into his mouth. Molly *didn't* hear a word Mrs. Green said. She was too busy with Tiger.

Lunch ended, and Mrs. Green prepared herself to go home. "I am pretty sure Snowball wants to venture from my warm pocket and stretch her tiny legs. Besides, she'll need to eat and drink a little, and I must set up her potty box." She stood up and excused herself from the table.

"Would ya like me to take you home, Maggie?" Samuel offered as he swallowed a mouthful of soup.

"Oh no, Samuel, I think I'll walk. I love the way the snow crunches when I step on it. Please stop by later though. I'd like to discuss the crate in the barn."

Samuel recognized Maggie's clever way of not explaining what they'd found earlier in the day, so she said her goodbyes and headed out across the winter field. She could see a small, thin ribbon of smoke rising from her chimney, and she knew it was time to stoke the fire again.

Molly and Jane helped Mary clear away the lunch dishes as the men went back out into the barn and rehitched Fiona to the sleigh. Wildfire was calm and friendly, so William grabbed a brush and gave her a good brushing as he spoke to Samuel. "Maggie had a good point at the table. I am going to have a talk with Molly about just jumping on Wildfire and grabbin' her mane like they're the reins. We don't need Maggie's horse gettin' hurt." William was right in discussing the conversation from lunch. The pony was Mrs. Green's after all. "I saw the saddles Mrs. G. was talkin' about. I'll swing one by to ya later. Sound good?" William took Samuel up on his offer, and the beginning of a good friendship was sealed with a handshake.

Samuel and Janie waved goodbye as the sleigh began its journey back to Maggie's house. The snow had melted during the warmth of the afternoon sun, and with no clouds on the horizon, it was fair to assume that the next day would be business as usual.

The Fitzwilliam's stood on the front porch and waved goodbye. Even Tiger had his paw in the action as Molly held him up to wave, though he'd rather have stayed in the warm, dark pocket of her sweater.

Momma set up Tiger's own place on the back porch and had Molly put him down for a while to drink, eat, and rest. Molly just lay by her kitty and watched him play in his new home. He was a little frightened at first, but soon he got used to the water, food, and smells. Momma check on her two little ones only to find that they had both fallen asleep in each other's arms—Molly curled up in the folds of her soft sweater and her kitty in the crook of her protective arm.

The afternoon quickly became a fond memory as the sun began to soften. Samuel and Janie stowed the sleigh back in Maggie's barn, grabbed a saddle and bridle from the loft, and walked over to Maggie's house. They knocked on the front door, and she answered shortly thereafter. "Oh, lovely," said Maggie with the pleasant sound of familiar friendship. "Please come in." She held the door open as the two entered the home. She offered them tea, and since they could already smell the cozy aroma, they said yes.

"Janie," said Maggie as she poured out some tea. "I thought about what you said in the barn today—you know, about the date on the crate. And you were right. It was delivered about a week after he passed, so it's no surprise that I didn't know about the Model T." Maggie seemed fine as she relayed her story, so Jane just listened. "I went through the rest of my father's receipts after lunch today, and this is what I found." She handed an unopened letter to Jane. "The handwriting is my father's. It's addressed to Johnny and me. I've never seen it before today." Maggie looked at Jane, and Jane could read her mind.

"Would you like me to read it, Maggie?" Her whole being was kind and gentle. Maggie nodded yes and led them both to a seat on the sofa.

"I am a little nervous," admitted Maggie as she sat wringing her hands. "My father and mother had their hands full caring for me, so I can't imagine what was going through their minds knowing a Model T was in the barn. I could be wrong, ya know ... but I could be right." Maggie took a deep breath. "Okay, Janie. What does it say?"

Jane took a minute to carefully look at the yellowed envelope. She asked for Samuel's pocket knife and opened the top of the paper with extreme care. She pulled out the fine stationery and read the words aloud.

October 16, 1908

> *Congratulations, Mr. and Mrs. Green! We wish you both the best of everything. Now that the apple orchard and farm are yours ... our gift to you both is a Model T. We know it will come in handy when it is harvest time. We love you dearly.*

Mom and Dad

Jane looked up from the letter and sat quietly. Samuel set his tea down, and they both waited for Maggie's reaction. "I didn't know the farm was ours too! I thought Mac had hired Johnny and me to work the place. I don't really remember, and now the car makes sense! Why, it would have been a great way to take the harvest to market." Maggie stood up and walked over to Johnny's picture. She lifted up her hand and touched the canvas as if tapping into another realm,

"Oh, Johnny, I had no idea."Her tone was dark and regretful. "I am so sorry I let our dream go. I remember you told me about some good news about the farm, but I urged you to go back and get the last bushel of apples you'd left behind. I warned you that they'd freeze if they were left out overnight!" She stopped and wrung her hands again. "Why didn't I just listen to you and not be so pushy?" She began to weep. "Oh, honey, I am such a fool!"

Janie stepped in and corrected her declaration. "You are no fool, Maggie. You were following your business instincts. You had no idea about the tree or the farm or the Model T. Those details were still unknown to you. You can't blame anyone or anything for what happened to you and your husband." Her tone was compassionate but firm!

"Tragic—that's what this is, Mrs. G!" added Samuel, defending her honor. "No one blames you. No one ever could! The McGregor's didn't lose the farm. They kept it. You weren't in any state to work it. Heavens! I'll wager they didn't even know that you hadn't been told about the deed. And the Model T ... well, Mrs. G, it's still yours, and you should be proud to use it. Why not drive it to school? It's a classic car now." He was smiling, though his effort to comfort her was a bit awkward.

Janie cut in and repeated, "You are no fool, Maggie Mae. You are a treasured member of our community, and you've punished yourself long enough by staying locked up in a house for a crime you couldn't and wouldn't commit! Now that's enough of that monkey business! Samuel and I won't hear another word spoken about blame. You, Mrs. G ..." She leaned in as if sharing a secret between friends. "You are the proud owner of a Model T, antique or not!" She flashed Samuel a look and continued, "We think you should do what makes you happy. When and if you are ready to get it out of the loft, let us know, and we'll arrange it. Otherwise, it can stay right where it is for as long as you wish." Janie sounded more like Maggie's mother than her friend, but Maggie needed those firm words to trigger her sense of self-forgiveness and acceptance.

She took Janie by the hand and said, "Yes, dear, you are right, and when did you become so much like my mother? For a moment there, I could have sworn it was her!"

The two ladies laughed with tear-rimmed eyes, but Jane was secretly glad that the strength of her words had struck the right chord in Maggie Mae's heart.

The couple finished up their tea, and then they informed Maggie about the saddle and bridle and the plan to drop it off with William. Samuel relayed the plan to get Molly on Wildfire the right way. Mrs. Green was relieved. "Oh, thank you, Samuel. I was hoping he'd heard my words. It'll be fun teaching the youngster to ride properly. Ya know ... there was a time when I was pretty good on horseback myself, though I haven't ridden in years and years."

"Well, Maggie," said Samuel with the look of an old Scot, "that is somethin' we shall have to remedy." He swooshed down from his six-foot-four stance and kissed her on the cheek. "Janie, I'm afraid it's gettin' dark. We'd best get a move on before its pitch dark. We are still riding Fiona, ya know."

Maggie hugged her friends with the arms of one who loves greatly. "It's been a glorious day, you two. Thanks for everything you have done!" She opened the door and walked out with them into the crisp, cold air. She wrapped her arms about herself and hollered, "Goodbye."Samuel and Jane climbed up onto Fiona, waved again, and then headed back to William's with the saddle and bridle.

Maggie returned to the nurturing comfort of her home. As usual, she stoked the fire and made her dinner. By the time she was done with washing the dishes, Molly was signaling goodnight, and of course, Maggie was doing the same.

The tiniest cry came from the back porch, and she remembered to go and see how her Snowball was doing. When she opened the door, there she was. Maggie bent over and picked up the purring ball of fluff. It was no bigger than a softball, and it was all eyes, pink nose, and tongue, "Well, I'd almost forgotten about you." She brought the kitten up to her face and gave it a little kiss. "I think you are a special gift from God. Yes, I do, my tiny Model C. Yes, I do." She sounded as if she was talking to a newborn baby instead of a cat. "You are a clever kitten, leading us to the Model T. Yes, you are!" The evening was all snuggles and cuddles. Snowball ended up sleeping with Maggie, and she slept with her from then on. Maggie and Snow-Snow, as she nicknamed her later, became the best of friends. When she was old enough, Maggie allowed Snow-Snow to follow her all over the farm. In fact, wherever you found Maggie Mae working outside, Snow-Snow was sure to follow.

The next few days slipped from the calendar like someone had ripped the pages away. Before they knew it, it was two weeks to Thanksgiving, and the whole town was agog.

It wasn't a surprise that Thanksgiving was the town's favorite. After all, there was a parade, a pumpkin pie contest, and of course, recounting the Pilgrims' history at school. Maggie was particularly excited this year because she was in charge of the school's play production. A handful of mothers had volunteered to sew and repair the used costumes, and their husbands took it upon themselves to repaint the old stage and spruce up the props. Maggie assigned the character parts to the children who wanted to act in the play, and of course, Molly and Becky were on the list. Myles Standish was a noted person on the *Mayflower*, and that part went to Tommy. Billy was cast as Samoset. Chief Massasoit went to Becky, and Squanto went to Michael. Since Molly had such a strong reading voice, she was cast as the narrator. A handful of kids played the pilgrims on board the *Mayflower*. The ship itself was a cardboard cutout manned by three hidden children who knelt behind it and rocked it so that it looked as if it were sailing on the ocean. They practiced every day after school for a week. The history of the voyage was what the children focused on retelling and how the Americans were here because of the settlers' bravery in 1620.

On show day all of the families were present and accounted for. As the audience took their seats, Mrs. Green kept a firm handle on her troop of actors and stagehands. When everyone took their places and was ready to begin the production, she stepped out onto the stage and welcomed them. "Good afternoon, ladies and gentlemen. Welcome to Pine Valley's annual Thanksgiving pageant. We shall be learning about a ship called the *Mayflower* and the people who journeyed aboard her and came to the new world. We shall learn about their trials and tribulations before and after the voyage in addition to learning about the very first Thanksgiving meal." She was doing such a great job. She didn't miss a word she'd memorized. "So it is without further ado, I present to the citizens of Pine Valley ... *The Voyage to Freedom.*" The audience applauded loudly as Mrs. Green bowed and left the stage.

A moment later you could hear the sound of ocean waves and the clap of wind filling the sails. Slowly and with great dramatic effect, the heavy blue curtains parted, and people could see the *Mayflower* rocking and rolling on the turbulent waves of the sea. Myles Standish is at the helm of the ship with his hands over his eyes as if blocking the wind and straining to see land. Then he began to speak. "We finally set sail. We travel alone. Our sister ship was sabotaged by a faithless crew, and so we depart a month later than planned from Plymouth, England." Tommy was excellent! Now it was Molly's turn, and she had a very long speech. "It is mid-September in the year of our Lord 1620.There are 102 people on board the *Mayflower*, and the living conditions are very cramped. Voyagers are at sea for sixty-six days and nights. Many people are sick and want to turn back and go home. Their ship suffers damage and begins to take on water. After some quick thinking, the damaged main beam is fixed, and they continued on. They arrived at the beginning of a harsh winter." Molly paused the narration and walked over to the next place on stage. Mrs. Green looked at her and nodded for her to continue. "A child is born!" Someone from backstage made the sound of a crying baby. "The very first child born to Pilgrims in the new world is Peregrine White. His parents, William and Susanna, are very happy! Soon the people on board are getting tired, but the ship couldn't land at its original place, so it is decided to anchor in an area later known as Cape Cod. And it is there that they wrote the Mayflower Compact. On November 21, the compact formed laws for everyone to follow. By signing it, the majority of people agreed to a harmonious lifestyle. After exploring the shoreline of the New World, they settled and began to build a common house. The winter was so harsh that many people died." Molly paused and allowed the sadness to impress the audience. Then she began again, "On March 16, 1621, an Indian named Samoset walked into the village of Pilgrims and said hello in English. They were so surprised. What do you think they talked about? Let's take a listen." Molly stopped and turned her attention to center stage, and Michael came out dressed like the Indian Samoset. "Hello. I am Samoset." He held up his hand. Then he said, "I can speak a little English, and I come in peace. I will bring another Indian chief later, and you will like him too."

A minute later Becky walked on stage, and she was dressed up as Massasoit. The headdress she was wearing was beautiful, and she looked like the father of the tribe. "Greetings, I am Chief Massasoit. Let's be friends. I will help you plant food and survive in our wilderness." Becky had disguised her voice to sound deeper, but she still giggled a little. "We are nervous about the white man coming to our world, so we would like to sign a treaty to show good faith in all men."

Now Molly's narration started again. "On July 2, the Pilgrims, led by Edward Winslow, create a trade agreement with Massasoit and Squanto. They are welcomed to the Indian village, and they share a meal and gifts. Later, Myles Standish ..." Then Tommy walked out onto the stage dressed like a pilgrim. He walked up to Massasoit, and they shook hands. "Myles Standish led another group of Pilgrims back to the Indian village where they continued to uphold the friendly trade agreement. In October 1621, the fifty-three surviving Pilgrims shared a feat with ninety of Massasoit's men. They serve waterfowl, turkey, fish, and venison. Today we think of that meal as the first Thanksgiving." Now all of the actors sat down around the large table on the stage.

It was set with pretend foods of all kind. Myles and Massasoit held up their glasses and said, "Happy Thanksgiving," to each other, and then they turned to the audience and said the same thing, "Happy Thanksgiving!"

In that instant, the room broke out with the same words. Everyone stood and shook hands with their friends and said, "Happy Thanksgiving!"

The play soon ended. Mrs. Green couldn't have been more proud of her kids. The parents were also very pleased with the performance, and they made sure to compliment her on her outstanding production. "I'd like to thank everyone for coming." She stood in the center of the stage as everyone milled about. "Tomorrow is the parade and pie contest. Festivities begin at ten o'clock in the morning." The noise level was a happy roar, and she knew they could hear her. "We meet in the church parking lot at nine in the morning. Be sure to drop off all pumpkin pie entries at the great hall. The doors will be open at nine as well." She was still shaking hands. "Have a wonderful evening, folks, and we'll see you bright and early tomorrow."

It took a little while to clear out the school auditorium, but Maggie was home and resting by seven in the evening. She'd already said goodnight to Molly, and she was done preparing for the next day. Since she was still a bit wound up from the day's play, she decided to read a little more of Johnny's journal. She sat in her usual chair and opened to where she'd left off. The next entry was all about apple trees and how McGregor and he had talked about the proper way to plant an orchard. The next entry was about how to bring water to the orchard and store it through the summer. Finally, she noticed some doodles he jotted down. At first Maggie thought he was drawing waterfalls, but when she read the scribbling below each picture, she realized he was drawing her hair and the way it fell down her back.

"It's like the sun has kissed her hair. The way it cascades over her shoulders and down her lovely back reminds me of the falls on Winter Mountain." Maggie stopped and marked her place in the journal. She looked up and closed her eyes. How could she possibly endure all of these secrets coming to light now? How?

Snowball showed up just in the nick of time. She jumped up onto Maggie's lap and curled into a purring ball of fluffy love. Maggie's hand naturally reached for the kitty and for the change of thought that the kitty brought.

"Well," she said aloud to Snow-Snow, "it's been a long day. We should go to bed. Daylight will be here before you know it, and we have a lot to do tomorrow." She slowly stood, forcing her pal to jump down and stretch. They walked together, Maggie shuffling in her slippers and Snowball scratching her back on every piece of furniture she passed.

It was silent. Not a breeze or purr or creaking bone in the old house. Maggie lay tucked in and staring at the ceiling. Moonbeams shone through the white lace panels over her windows, but the light was so soft that it really didn't disturb her. She turned over and over and over again. She was restless, but why? She recalled being the same way after the plays she acted in when she was younger, but this was different. There wasn't a way she could identify this restlessness. She just knew something was up, and what that something was would stay a mystery until the time was right.

Again, she said her prayers, and then she finally fell asleep. Outside on the pasture, Wildfire roamed. It seemed she was anxious too. Though the filly was quiet enough not to cause alarm, she was trotting along the fence line and snorting at the shadows. After a while she seemed to relax; however, one snap or crack of wind in the trees seemed to alert her protective instincts, and then she was back on the pasture again. Something was up on the meadow of Winter Mountain, and it was about to thunder!

"Rise and shine and sing out your glory-glory! Rise and shine and sing out your glory-glory! Rise and shine and sing out glory-glory, children of the Lord!" The parking lot of the church was overflowing with voices raised in song that Saturday morning. The great hall was opened and almost filled with pumpkin pies by the time Maggie Mae and the Fitzwilliam's arrived. As before, William dropped the ladies at the front door and then parked the truck. The only difference this time was whose pie was entered in the contest. Now that Maggie was on the Ladies Church Council, she declined entering a pie and instead volunteered to judge the entries. Mary had made a pie, and Maggie simply had to comment on the lovely aroma as Molly carefully carried it into the hall.

"Some of the spices in your pie are new to my nose, Mary. Perhaps after the contest, you could tell me you're secret because your pie smells scrumptious!" Mary promised she'd write the ingredients down as they walked through the fragrant hall. There had to be fifty pies, and to tell the truth, Mary had her doubts.

The staging line was beginning to take form as Maggie and Pastor Smith walked out of the hall and into the rear parking area of the church. One volunteer was busy checking off the entries. Another was passing out their call numbers so that the parade announcer could check each one off as they passed down the street. Samuel was leading the last-minute entries to a table where volunteers could take their information down. Altogether the assembly of participants went smoothly and within the hour, the parade was ready to go.

"A model T would sure be a nice addition to our parade, Mrs. G." Samuel was smiling and looking up into the sky as if those weren't his words. "I can just see it now ... all polished and—"

"Now, Samuel," commented Jane with the sound of a parent correcting a child, "please take this list to the announcer. He's waiting for you." Samuel nodded and walked away with a grin.

"Don't you worry a bit, Maggie. The parade has plenty of entries." Jane's statement was meant to be protective and gentle. "But he does have a point!" The ladies smiled brightly at each other. Janie kissed Maggie on the cheek and promised they would meet up later as the rest of the parade organizers began to stroll downtown.

Though Main Street was only a short ways away, you could hear the murmur of people standing on the curb, waiting for the festivities to begin. The smell of hot chocolate was in the air. Burn barrels had been set up along the parade route and each barrel was loaded up and cracking away with a warming fire.

Maggie Mae and Pastor Smith entered the crowd, and a small round of applause rose from the citizens of Pine Valley as the two took their seats of honor in the announcers' booth. The pastor took out his pocket watch and checked the time. Seeing that it was ten o'clock, he nodded to the master of ceremonies and then rang the bell.

Somewhere, a dog barked, and a rooster crowed. The horses pulling wagons were rearing to go, and the band was keeping warm air flowing through the mouthpieces of their brass instruments. The crowd hushed, and then the announcer began. He held a large megaphone up to his mouth and said, "Good morning, citizens of Pine Valley. Welcome to our annual Thanksgiving parade!" The people clapped and cheered. Somewhere off in the distance, that rooster crowed again. The pastor said, "Let the parade begin!" This time he rang the town bell with three distinct clangs, and you could hear the snap of the reins and movement of the wagon wheels on the cobbles of the old street. A moment later the town's historic horse-drawn fire wagon rounded the corner and headed downtown. Two men sat on the wagon dressed in fireman's costumes, and between them sat their dog. The old fire engine was a real treasure. It stopped in the middle of the street and in front of the grandstand, and a group of local men jumped up and took their places to demonstrate how the old pump engine worked. On the count of three, a whistle blew, and the hose came alive! As the men rocked the old engine's wooden arms up and down, the water spewed forth with enough pressure to cross the road and hit the middle of the field. Everyone clapped as they commented on how nicely the equipment had been preserved. Just as quickly as the men came out, they stowed the hose away, and the parade continued. Next was the Ladies Library Committee. They were all walking and wearing the fanciest hats you'd ever seen. They carried a sign high up in the air, and the names of all the new books in the library appeared on it. Molly got excited when she saw the book titled *Little House in the Big Woods* because she remembered what Maggie had told her about Laura Ingalls Wilder. Everyone clapped as the ladies gracefully passed, especially their husbands. Next in line was the hardware and grocery store float. They had decorated their entry to look old-fashioned and homey. There were bushels of apples and stalks of corn, barrels of nails and planks of pine. Old cans of paint and tools were hanging from the edge of an old farm table, and a butter churn sat on the table with a bunch of flowers tucked next to the paddle arm. Janie and Samuel drove the truck that pulled this entry, and they were happily waving from their window seats. Next, some mountain men were riding on horseback. Their buckskin clothes were sewn with thick sinew, rabbit pelts, and beads. Across their backs they carried black powder rifles and knapsacks. Tucked at their waists, they carried antler-handled knives they'd stowed tightly inside their leather belts. Many said that some of the costumes were more than one hundred years old, and from the looks of them, the rumor was true.

The feed store came next. Aboard its clapboard rig were crates of squawking hens and honking geese. A lamb and a year-old calf were tied to the back and walking along. As this float was led through the crowd, it littered the street with bits of straw and hay. No one seemed to mind though. That was just part of the country lifestyle. When Molly saw the lamb, she tugged at her Papa's side and whispered into his ear. When she pulled back to see if he'd heard her request, Papa had that face, again, and he patted her on the head with a smile and nodded yes.

When the parade seemed to be winding up, and everyone was looking to see what was next, a young man rounded the corner, blew a shiny brass whistle that hung from a chain around his neck, and began to march in stiff formation toward the patient crowd. He was dressed in a magnificent uniform of royal blue and white. He wore a tall hat of white too, and across the brim was a wide band of blue and gold. In the center of the band was a brass oval medallion and stamped into the middle was an eagle, its wings spread open wide as if it were about to take flight. He held a long baton out in front of himself, and he used the baton to instruct the band that followed behind. He turned around and faced them as they walked around the corner and onto the street. When the entire group was in place, he blew the whistle three times, and the drums rolled. The cymbals crashed together with enough force to make you jump, and then they began to march as they played "It's a Grand Old Flag," composed by George M. Cohan. The music filled the air with more than sound. It filled the hearts and souls of all those who attended that morning. It inspired a choir of voices to join in and sing along. Children who held American flags waved them high up into the sky. The melody was infectious and patriotic. You couldn't help but sing along. "You're a grand old flag. You're a high-flying flag ... and forever in peace may you wave. You're the emblem of the land I love. The home of the free and the brave. Every heart beats true 'neath the red, white, and blue, where there's never a boast or brag. But should auld acquaintance be forgot, keep your eye on the grand old flag."

There wasn't a dry eye on the street. Everyone was singing and beside themselves with joy. The band kept playing until it rounded the last corner and was out of sight. Then the announcer spoke into the megaphone again. "Thank you for being here, folks. May I say from all of us, to all of you, God bless America, and Happy Thanksgiving!"

The citizens cheered and clapped. As they slowly collected themselves and prepared to walk to the great hall, Maggie Mae and Molly walked together hand in hand and heart to heart.

"Papa said we can get a lamb, Maggie Mae." She was beaming again. "We're gonna have a real farm."

"I think you already do, Molly," replied Maggie with a smile in place.

By the time they got to the hall, people were everywhere. The afternoon sun was warm and inviting. Warm apple cider and fresh pumpkin pie filled the air as everyone visited and reminisced about the parade. Jane and Mary were busy at the table with all the spectators passing by, and of course, Pastor Smith was busy attending to all the questions people seem to need to discuss. Seeing this, Maggie Mae stepped into her role as one of the judges and rescued the pastor from a long, drawn-out conversation. "Pastor," said Maggie as she waltzed up to the flock of chatting ladies, their feathered hats bouncing with enthusiasm from the topic of the conversation. "Ladies, how lovely you look this afternoon, and may I add how remarkably well you did in our parade today. This township is blessed by your tireless contributions. May I borrow Pastor Smith? His contributions are needed to judge the pie contest." Maggie's diplomacy was spot on! "So if you please, ladies."She took the grateful man by the arm and whisked him away.

"Oh, thank you, Maggie. I was beginning to wonder how long they were going to go on about the latest washing machine." He was going on himself. "We'd best get to the judges' table and take our seats." Maggie just nodded. That had been the plan all along.

Soon the hall calmed down, and Pastor Smith stood and addressed the township. "Once again, greetings, and welcome to our annual pumpkin pie contest. I'd like to take a moment and thank all of those who participated in our parade today. It was a fine showing." He paused a minute, and they all began clapping. "We truly have a remarkable community." Everyone joined in and looked about in agreement with his kind compliment. "Now without any further delay, let us taste the pies." The judges stood and walked over to the bountiful table display. Nobody knew whose pie was whose, so it made the judging very fair. Some crusts were elaborate, while some cut like butter. Some looked hurried, and some chewed like rocks. The ladies held their clipboards tight to the breast as they tested and tasted. Some pies had a smooth texture in comparison to others that weren't cooked enough and had a stringy quality. A few had too much sugar, and some didn't have enough cinnamon. It was even fair to say that some tasted bland while others lacked the balance from a pinch of salt. Maggie and the others had their work cut out for them, and when they finally finished, they took their seats. The pastor rang the bell again, and everyone gathered to hear the results.

"Again ladies, an excellent showing this year! I am sure the men-folk around these parts must be pleased to have so many good cooks in the neighborhood. I am stuffed!" Everyone laughed at his comment because they knew that pumpkin pie was his favorite.

"Let's begin with third place. For a lovely crust and a tight, smooth pumpkin texture, the ribbon goes to ... Mrs. Dickens." He looked out into the audience and applauded as she walked up to take her ribbon. Mary and Janie stood side by side, each one swallowing back their nervousness.

"Our second place ribbon is awarded for the lovely caramelized sugar top on the butteriest crust." The pastor sighed. "Oh, it is delightful. And the winner is ... Miss Agnes Erstwhile." She stood up with the slip of a squeak from her lips. She covered her mouth with her hand and walked to the pastor in humble thanks and surprise. Everyone clapped again, and she blushed all the way back to her seat. Mary and Janie swallowed hard and looked at each other with understanding eyes of resignation. "And lastly," the pastor continued, "first place for the annual pumpkin pie contest goes to ..." He stopped and looked at the paper in his hand. He looked up and over to Maggie Mae. She nodded yes with her eyebrows speaking the same fact. "Well, folks, this is our community's first! We have a tie!" He cleared his throat and said, "First place goes to our very own Mary Fitzwilliam's and Jane Collier!" The room roared! The two friends looked at each other in complete disbelief and then hugged each other. Janie took Mary by the hand, and the two ladies walked up together. All of the judges left their seats and joined the fun. Since there was only one first-place ribbon, Samuel found a pair of scissors and cut the ribbon right up the middle. The ladies loved it! They laughed and hugged the roomful of adoring fans. Molly grabbed her Momma by the hand and pulled her down for a kiss on the cheek. "I knew you could do it, Momma! I am so proud of you!" Molly's toothless grin stretched from ear to ear.

Maggie made her way through the crowd and told Mary she knew it was a grand pie. Janie, too, was congratulated like a movie star. Samuel stood back and accepted the praise as if his wife were a real thoroughbred.

Winter was in the air. While they were busy cleaning up the hall, large puffy clouds had managed to creep into the sky. The crags on Winter Mountain looked as if they had been topped with spoonfuls of whipped cream; the suspended ribbons of white covering them completely and keeping them from view. "Molly dear, I think it may snow soon. Can you feel the chill and smell the moisture in the air?" Maggie was looking around in awe at the environment as they approached her home. The two quickly inspected the farm for anything that needed tending, and then they walked inside to get warm. "It was a grand day, Maggie Mae. Momma is so happy," started Molly. "I don't think I saw her stop smiling."And saying so brought a smile to her face. "Momma and Papa wanted me to invite you to Thanksgiving dinner Thursday. So if you are available, my darling," Molly said, trying to sound English and fancy, "then please join us. Momma roasts the best turkey!"

Maggie took her in her arms and gave her a big squeeze.

"Of course I'll join you, my darling." Now Maggie was pretending. "I shall bring a batch of my mother's cranberry relish. It won first place at the county fair!"

The two best friends giggled and finished planning the feast as the sun began to set on yet another wonderful day. Maggie buttoned up Molly's coat and walked her to the back door. "You'd best be gittin' on now, dear." She paused as she looked up at the incoming clouds. "I am thinkin' they'll be a fresh batch of snow on the ground by morning." She kissed her Molly on the cheek. "Won't that be lovely when the church bell rings … and town's all covered in snow? Take good care of our pony, and don't forget her blanket tonight. It's gonna be a cold one!" Molly turned around and hollered that she'd be sure to check on the filly and that she'd take an extra flake of alfalfa as well.

The chill was biting. Maggie waved, and so did Molly. Next thing she knew, Snowball was rubbing and purring at her feet as Maggie closed the door.

Halfway across the open pasture, Molly jumped on Wildfire's back and began to ride her home. The wind was picking up, and the muddy gray clouds began to block her view of the house. She clicked her tongue, encouraging the pony to pick up the pace, but Wildfire resisted her. She kicked her in the flanks with both of her heels and used her tongue again. Wildfire stayed calm. Molly grabbed her tighter by the braided mane, the braid making a good, strong strap. The two continued moving forward, but the clouds had a different idea. Without warning, they touched down to the ground and became more like a thick fog. Neither one could see the stable or the house. Neither one could pick up those cozy smells of home either. As they continued to walk toward what they thought was home, they went too far and missed the target altogether. By the time Molly realized her mistake, the clouds lifted like the curtain on a stage, and the two were faced with terror! They were standing on the edge of a cliff! One more step and they would go off the edge and tumble into uncertainty! Wildfire reared up and let out a horrible cry of panic! In that instant, Molly lost her grip on the braided mane and was thrown off the back of the pony. The horse that was too young to ride! The horse that Mrs. Green said not to ride! The horse that was her best friend! The horse of Winter Mountain!

Maggie followed her usual evening ritual—kettle on, fire stoked, and dinner prepared. She took down Johnny's journal and began to read again.

> Maggie and I went fishing today. The rascal caught more than me! She isn't afraid to touch the worms and casts like a champ. She's lovely, and I am in love. I think about her day and night. I can't stop myself. Next week there's a dance in town. I am gonna ask her to go. It'll be our first dance. I'd best practice in the barn. I wonder if Dad could teach me how to dance? Time for chores. I love you, M!

Maggie closed the journal and pressed it to her heart. She still remembered that day—the day they went fishing. And come to think of it, she usually caught most of the fish! Honestly, she thought he had let her. He'd always be doting on her and not paying attention to what he was doing. She smiled and found these private discoveries to be comforting in a special way. He was the kindest man she'd met in her life.

A knock at the door. It is William.

"Good evening, Lady Green." He was being silly. "I am here to collect my Molly dear. Do you mind telling her that Papa has arrived?"

Maggie's face dropped, "William," she said and ushered him into the house, "Molly went home over an hour ago." Now his face dropped. "I sent her home when the clouds began to look like they were going to snow."

They looked at each other. The two ran to the back door of Maggie's house. When they opened the door, a stiff hard wind nearly blew them over. The clouds were still down to the ground, creating a wall of gray, and they couldn't see anything. They both yelled Molly's name, but there was no reply. They both walked out into the muddy night and yelled again. Nothing. "You stay here, Maggie. I'll go back home and see if we just missed each other. I'll let you know what I find out when I get there." He sounded commanding but kind. "Say your prayers, Maggie. We may need them tonight!"

He was out the back door and over the fence and headed across a pasture, lost in the clouds. Maggie thought it best to say those prayers now, and she was sure to include William's safety in them. She closed the door and walked back into the living room, her thoughts completely absorbed in the possibility of a problem. The fire was crackling and warm, and she began to pray aloud. "Heavenly Father, please keep our Molly and William safe in this storm. Guide them and protect them from the things they can't see. Fill their hearts with the power of your goodness and lead them home to the safety of Mary's arms." She opened her eyes and looked at Johnny's picture. "Help them, Johnny. Help them." She closed them once again and added, "In Jesus' name, amen." Another wind hit the house. It rattled the windows. Maggie jumped and then tightened her shawl around her shoulders. Instinctively, she knew something was wrong. She walked into the kitchen and looked out the window and across the pasture. The lantern stood in its place, cold and dark. Her hand gravitated over to it, and she thought of her mother. "Oh, Momma, help us. Find Molly dear and get her home."

Another blast of wind hit the window she was standing in front of, and the sound snapped her attention away from the lantern and back to the outside. The window was beginning to fog up from her rapid breath. She lifted her arm and used her sleeve to wipe away some of the condensation. When the window was clearer, she noticed the clouds had lifted, and she could see across the field and all the way to Molly's. Her heart lightened. Then the massive layer of lingering cloud began to move. It began to swirl in a clockwise pattern. She first thought it was a tornado, and then she thought it was a whirlpool. Her eyes were transfixed. As she watched, the movement sped up ... faster and faster until Maggie was sure a twister was about to touch down. She couldn't move. She became mesmerized by the undulating pattern of the cloud, and in her hypnotized state, she saw the miracle. Down from the middle of the spinning soup, a single spout of mist extended and touched the ground. It deposited a solitary body of electrical static energy. Maggie rubbed her eyes and continued to watch. The phenomenon moved toward the house, and Maggie stayed still. Its graceful motion hovered across the ground as effortlessly as it came down from the ceiling of gray. Then it came right up to the kitchen window and stopped as if poised and waiting for Maggie's reaction. As she watched, she beheld an act of God. She beheld ... Johnny! Slowly, the static dots collected into the form of his face, every speck of light energy taking its place as if put there by the hand of Monet. She knew what was happening and became humbled by what she was about to receive. After a few minutes, the reconstruction was complete. They looked into each other's eyes and souls. Words weren't necessary. She knew his time was limited and listened to her intuition. In a flash she grabbed her lantern, bundled up, and was out the backdoor. Johnny met her there, and without a word, he swept her away from the house and across the field. They moved swiftly. Maggie stopped at Molly's and rapped her hand on the side of the house. Instantly, William and Mary responded. They dressed and followed Maggie and Johnny out into the darkness. Mary carried Molly's lantern just like Maggie carried hers, and together, they disappeared into the black of night!

Johnny led the way. No one asked any questions. No explanation was needed. The four of them moved toward finding Molly, and what they'd find was anybody's guess.

They heard a horse galloping at high speed "That must be Wildfire!" said William, redirecting his attentive ears. "I can hear her gettin' closer. Hold up the lantern. Maybe she'll see it." Maggie did just so, and the powerful noise came quickly. Only it wasn't Wildfire. It was Samuel, and he was riding Fiona! The search team gathered in a circle. The sense of panic was unmistakable.

"Where's Molly?" asked Samuel out of breath. "I was sitting in the living room reading a book when out of the blue, a red cardinal started pecking at the window. It kept tapping at the glass and fluttering like it was on fire. Call me crazy, but I could hear words in my head. They sounded like, 'She's gone! She's gone! I knew something was wrong, so here I am.'" William walked around to his right side and explained what they knew. Molly hadn't come home, and they assumed Wildfire was with her. They'd left Maggie's about two hours ago and hadn't been seen since.

"We're following Johnny's lead at this point." He pointed to the angelic presence that was standing next to Maggie and ran his fingers across his mouth and face. "We have an angel, Samuel." William choked up, but he caught himself before he burst into tears. "We have an angel to guide us!" Samuel nodded with respect and without doubt. After all, the red cardinal spoke to him. When God raises his voice, *you listen!*

Without a word, Johnny began moving forward again. Samuel had the advantage of riding Fiona, so he moved ahead of the group and continued to holler for Molly and Wildfire.

The lantern light was better than nothing, but the light they cast was simply not enough. In that instant, beams of moonlight broke through the canopy of cloud cover and streamed over the mountains ahead. They could suddenly see everything! They had traveled farther than they realized when they heard Samuel shouting, "Over here! I can hear Wildfire. Over here!" They raced without care over the rocks, through frozen puddles of slippery ice, and across the uneven mounds of forest debris.

Johnny and Samuel reached the cliff edge first. When the rest finally arrived, Samuel was already off of Fiona, and he tied a rope around the horn of the horse's saddle. He looped the sturdy rope around his waist and was halfway down the cliff-side where Wildfire lay. She was still making a horrible racket, and Molly was nowhere to be seen. As Samuel approached the pony, the moon seemed to brighten. He slowly walked up to the frightened animal, and with a soft, calming tone of voice, he said, "Easy, girl. Easy, now." He reached out to her and placed a comforting hand on her neck. He stroked her nose and forehead making sure that the pony made eye contact with him first. Wildfire calmed. She snorted out with a sense of relief.

"That's a girl," Samuel said gently. "Are ya hurt, lass?" He looked at her legs and her belly and didn't see any outward signs of injury. Then he saw the small pool of blood by her front leg, "its okay, lass," he said in the same calm voice. "Let's get ya up and see where you're hurt."

"Do you see Molly?" asked a breathless Maggie from high up on the cliff's edge. "Where's Molly?" Maggie and Mary were holding each other now, the fear taking hold of their strength and rendering them hysterical.

Johnny stood silently and watched from above. Without hesitation, he began to go down the steep embankment and over to where Samuel stood. The closer he came to them, the brighter he became. When he was finally close enough to reach out and touch Wildfire, it was as if he'd become a beacon of light! Johnny held out his slender hand to Wildfire, and with the touch of a single finger, he coaxed her to stand up and walk over to the side of the ditch. Samuel was silent. He quickly checked over the pony for any injuries, and then he saw … Molly! Wildfire had been lying over the top of Molly, keeping her safe and warm. Johnny moved over to where she lay and then looked up to Maggie. The ladies gasped! Samuel rushed over to her still form and discovered where the blood had come from. When she had fallen, she had hit her head on the boulder. Molly was seriously hurt, and she wasn't waking up! By now, William was down at the scene. The night air was ice cold, and he knew that without the heat from Wildfire's body, she would soon be ice cold too. "Take the blanket off of Wildfire!" commanded William, his daughter getting paler by the second. "Got it!" replied Samuel. "Mary, call Wildfire. Try and coax her up to you, and Maggie, throw your extra wrap over her back. She'll need to stay warm. I think she may be in shock!"

The ladies, relieved to see Molly, listened to Samuel and began to call for the confused pony. Johnny moved over to her, and once again, he touched her on the forehead with a single finger. Wildfire met Johnny's eyes and instinctively knew what to do. She found the path of least resistance and walked up the cliff-side and over to the ladies.

The men put the warm blanket on the ground, and then with great care, they lifted Molly's listless body up and onto the blanket. They folded the thick cloth around her and then secured the edges with a soft cotton rope. A second later William carried her up the same trail that Wildfire took and prepared to get her home. The moon was still bright enough to see by. William mounted Fiona, and Samuel handed Molly up to him so that he could carry her home on horseback. Everyone moved at a hurried pace. Wildfire tagged along behind, her movements exhausted and slow. Johnny walked alongside Maggie and Mary, staying consistently calm and quiet. As they got closer to the house, Johnny's light softened. When they finally reached the gate, Johnny lingered behind. Maggie turned around and met his gaze. He held up his hand, and in doing so, he invited her to walk with him. She turned back and looked at Mary and William, her expression strained by which way to go. "Maggie, we'll be fine. You go. Go with your angel. Thank you, Johnny," said Mary, her eyes brimming with grateful tears. "Samuel's gonna get the doctor. All we need to do is get her inside and keep her warm, so go, Maggie. *Go!*" Maggie knew that she was meant to be with him at this moment in the miracle. She waved goodbye and walked away with the love of her life.

It wasn't long before they were back at the house. Johnny, still silent, reached out and touched his true love's face and blessed her with his thoughts. "My love, I am glad you are reading my journal. Our love was—and still is—genuine and good. I am with you always. I am in the way you see the world. I am in the way you smile and in the way you love children. We love with a timeless connection, every day brimming with truth. You have many more years ahead of you. Please—for me—live them to the fullest. Remember, I hear your prayers, and so does our heavenly Father. Strive for joy! Live for love! Share your wisdom, but most of all, live for love. Lonesomeness breeds despair, and you deserve to love again."

As his final words strengthened her thoughts, he began to fade away. Slowly and with great finality, the static energy, which only moments before was collected into the face of a man, scattered apart and rose up toward the cloudless sky, once again becoming golden light in a starry night.

Maggie stood there and waited. She didn't know what for, but she stood and stared and thanked God. Soon, she began to shiver, the gravity of Molly's situation taking its toll on her. She heard a truck driving down the road toward the apple orchard and watched it head up the drive to Molly's house. Good! The doctor had arrived. Maggie walked inside and immediately went to bed. Snowball comforted her as if she knew she needed a little extra love. Like a child again, Maggie Mae Green simply wished she had her momma to hold her and tell her everything was going to be all right. Thank goodness for sleep.

When the doctor and Jane arrived, the horses were in the warm barn. Fiona was nuzzling and doting on her filly, giving Samuel a parent's peace of mind. The animals looked as if they could take care of themselves now, so Samuel joined the other concerned parents inside of the house. Molly lay still and warm in the living room on a makeshift bed by the fire. Tiger had found a warm spot to curl up by her side, and the orange fluffy cat laid there purring until he, too, finally fell asleep. Mary was sitting calmly by her side, while Janie held her thin, shaky hand. William paced the floor. Samuel entered and then took a seat. The doctor stood silently looking down at his pint-sized patient and thinking deeply. The old clock was the only sound one could hear, each tick prickling the skin with every unspoken fear. The doctor took a deep, exasperated breath and exhaled with a frustrated guess. "The good news is the wound is small. She landed on her head, but she landed in an area where the chance of brain damage is very small. I cleaned and stitched the gash and put on a soft bandage. Now … we wait." He looked up from Molly and into a room full of concerned people. "She is remarkably healthy, I dare say. She needs to rest, undisturbed, and if by dinnertime tomorrow, she hasn't …" He stopped and checked the delicacy of his next words. "If she hasn't stirred or moved … well, then we will decide what actions to take." He walked to the door and put on his coat. William met him there and handed him his hat. He took the doctor's hand and shook it, "Thank you for coming, Doc, especially at this time of night." He tried to smile while speaking, but exhaustion and sadness simply filled his eyes with volumes of emotion. The doctor patted him on the back and looked around the room at everyone's need for comfort. "I'll come by after church tomorrow. When word reaches the townsfolk, you can count on many well-wishers stopping by to see how our little Molly is doing. I dare say many friends, indeed." He tipped his hat and left.

Mary sat silently and watched Molly. There wasn't much anyone could do at this point, so common sense demanded that everyone get some rest and prepare for the next crucial day.

Samuel and Jane agreed it was best to leave Fiona with Wildfire overnight. William gave them the keys to the truck and insisted they go home and rest. "Mary and I can manage now. Please know how grateful we are to ya both, not just for tonight's help but for your friendship. You have both become quite dear to me and my ladies." He held out his hand, and Samuel grabbed it. The men hugged, and so did their wives.

"We'll stop by after church and return your truck," said Janie as she slipped on her coat. "I'll be including Molly in our prayers at church tomorrow." She stopped and looked directly at Mary. "If that's all right, Mary?" She stood and walked over to where Janie stood and hugged her tightly. "Of course it is, Janie. Of course it is!" A few tears flowed as everyone said their final goodnight, and when the Colliers were finally gone, William held Mary in his arms for the rest of the night. They stayed on the sofa and kept watch over their darling girl, alternating between them, one dozing while the other stayed alert. Soon they both slept a hard, deep sleep, and that was when God spoke to Molly, "You have been given a very great gift Molly. The chance to glimpse *the land of awareness* is usually reserved for those souls who have passed out of physical form and no longer require the use of a human body." The voice, deep and rich, resonated all around her. "Johnny tells me that you are an angel on earth already." Molly could sense the warmth of a smile. "He says that you have shown Maggie Mae unconditional love and understanding. I also understand that through your example of faith in Me, she has chosen to come back into the light. Your belief and courage inspired her to wash away years of lonesomeness and despair." Molly was listening intently! She was not familiar with her surroundings, but she knew she was safe. The tone of the voice she was listening to made her feel peaceful. As she looked around herself, she could feel a desire to explore, a need to understand, a yearning to stay. There wasn't any way for her to describe what she was experiencing because she'd never imagined anything like this before. God continued, "Your curiosity is very thoughtful, Molly, but it isn't time for you to stay." It was as if he could read her mind. But of course, He could. He had created her! "I am very proud of you, my dear, but you must go back. You must continue to thrive and love and create. Know in your heart that the land of awareness dwells inside of you. It dwells inside all of mankind. An experience of this profound nature is rare for someone so young. Therefore, I ask you to continue sharing My truths. I ask you to continue to be an example. I ask you to continue to grow." The gentle voice softened and calmed.

In a moment, Molly replied, her lips pressed together, her mind alert and responsive, "Father, thank you. I only live the way You've taught me. I share Your love and sing Your songs. I walk in faith because I feel your hand in mine. I am *because* You are. And Father, I will go back, and I will thrive and love and grow." She paused her humble thoughts. "Yes, Father?" Her angelic head tipping to the side in anticipation of what she was receiving. "Yes, Father, I remember. God is love."

The conversation ended as subtly as it began. Molly felt a warming sensation begin to tingle all over her body as if a million tiny fingers were tickling her skin. She felt her consciousness lift and engage with an electrical flow. Along that charged river, she felt another hand slip into hers. When she looked to see who had grabbed her other hand, she saw his eyes—a pair of the clearest blue eyes. They were large and kind and deep. As she was drawn into his stare, she just knew it was Johnny. He smiled, and in his own wordless way, he thanked her for bringing *his love* back to God. Johnny truly touched Molly's heart as he guided her back into the bosom of her family and home. He stayed with her as her parents continued to sleep, holding her hand until he had to let it go. And when he let it go, it was because Momma had taken a hold of it and had started to cry.

"Oh, my dear, sweet Molly. Please, God, protect her," she prayed out loud. "Bring her back to us, to all of us. She is our sunshine! She is our only child and a precious reflection of You, God." Her tears flowed freely. Molly stirred! She groaned and softly moaned. Mary sat up and called out William's name. He bolted off of the sofa and rushed over to where Molly lay. They looked up into each other's eyes. Morning smiles began to tease at the corners of their mouths.

"Momma? Papa?" Molly said in a groggy tone as she reached up to rub her face. "Momma, I am hungry! Is it Thanksgiving yet?"

The Fitzwilliam's hugged each other as they began laughing at the first words out of their daughter's mouth. As the morning sun crested over the distant hills, glorious rays of sunshine shone through Johnny's wings as he lifted himself up into heavenly peace.

The congregation was dumbfounded. The room was full to the brim with excitement until Samuel put in a prayer request for Molly. Without going into too much detail, he explained what had happened the night before and how the young lady was still unconscious from her fall. The doctor stood up and added to Samuel's recounting that Molly would be fine in his opinion, but there was no reason not to say a prayer for a little girl who had done so much good in their small town. Needless to say, the congregation lost its sense of excitement when the news had been delivered. Maggie Mae was there too, but the spark in her eyes was gone. Her thoughts were somewhere else, and now that the news had been delivered, everyone knew why. The pastor changed the direction of his planned sermon and asked everyone to join him in prayer for Molly Fitzwilliam's. He held his hands up, signaling that everyone hold each other's hands. When the room was ready, Pastor Smith led them in prayer.

"Heavenly Father, we ask you to protect our Molly from the injuries she received last night. Father, we humbly ask that she be healed quickly and with as little pain as possible. She is a darling girl, Father, and we all love her dearly." The room was quiet, and Maggie softly wept. "Please help her friends and family cope with the challenge ahead of them, and allow them to work from a place of peace. In Jesus' name, amen." Amen quietly echoed through the church. Maggie Mae looked up at the pastor. She did her best to thank him with a smile, but the pastor knew how hard she was struggling at the moment. He was at a loss for anything else to say. He couldn't imagine how she would cope if she lost Molly. She'd just recovered from the loss of Johnny. How would she ever heal if Molly were to pass away? The pastor put those thoughts out of his head, and then he suggested that the service end early because of the news about Molly. Suddenly, the front door slammed open! William stood there. His eyes were puffy, and his face was red. He was out of breath as if he'd run all the way from the orchard. He looked frantically around the room and then finally clapped his eyes on Maggie Mae. She slowly stood up during his startling entrance and clasped a hand to her mouth. William entered the church without regard for anyone else in the room. He walked straight over to her and grabbed her by the shoulders. Maggie's knees went soft, and it looked like she was going to faint! William's powerful arms held her up, and he looked into her strained eyes. A single tear streamed down his cheek and then he said, "Molly asked me to apologize to you for not lighting her lantern last night." He began to grin. "She hopes you can forgive her." William turned and looked out into the congregation and said, "Molly woke up this morning at dawn. She's gonna be fine!"

Maggie looked dazed at first. Then she began to comprehend what William was really saying. "You mean, she … Oh, William! Molly dear is going to be okay?"

"That's exactly what I mean." He hugged her like a man on top of the world. The entire church cheered! Everyone was out of their seat and shouting hallelujah! Half the town was crying, and the other half was laughing. The pastor had to sit down, the overwhelming news rendering him speechless. When the noise level had dropped a bit, William added, "She asked me to thank everyone for their prayers. She said God told her that everyone needed her here in Pine Valley, so she had to come back!" He looked down into Maggie's eyes and quietly added, "She also said that Johnny thanked her for bringing you back into the light of God!" William kissed her on the wet cheek. "Thank you too, Maggie Mae." He squinted his eyes. "Thank you for bringing your miracle to my family."

He kept his arm around her shoulder while the township filed by and expressed their relief about Molly. Over the course of the next thirty minutes, about the time it took for everyone to head home, Pastor Smith came up to the two of them and offered his best wishes.

"It really is wonderful news, William. We are so glad you came in today and put all of our minds at rest. I'd imagine that little one of yours better prepare herself for many cards and treats over the next few days." He seemed truly relieved. "Be sure to let me know if there's anything I can do to help you and the missus." Then he stopped and directed his attention to Maggie. "As for you, young lady," he said as he slipped his arm through hers and began to pat the back of her hand, "you take care of yourself." He looked at her with fatherly concern. "Do you understand what I am saying?"

She leaned her head against his shoulder and heaved out a sigh of relief. "Yes, I do, and yes, I will."

"That's a good girl. Now be gone with yourself and get along home." His dedication to his friends was unmistakable. "I am here if need be, but something tells me you have a guardian angel!" He winked and smiled. As the two headed for the front doors, they looked at each other and smiled. Little did he know!

By the time William and Maggie reached the orchard, three cars were already leaving, the drivers smiling and waving happily, and four other cars were parked alongside of the barn and house. From where they sat, you could see a living room full of people standing and talking to Mary and Molly. It seemed Janie was stationed at the front door and Samuel was in charge of parking. They looked at each other and began to laugh."Looks like we have a celebrity on our hands, Maggie. Do you think there's room in there for the likes of us?" Maggie, still a bit overwhelmed by the last twenty-four hours, chuckled and replied, "I think we are all star struck!" She winked at William, and he knew exactly what she was getting at.

They cautiously walked into the house and were greeted by many of the people they had just left at church. Maggie bee lined for Molly and gave her a tight but gentle hug. Molly was so happy to see her best friend that she practically jumped off of the cot! "Oh, Maggie Mae," started a jabber-jawed Molly, "I am truly sorry I didn't light my lantern last night. I was busy talking with God. I hope you understand? I won't let you down … tonight."She took a deep breath. "Momma said she'd help me if I needed her help. Oh, and Maggie Mae, I am sorry I rode Wildfire yesterday. I knew better, but when the big cloud came down from the sky, I got scared! I figured Wildfire knew how to get me home. I guess she got scared too. I'll listen better. I promise!" She beamed again. She had no front teeth, but she beamed nonetheless.

"Don't you worry that tough little noggin of yours," reassured Maggie Mae. "God has just as much right to talk with you as I have. We'll teach you how to ride Wildfire in the spring, Molly."She leaned down like she was telling a secret, "And I fell asleep before I lit my lantern too."

The room of well-wishers all *awww'ed* at the same time when they heard them speaking. Mary stepped forward and placed a hand on Maggie's shoulder and looked down at her with loving eyes. "May I bring you some tea?"

"Oh, yes, please. And come to think of it. I am hungry too."She paused and asked Molly, "Are you hungry too, Molly dear?"

Mary chortled. "Come with me for a second, Maggie."She led her to the kitchen. "Hungry isn't a problem around here anymore!"

The kitchen was filled with so many different kinds of foods that the two ladies just looked at each other and began to laugh! There were pies. There were casseroles. There were loaves of warm bread and jars upon jars of jams and jellies. One corner of the counter was loaded up with smokehouse hams, and on the drain board was a wooden box filled with carrots and beets and squash. The kitchen truly looked like Thanksgiving had already started, and in a way, I guess you could say it already had.

In an hour the Fitzwilliam's house emptied of their guests, and Molly dozed off. A handful of thankful but exhausted friends sat at the dining room table. Janie was next to Mary, and William was next to Samuel. Maggie was more or less the mother of the group, and that was fine with her. They all chatted and nibbled from the marvelous feast donated by the citizens of Pine Valley. Each person touched on the day before and the phenomenon they had all been a part of. "Ya know, it never did snow or rain," observed Samuel as he took a sip of his tea. "I thought it was going to be white in the morning, but it never happened. And don't the cardinals go south in the winter?" He'd forgotten about the red cardinal at his window until then. "It was like nothin' I'd ever seen before. *The bird was frantic.* It kept tappin' till I got outta my seat! 'She's gone! She's gone,' kept ringin' in my ears!" He slowed down a little, hoping that his loud voice wouldn't wake up Molly. "Well, it's fair to say they're my new favorite bird. Right, Mary?"

"Right, Samuel." She nodded as enthusiastically as she could, but she was ready for some sleep too.

Maggie looked at Samuel and gave him a little wink and sideways nod of her head in Mary's direction. She was beginning to doze at the table. Seeing this, William said, "Maggie, let me take ya home. You must be ready for a nap yourself."

"You are absolutely right, William," agreed Maggie as she stood and pushed her chair under the table. "That sounds like a lovely Sunday afternoon to me."

"Thanks for the lunch," added Janie as she, too, took the hint and prepared to head home.

"We'll saddle up Fiona and ride her back to the ranch, William," offered Samuel. "She's ready to stretch a bit, and so am I."

"Oh, don't leave on my account," begged Mary through one more yawn. "We haven't had any pie yet."

William walked over to his lovely wife and kissed her on the cheek.

"Our friends need to go, darlin'. They are ready to relax too." His smile was tender and kind. She agreed but insisted that they all come back for Thanksgiving dinner.

"Thursday at four in the afternoon… does that sound okay?"

Everyone accepted the invitation and promised to bring a special dish that had been a favorite in their family's traditional meal. Maggie would bring the cranberry relish, and Janie would bring sweet potatoes. "That would be great," said Mary, standing up and checking on Molly. "Thanks again for everyone's help. I must admit that I am still reeling." She hugged them one at a time and said goodbye. William took it from there and escorted everyone outside. A moment later the house quieted down as everyone headed home. William put Wildfire out in the pasture, and she pranced around as if it was the first time she'd been freed. Fiona and the Colliers were down the road quickly, and Maggie was soon waving goodbye to William as he dropped her off at home. In no time her kettle was simmering, and her slippers were on. It didn't take long for Mary to drift off, though she still had a conscious ear awake for Molly. About half an hour into her nap, she felt her honeybun's tiny fingers tapping on her shoulder. "Momma, are you okay?"

Mary slowly opened her eyes to see Molly standing at the side of the chair. Her hair was tousled, and her face looked concerned.

"Molly, I am fine," said Momma, sitting forward with a catlike stretch. "I was just taking a short nap. Are you okay too?" She awoke instantly. No sign of tiredness lingering, she said, "Let me see you," as if she were appraising a genuine treasure. She casually grabbed her hand and turned her in a pirouette like a ballerina, being clever so that she could check on the bandage at the back of her head.

"How is—what did Maggie Mae call it?—your noggin feeling?"

"I am fine, Momma. Kind-a sore, but not so bad." Molly climbed up onto her Momma's lap and snuggled in closely. "My knee hurt worse when I tripped in the rocks. Remember, Momma? Papa said I howled like coyotes at the moon!" She was her old, dramatic self again, much to Momma's relief. "That cut bled and bled! It made the best scab I had ever had! Remember, Momma?" Mary had to laugh to herself. Her little jabber-jaw was just fine, and her memory was sharp as a tack!

"One thing I wanted to tell you about is God." Molly sat forward and looked around at her momma. "He said I was important. He said I was an angel on earth, Momma. Wasn't that very nice?" Her face was young, but her wisdom ageless. She giggled and then added, "Momma, He even said He was proud of me!" She continued, and Mary didn't stop her. "Johnny had been telling him about me and Maggie Mae, but I think God already knew because I just shared God's truth with my friend. Ya know, Momma, that's why he told me to come back. He said I should always share his truths. He said I was only visiting the land of awareness, and I was lucky to be there." She paused and then asked a question. "Momma, what's the land of awareness?"

"Well ..." Mary had to stop and think about this one. "I am only guessing, Molly, but I'd say it is a place somewhere inside of us all. A place where, if we make the effort to learn like we do in school, we can discover how really remarkable we are as human beings."

"Re-make-able!" Molly grasped her meaning. "Exactly, Momma! Just like when I met Janie and Samuel. We talked about things being re-make-able like Maggie Mae. Ya just gotta want to be re-make-able. Right, Momma?" She looked so proud of herself that Mary didn't have the heart to correct her use of the word, and really, both definitions made sense. Molly became quiet and changed the conversation. "I am sorry I rode Wildfire, Momma." She looked sorry too. Her head dropped, and she cast her eyes down. "I got scared of the clouds. I figured Wildfire knew the way, even when she couldn't see, but I was wrong. I am sorry to make everyone scared and worried. Please forgive me."

Mary choked up but didn't let her tears show. "Ya know, honeybun, some of the best lessons we learn from are the ones that cause us the most pain. Making mistakes is part of life. The trick is not to make the same mistake over and over again." She stopped and let her personal experience resurge in her memories. And she was right!

"Yes, Momma, you are right, and you can bet a big piece of that apple pie I can smell in the kitchen that I won't be making that mistake again! The land of awareness is right here." She pointed to her heart and placed a hand on her bandage. "But right now, I think I am ready to have a piece of pie. How about you, Momma?"

Who knew a piece of pie could feed more than the tummy? Mary and Molly giggled all the way to the kitchen, and Mary cut them both a big chunk. One icy glass of milk to wash it all down and the two were as happy as they could be. *Somewhere from a nook in the sacred space of limitless time, Johnny smiled in his soulfulness. "Well done, Father." His admission suggested a plan had been fulfilled." Thank you," he said.*

School vacation began with sleeping in and eating French toast for breakfast! The Fitzwilliam's were glad Molly didn't need to wake up Monday and go to school. The doctor had stopped by like he had promised, and he suggested they keep her inside and cozy for the next few days. Since school was out for the holiday, they all spent the time resting and recuperating. Monday came and went. Tuesday came and stayed. A few people managed to drive up and visit and leave even more yummy treats, including six bales of alfalfa for Wildfire! All in all, Pine Valley's faith in Molly's recovery was well rewarded, and their attention to her recovery became a wonderful way to celebrate the Thanksgiving holiday. The doctor declared she'd healed faster than any patient he had ever had, and that it would be fine for her to go outside and play again. "Now, young lady," he said, looking over the top of his glasses, a professional and serious sound in his voice, "I expect you to learn to ride a horse properly before you jump on the back of one ever again!" He sat up, his own back straightening as if he was sitting in a saddle himself. "There are plenty of people around town who would be glad to teach you how to ride." He stood up and adjusted his hat. "Do you hear me, young lady?"

Molly smiled and rushed at him. She wrapped her arms around his legs and hugged him tightly. "Yes, sir, I hear you, and I promise I will learn to ride. I am re-make-able, ya know!" She looked up at him, her toothless enthusiasm lighting up her face.

"Yes, yes." He patted her on the head. His old age rendered him impatient. "Yes, now where is your mother?" His dismissive tone was not at all offensive, but it was quite normal for one who didn't tolerate any monkey business.

Molly took him by the hand and led him to the kitchen. Mary had put a basket of food together and thanked him profoundly. "William and I are very grateful!" She put a hand on Molly's shoulder. "Thank you for everything." She kissed him on the cheek and handed him the basket.

"Well, well. You are welcome." He looked up bashfully as if kisses didn't come his way often. "The missus will appreciate the goodies, I dare say. Thank you kindly, Mary." Then he said again and in front of Momma, "Remember, Molly must learn to ride properly." He smiled and walked to the front door. "Give my best to your husband." He tipped his hat and walked out to his truck. Mary and Molly followed and stood on the front porch. Wildfire was out in the pasture as usual. As the doctor began to pull out of the drive, he rolled down the window and hollered, "Fine animal there. Sure am glad she wasn't hurt either. I heard ya found her protecting Molly from the cold. That's remarkable, Mary. Simply remarkable! Good day!" And he drove away.

Molly tugged at her momma's apron. "Did ya hear that, Momma? Re-make-able. We can teach Wildfire, too." They looked at each other as if they knew a secret.

With Thanksgiving only two days away, the townspeople seemed to be out in force patronizing the local businesses. The grocery store was a dizzying array of cheerful people as well as an abundant stock of harvest goods! Turkeys hung at the meat counter. Bushels of apples and sweet potatoes lined the walk through the produce section, and freshly baked pies seemed to say, "Take me home. I am delicious too!" Maggie Mae was in town for the morning, seeing to her simple grocery list. So many people stopped her to chat that it took an hour just to collect the items on her list and head back home. Being acknowledged again was a lovely feeling, and Maggie relished every hello. She enjoyed the walk to town (which was only around the corner from her house), and the crisp, fresh air always seemed to stir something in her soul. She'd finished reading Johnny's journal the night before, and it seemed to have revived an interest in her dormant mind. The recent changes she'd chosen to make in her outlook had spawned all sorts of possibilities in her thinking, and the first change she was going to make was to get the Model T out of the barn. The letter her parents had written to her and Johnny claimed that the automobile was destined to be used in the orchard business. The more Maggie thought about it, the more she realized that the Model T could still be used at the orchard, and because it was now a classic car, the novelty of driving it would cause quite a sensation. She thought long and hard on the subject and finally came to the conclusion that the Fitzwilliam's should have the old car. In fact, Maggie felt her parents' intentions should be honored and there was no reason not to fulfill their wishes. On linen paper she wrote down some business ideas, ones she had come up with when she was working at the farm, and she tucked them into a fancy envelope. She wanted to make the car a gift on Thanksgiving Day, and a little formality couldn't hurt.

She contacted Samuel and shared her plan with him. He offered his services, a few ideas of his own, and set an appointment to meet at the farm and get the vehicle out of the barn as soon as possible. Secretly, they needed to relocate the Model T to the auto shop that morning so it could be assembled and prepared for the Thanksgiving holiday.

There was a knock at the door. She tucked her project away and answered it. "Oh, Molly and Mary, how lovely to see you. I must say you are looking very well today." Maggie gushed a little, but that's what grandmothers were supposed to do. "Please come in, ladies. May I put on the kettle?"

"Oh, not today, Maggie Mae," announced Mary. "We are getting a little exercise. We stopped to invite you to join us. Would you care to take a stroll?"

They were quite precious-looking. Molly and Mary had large floppy hats on. They looked more like something you'd wear to the beach, but they were decorated with fall leaves, ribbons, and crab apples. "Do you like my hat, Maggie Mae? Momma and I made the hat bands this morning. We brought you a band for your hat too." Molly held it up and handed it to Maggie Mae. "Does a short walk sound good to you?"

Of course, Maggie said yes. She grabbed her sunhat, put on the charming hat band, and joined the ladies for a stroll. The day was still young, so Maggie knew there was no harm in putting off her secret chore for a little while. They walked up one side of Main Street and down the other. Citizens and visitors were everywhere, and the ladies' hats attracted all sorts of attention! "What lovely hats, ladies," one commented. Another friend commented on the brightly colored apples and ribbons that caught their eye. Mary and Maggie just followed behind Molly as she paraded them through the quaint town. She seemed to truly enjoy all of the attention, and then they saw why. On the back of her hat in the same place where she'd had fallen and gashed her head, there was a bandage. She had taped it to the outside of the hat, and on top of it, she'd drawn a smiling face! It was Molly's way of showing the town that she would be okay. The two ladies looked at each other when they finally realized the clever way Molly said thank you to her townspeople.

"Mary," Maggie said, "that gal of yours is something else. Something else, indeed!"

Midmorning approached, and Maggie said she needed to get home. Since there were still chores to finish and relish to make, she knew every minute counted. "Thank you for including me today, Molly. It was a lovely walk, and thank you again for the hat band." They'd already made it back to Maggie's house and were saying their goodbyes when Samuel pulled into the driveway. "Oh, there's my handyman now. I really must go." She kissed each one on the cheek and waved them on. She and Samuel had a big project to begin, and she didn't want Mary or Molly to see what was going on.

Within thirty minutes a long-bed wagon pulled by a team of horses parked in Maggie's yard. Four men jumped off and walked over to Samuel and asked for instructions. In no time, there was a commotion in the barn. From where Maggie stood, she could see dust escaping through the old wooden walls along with tidbits of straw floating out from the opened windows. A few minutes later, an old block and tackle was set in place outside of the upstairs delivery doors, and the old dirty crate could be seen hanging from the secure but rusted hoist. The men knew what they were doing, and it showed. The hand signals they used were almost like a waltz. Without a word or melody, one arm went up and the crate swung to the left. A hand closed, and the movement stopped. A thumb went up with a shrill whistle in the wind, and the reins were snapped, triggering the team of horses to move in closer with the wagon in tow. Another handed opened, and the crate lowered. A hand closed, and the crate stopped, all of the men taking notice of the movements to assure all of the ropes were still secure. A man's hand opened, and his other hand waved in a forward motion, spurring the team of professionals to coax the crate onto the bed of the sturdy wagon. One loud *shout* and the Model T crate was set down with a dusty thump! Samuel took his handkerchief from his pocket and wiped the back of his neck as he ran over to where Maggie was standing. "Well, Mrs. G, she's all loaded." He was huffing a bit, but he was charged by the accomplishment. "Joe should have it assembled today. He said they're pretty simple to put together." He was looking at the fellas, and with a wave, he granted them permission to get a move on. "What you're doin' here is a real nice thing, Mrs. G." He looked down at her with the love of a son in his eyes. "It'll change their lives, but I think ya already know that." He bent down and kissed her on the cheek. He took off his hat and rearranged his mop of straggly hair. "I'll keep ya in the loop, Mrs. G, and thank ya again. You sure know how to make a Thanksgiving extra special." He tipped his head, threw her that handsome smile, and ran to catch up with the wagon. By the time he reached it, William came around the corner with two bales of alfalfa on the bed of his wagon. He pulled into Maggie's yard, and jumped down from his seat while craning his neck toward the men who were leaving. He asked what was going on.

"Ya should have asked me, Maggie. I'd have helped ya too." Maggie smiled down and kicked an invisible rock out of her way. "No worries, William. I had some old junk to clean up, and they came by to take care of it for me. Besides, I need you to be keepin' an eye on that lil' one of yours." She managed to change the subject without him asking more questions. "We went for a walk today, and Molly's just fine." She took him by the arm and led him to the barn. Since the doors were still open, she suggested he toss the bales inside. "In fact, William, I'd venture a guess she's even better than before. Now mind you, I don't think gettin' hurt is a good thing," she said, rambling. "But the whole accident seems to have triggered something more grown-up in her spirit. I can't put a finger on it, but I am sure we are gonna see our girl accomplish more amazing things." William unloaded the bales and listened to Maggie. She was on a roll. "I am lookin' forward to her learning to ride this spring. I know it's a lil' early for Wildfire to be ridden, but my instincts tell me she's ready." She looked up at him and smiled. "I love ya, son. Thank you for all of the miracles your family has awakened in my life. I am still reeling about Johnny Angel, as Mary called him. I don't quite know how all that came about, but I learned one thing recently. Don't question an act of God. Just go with the flow. The answers will come to ya later."

"Mrs. Maggie Mae Green, you are a miracle in our lives too! Times were tough before we came to Pine Valley. It's almost like Johnny brought us to one another. Mary and I are overwhelmed every day, and thank you doesn't even begin to describe how blessed the three of us feel." He took her in his arms and squeezed her tightly. "We love you, Maggie Mae." He looked as though he was about to cry, but he choked the tears back once again. "Now I had so much extra alfalfa that I thought you could use some too. If there is anything else I can do for you, don't hesitate to ask." He stopped, smiled a clever smile to himself, and added, "You know where we live."

He closed up the barn and walked her back to the house. The afternoon was ticking away and both knew that they had additional chores to finish up. "I'd best get a move on, Maggie Mae. I know my ladies will have a list a mile long if I stay away too long." He smiled, blew her a kiss and headed down the road to home. Maggie sat down on her front porch and pulled a tied-up bundle out from her pocket. She knew what it was. She rocked for a moment, holding the bundle of letters in her hand. There was no need to open them. She had written them, and there was no way she could ever forget what she had written. The passage of time filled her mind. In the blink of an eye, forty years had passed. Old feelings of regret and bitterness reentered her mind, but she dismissed them. Thoughts as comfortable as slippers knocked on the decrepit door of shame, but now she only answered the call to truth and freedom, and for that brief but enlightened moment, Maggie knew that she was truly blessed. Her years of melancholy had been completely washed away.

A cardinal landed on the railing of the porch. She sat, quietly shocked by its sudden landing. They looked at each other, neither one budging. Maggie recalled Samuel's story about the red bird frantically tapping on his window, and she chose to believe that this bird was one and the same. It chirped! Like a perch, Maggie calmly held a finger out toward the patient visitor. She knew it was a long shot, but so many miraculous things were happening these days that she figured it was worth a try. She sat motionless and waited. It chirped again and flew away. She softly laughed to herself and stood up. As she headed back into the house, she heard it chirp again and turned back around. There it was, only this time there were six more. Within seconds, they were all chirping and making quite a racket. Maggie opened the front door of the house and ran into the kitchen, "What can I feed them?" she asked herself. She went to the pantry and pulled down a container of oats. "This will do the trick!" She walked back out onto the front porch and tossed a handful of oats onto the ground. The red cardinals swooped down and began to eat. She tossed handful after handful out to the birds, and as she did so, she thanked God for bringing the one cardinal to Samuel on the night of the accident. The vibrant red color of their feathers was in bright contrast to the white paint on her house. They really stood out against the few patches of old snow that lay clumped on the barren brown grass. You'd have thought they were having a Thanksgiving celebration of their own, and in a way, they were. Maggie continued feeding her friends when she felt something land on her shoulder. She moved her head to the right and saw a cardinal perched just there next to her ear, resting. It was as if it was taking stock of the rest of the flock and enjoying their feasting as much as Maggie Mae. It didn't panic or flutter about. It just sat, beak forward, looking side to side. Maggie felt a sense of genuine privilege. She sat back down and committed the moment to memory—the gentle tickle of its weightless movement, how it clicked and chattered as it calmly sat and observed the others. It snuggled in closer and actually nestled against her cheek, the satin-like texture of its feathers rubbing against her skin. Maggie instinctively knew the cardinal felt safe in her care, and she also knew this was the *The Bird* that sounded the alarm to Samuel only a few nights before. The two rested for only a few minutes longer, and when the flock had finished feasting, they all flew away. Maggie left the oats on the front porch table and walked back into the house. It had been quite a day already, and she still had relish to make!

The room was cozy but a little neglected. She built a fire, fluffed a few pillows, and added birdseed and a feeder to her shopping list. She took the love letters out of her pocket and placed them back on the fireplace mantle and then headed into the kitchen. The clock struck two, so she got busy and made the cranberry relish for the party. There really wasn't much to it, whole cranberries through the grinder, a few ripe oranges peeled and the seeds removed, and of course, a cup of sugar. She added a splash of almond extract and gave it all a good stir and then put it into a bowl to marinate in the refrigerator. When she was all done, Maggie had a large portion of simple deliciousness. Just as she was tidying the kitchen, she heard a yoo-hoo at the back door. It was Molly, and she had a basket of goodies to share. "Momma said you should have these treats to eat. We still have so much that some will go bad before we have the chance to eat it all." Molly was beaming as usual. She held up the brimming basket and Maggie took it from her with a smile and a thanks. "I see Wildfire's followed you over," said Maggie as she closed the door behind Molly. "I was just talkin' with your papa today, and we are both very excited to teach you how to ride her this spring." Maggie continued to talk as she walked into the kitchen with the basket in her hand. "I think Wildfire will be ready to ride earlier than a regular horse. I see very mature lines in her build and in her actions. She is very much like you, young lady, very grown-up for her age."

Maggie stopped and noticed how Molly was looking at her apron splattered with cranberry. "Is everything okay, Molly dear? You look kind-a puzzled." The question was fair since Molly had stopped paying attention to Maggie, completely fascinated by the dirty apron hanging from a nail on the kitchen wall. Maggie walked up to where Molly was standing and took a closer look at all the splattered red dots on the front of the apron. "What are you looking at, dear?"

Maggie was dumbfounded. It looked like a used apron with cranberry stains. A second later Molly spoke, much to Maggie's relief, "Oh, I just think it's kind-a pretty. Look here." She pointed to how the red dots clustered in one spot and not another. "They remind me of birds ... red birds in the snow." Maggie swallowed. She couldn't believe what she was hearing. "And here it looks like strawberries in cream. I love strawberries. Maybe we should grow some this spring when I learn to ride. That would be a yummy treat after a long day on Wildfire." Molly paused and looked up at Maggie Mae. "Are you okay, Maggie?" she asked with concern. "You look so serious." Molly was right. Maggie did look serious, and she needed to sit down.

"I am all right, dear. Just a busy day." She patted the chair next to her. "Come and sit down by me. Tell me more."

Molly took her seat, and with a great focus on her words, she said, "Well, everything is different now, ya know, since I was naughty and rode the horse. I see things differently." For a moment, Maggie thought she was listening to a wise woman speaking. Molly sounded older and wiser. There was no mistaking that. "Take the dots on the apron, Maggie. I've been having this dream about big red birds, and the berry stains reminded me of the dream. Silly stuff like that. Sometimes ..." She laughed at herself and leaned back in the kitchen chair. "Sometimes the clouds have faces in them. Like an angel is watching over me. That's a good idea, huh, Maggie? An angel to watch over ya and keep ya safe."

Her innocence and matter-of-fact comment was priceless, and once again, Maggie just listened. She felt it was best to let her speak. "Do you remember your red bird dream, Molly dear?" asked Maggie.

"Oh, sure. I have dreamed it a few times since Saturday night, and it's always the same. A bright red bird is flying through the forest, and it keeps tweeting. I can hear it say, 'She's safe! She's safe!' It's kind-a silly, really. But it makes me feel like the bird is talking about me, and I like how it makes me feel." Molly stopped and took Maggie's hand. She started to speak but paused. After she'd collected her words and put them into place, she said, "Ya see, Maggie Mae, since Sunday morning when I woke up, I see everything in a different light and by a different light. That dirty apron speaks a different language now. Instead of it saying it's messy, I see it as a thing of beauty, and then I find the lesson. You know what Momma said?" She paused and looked at Maggie to see if maybe Momma had already told her. Maggie shrugged her shoulders, so Molly continued, "Momma said that the mistakes we make while we are alive are some of the ways we learn to grow and get smarter, and that we should learn from our mistakes and try to not repeat them." She stood up and walked to the kitchen window. Wildfire was out in the pasture, and it brought a smile to her face. "So ya see," she said and turned and faced Maggie, "it was okay to have the accident and learn the lesson. The trick is not to make the same mistake again." She laughed again as she rubbed the back of her head with her hand. "I really don't want to repeat that lesson again! My noggin is still a little tender." Maggie stood up and walked over to where she stood. She put a grandmotherly arm around her tiny shoulder and squeezed her tightly.

"Molly, darling, I couldn't agree with you more." The two gazed out of the window and chatted about how Wildfire had matured into such a fine horse. Maggie didn't feel she should tell Molly how Johnny appeared and helped them to find her. Then the clock face showed 4:44.

"It's getting late, Maggie Mae. I promised Momma I'd be home by five o'clock." She walked to the back door, opened it to leave, and then stopped. "I almost forgot. When I talked with God, I talked with Johnny, too. He thanked me for bringing you back into the light." She looked up into the old woman's eyes with a special knowing. "Maggie Mae, his eyes are the bluest blue, and he wants me to remind you that he is always with you." She kissed Maggie on the cheek and said, "Night night, June Bug." Maggie flinched. "Johnny said you'd recall those tender words since he said them to you every night before you went to sleep. Remember, angels are everywhere ... all the time." Molly waved goodbye and walked back across the pasture with Wildfire trailing behind. Maggie stood at the open door only a moment longer, and then the clock showed 4:45.

amuel arrived the next morning as the first rooster crowed. The sky was off to a glorious start as wispy clouds filtered the morning sun in a way that reminded him of a spider's decaying web. A chilly breeze teased at his neck while he rapped at Mrs. G's door.

"Joe is done with the model T," he said as she opened the door to a frosty morning.

"Oh, that is wonderful!" she replied as she let him into the house and straight away to the kitchen. "Here's a cup of tea." She handed him a mug that he happily accepted. "Was Joe able to get the picture painted on it in time?" she asked as she placed a tempting plate of scones down in front of him and took her place at the kitchen table. "He and Smitty worked all night on it, Mrs. G." Samuel added with a mouthful of warm, buttery scone. "They managed to finish it about five this morning. I do believe you are gonna be very happy with the colors too. They really stand out on the matte black paint."

Maggie caught herself smiling as she thought about the surprise to come, and she thanked Samuel for helping her find the right men for the job. "So you think tomorrow about three-thirty is the best time to have it delivered, Samuel?" Maggie sounded a little nervous. "We will already be at their house for dinner, so everyone will be there to share in the joy." She paused and asked Samuel again, her nail tapping on the table giving away her anxious feelings.

"Yes, Maggie Mae." The fact that she said her name surprised her! She'd become so use to Mrs. G, his proper address took her by surprise. "Everyone will be really happy and surprised. Joe offered to drive it over, and I told him yes. Now ..." He grabbed another scone and stuffed it into his coat pocket. "I have a busy day too. I best get a move on." He stood up, thanked her for the breakfast, and headed to the front door. Mrs. G followed and thanked him one last time for all of the wonderful things that had happened in the last few months. He bent over and kissed her on the cheek. Think nothin' of it, Mrs. G. Janie and I are glad to help."

The cold morning snap chilled them both as Maggie opened the front door. Samuel tightened his collar and walked out to his truck. He gave the horn a short toot and pulled away. She stood for a moment longer and mulled over her chore list for the day. The sky was basically blue, so she didn't need to concern herself with rain or snow just yet. She stoked up the living room fire, topped off her tea, and finished dressing for the day. Snow-Snow followed her around. Maggie always welcomed her loving attention, so the two began to tidy the house, and then they headed to the barn to feed and water all of the farm animals.

Abner and Daisy were standing in the fenced yard waiting as usual, their winter coats coming in thick and wiry. Maggie was still convinced they ate more than any other goats she'd seen before, but she took delight in the fact that they looked healthy and happy as she tossed them another flake of alfalfa. As she finished up her farm chores, Molly came bounding around the corner, her face smiling and her hand toting a basket of carrots and zucchini.

"Mornin', Maggie Mae," she said with joy. "Momma asked me to bring these to you too. We have so many vegetables, and we can't eat 'em all. Besides, Papa isn't very crazy about zucchini, and Momma keeps trying to make him eat some." She laughed like he was gettin' tattled on. "And to tell ya the truth, it's not one of my favorites either."

"Well, Molly dear, let's head to the kitchen. My animals are fed, and I just happen to have a recipe for zucchini bread. I'll bet your papa won't even know there's squash in it." Maggie took the basket and looped her arm through Molly's. "Can ya stay and visit for a while?" Molly nodded yes and walked with Maggie to the house.

It was warm and toasty inside, and in no time at all, they had loaves of fresh bread baking in the oven. "I think Papa will like this bread very much, Maggie Mae. Cinnamon and sugar in a bread batter is always yummy."

The two managed to stay quite busy on that Wednesday before Thanksgiving. Maggie showed Molly some of the more refined ways of cleaning the bathroom and kitchen floors as well as the proper way to polish antique furniture. Much to Molly's surprise, Tiger had followed her from the apple orchard, and they could hear her meowing at the back door. The racket he made caught their attention, and before too long, the kittens were reunited in a purring ball of paws and tails on the warm living room rug.

"Maggie Mae," Molly said as she began to move a few of the papers around the work space of the old roll top desk, "I need to move these papers if I am going to get the dust inside of your desk. Is that okay? It looks really organized, and I don't want to mess anything up."

Realizing that the Model T work order was on top of her to-do pile, she walked over to Molly before saying, "Oh, the desk is fine for today, Molly dear. Thank you for being thoughtful enough to ask first." And she closed the desk panel with a solid click.

Molly continued to tidy up until she was finished. "Well, Maggie, I think that does it in here," Molly said with one smear of dust across the apple of her pink cheek. "Is there anything else I can do to help you? "She paused and then lifted her nose toward the kitchen. "Maybe I could test our zucchini bread. I am a pretty good judge too." Maggie couldn't resist her darling request, and in a snap, the two had the kettle on and a plate of steamy-hot zucchini bread cooling in between the two of them.

Then there was a knock at the door!

"Wait here, Molly dear. I'll be right back." She sat down and patiently waited as she inhaled the decadent aroma.

"Well, look who's here," announced Maggie as she walked back into the kitchen. "It smells wonderful in here, ladies!" Papa spoke with a silly English accent, and his eyes were glued to the bread on the kitchen table. "I see you two lovelies have been very busy. The living room sparkles, and the kitties are snoozing by the fire." He looked about the room and then asked if he could sit down. Maggie had already grabbed another mug, placed it in front of him, and secretly winked at Molly. "Perhaps you'd like to join us for lunch? We were just getting ready to test our special recipe. Should I get you a plate?" Her suggestion was happily accepted. Maggie and Molly bit their tongues as Papa took a big bite of the hot, maple-buttered zucchini bread. He sighed as he breathed out through his nose. "Oh, ladies, how is it that you two can make such delicious food?" He took another bite and sat back in his chair as if he were eating the finest food in the world. "This is really the best bread I have ever eaten." His silly English accent had taken a back seat to his enthusiasm for the new flavors in the bread. He looked at Maggie after he took a sip of the spicy tea. "I should think it would be okay if you were to bring a loaf of this bread to our Thanksgiving feast tomorrow." He popped in another bite. Molly was giggling to herself. Papa checked her on her reaction and asked her why she was laughing.

"Oh, Papa," Molly said, thinking quickly, "you just have maple butter smeared all over your chin." Her fib fooled him! "You are a mess!" She walked to his seat and handed him her napkin. "Here, Papa. If only Momma could see you now." The three laughed as he finished up his chunk of bread. They talked a little about the day to come and about how nice the weather had been lately. Papa related that he'd sowed some potato seeds in an acre of soil out behind the orchard and that he was excited to see how they'd do through the winter.

"Johnny had the same plan, William. I believe you are on the right track." Maggie looked pleased with his decision to plant the potato seeds. "Ya know, we had great plans for the land surrounding the orchard too. I am so glad to know you and your family are thinking along the same lines." She stood and walked to the sink, her smile not giving away the big secret she'd be sharing the next day.

"Well, Maggie, I'd best get a move on. I just figured I'd stop by and see how you were doing," William said as he, too, stood and pushed in his kitchen chair. "Thanks again for a chunk of that amazing bread. It was really delicious. What did you put in that batter?" Maggie walked over to him and looped her arm through his. Molly's eyebrows raised as she stood by, wondering how Maggie was going to handle his question,

"You just never mind that, love," she said, using her English accent. "You know us pastry chefs never give away their secrets, and if they did, you would have to clean the kitchen." She batted her eyes up at him, acting so silly and clever at the same time.

"I know how to take a hint," replied William, putting his hat on and walking toward the back door. "Now don't wear out your welcome, Molly. Maggie needs time to herself too. Besides, Momma needs you at home pretty soon. I think she is also cleaning house." He looked back to Maggie as she wiped the crumbs from the table. "We'll see you tomorrow, Maggie Mae. Mary said to come over as early as ya like. Janie will be there about two o'clock. Mary found the finest turkey, Maggie." His smile said it all. "We even have chestnuts for the stuffing. It's gonna be the finest feast we've ever served!" He winked at Maggie, "Thanks again, ladies." He looked down at Molly and said, "Thirty minutes, honeybun."

"Gotcha, Papa. I'll be right behind ya."

He opened the back door and stepped out into the chilly afternoon. When he reached the gate to the pasture, Wildfire nearly pushed him over with her curious nose. William produced an apple from his pocket, fed it to the horse, and the two walked home together. Molly and Maggie watched from the window in the kitchen, each one admiring how beautiful Wildfire had become. She was eleven hands high now and every bit her mother's daughter.

"I am so glad ya stopped by for a visit, Molly dear. We always have fun, don't we!" said Maggie with genuine affection. "Ya know, this will be the first Thanksgiving I have left my house in forty years." She stopped and looked into Molly's surprised eyes. "You know the story." Maggie began to speak to Molly like grown-ups talked to each other. "After Johnny died, I quit living. I stayed locked inside of a jail I made myself." She stopped talking for only a moment as Molly took her hand. "Well," said Maggie, brightening her smile and looking dreamily out of the window. "That's over know, and I am very glad to say so." Both ladies smiled at one another, and they both understood why.

The afternoon was quickly becoming the early evening, and Molly knew it was time to head home. Maggie walked her to the back door as usual and helped her button up her coat. When she was all bundled and ready for the short walk, Molly shared with Maggie the lesson she'd learned that afternoon. "I didn't know that zucchini could be a teacher," commented Molly as she slipped on her mittens. Maggie looked at her *without* surprised eyes. "When I brought the basket to you today, I knew I was glad to share something that Papa and I didn't like to eat. But when you changed the way to use the zucchini, we both changed our minds and decided we liked it." Molly was making a very profound point. Just because one recipe didn't taste good, that didn't mean every recipe would taste bad. "Remember, when other people in town tried to help you, Maggie Mae, and no matter how they tried to get you to see God's light, you kept your eyes closed?" Maggie nodded yes with a sorrowful look. "Well, when I tried to help you, you liked my recipe for God's light better." Molly continued with a grin. "It's just like zucchini!" Then she said with a triumphant ring, "Zucchini and God are good for you, but if you don't like the way it's served, you simply have to change the recipe!" She was beaming up at Maggie. "Do you understand, Maggie Mae? It's re-make-able! It is all re-make-able! If ya don't like the way life is going, change it! Try a new recipe! If your clothes don't fit, find ones that will. When you feel your skin starting to burn, get out of the sun. There can be a better way to find answers to questions, so read! Make the effort. Spend time learning, and you won't waste your precious years wondering what could have been. Eat the zucchini when you find your favorite recipe and listen for God when you find your ears."

Maggie didn't know what to say. She wrapped Molly in her grandmotherly arms and held on tight. "You ...are a very wise little girl," she said while she snuggled. "Thank you for sharing your zucchini wisdom. I think it's the best recipe of all." With those words, Maggie Mae handed back the empty basket and opened the door. Molly called for Tiger, and the two headed out into the pasture. "See ya tomorrow, Maggie. It's gonna be the best Thanksgiving ever!" They waved for only a minute, and then the frigid air forced Maggie to close the door. She walked back into the kitchen and washed the few dishes they'd dirtied. Maggie had to laugh to herself. "She really is somethin' else. Leave it to Molly to use zucchini as a metaphor." When she was done tidying, she was reminded of a famous quote by William Shakespeare. "Nothing is good or bad, but thinking makes it so." She thought a little longer and then changed one word. On a piece of linen paper, she wrote down the revised quote. "Nothing is good or bad, but zucchini makes it so!" When she finished her writing, she sat back, chuckled a little at her cleverness, and looked up at Johnny's portrait. It was a comfort to have his presence in the quiet room. Now that her sadness was completely gone, she enjoyed whatever she had left of him and thanked God for those blessings.

Snow-Snow purred by the golden coals, and the room glowed from its earlier polishing. The fire needed to be stoked, so Maggie saw to it. Her life lacked the sting she had once felt, and she stood warming herself and looking out the picture window. The setting sun was glorious! Huge puffs of cotton-white clouds hung in front of the sun as it slowly faded behind a distant mountain range. Bold streaks of orange, pink, and steel blue burst out from behind the billowing plumes decorating the sky in a last-ditch effort to say, "Life is good!" Somehow, Maggie Mae felt the display of grandeur was just for her.

Molly was right on-time with her lantern that Thanksgiving eve. Maggie was already waiting when her darling came through with their traditional three flashes of candlelight. Somehow "I love you" meant more to Maggie than it ever did before. She held up her lit lantern, opened the panel, and sent back her goodnight greeting. Molly responded two more times as did Maggie, and then each one headed to bed.

Meanwhile, out in the orchard, a flock of seven red birds gathered on the barren branches of the oldest apple tree, its trunk thick and gnarled as if it had been through many years of trial and tribulation. They perched at attention, not a feather out of place, not a chirp to be heard. A moment later Wildfire walked up to the fence line and hung her large head over the tightly stretched wire. Thickly pelted rabbits and furry squirrels popped up out of their burrows, and when the time was right, an old snow owl swooped down out of a tall sugar pine and landed on a podium-like stump that faced the audience of listening guests. The owl craned his limber neck as he acknowledged the collection of forest creatures. The wisdom in his eyes shone out into the assembly and commanded complete attention. The sky was lit by a billion bright stars, each one sparkling as if they, too, were standing at attention for the wise owl. No wind rustled the leaves that littered the orchard floor. Peace stood guard as the owl spread out his enormous wings and exposed his powerful feathered breastplate for all to see. When all had bowed in respect, he lowered his wings and sent his thoughts out into their deserving minds.

"Behold a change in the forest. Our prayers have been fortified by our faith in her. Through this divine connection we all share, we will continue to thrive. She has talked with the one." The owl paused his thought. "She shares his love and lives his divine law. She will not falter. We will not falter. We are one, with the one, by the grace of the one, and from these truths, we live for the purpose of the one." The forest stayed motionless. Not a single creature made a noise or a sound.

"Go now and live for the one. I shall go and live for the one. Protect her. She is Molly." The wise owl looked directly at Wildfire and nodded his head in thanks. "Protect her always. She is a key. Her heart speaks universally, for she judges not. She is the hand of the one."

A soft breeze picked up. Slowly and with great reverence, the owl lifted his wings and thrust himself off of the stump and out into the crystalline night. Far off in the shadowed distance, Wildfire could hear someone calling her name. She looked at the animals and bowed her head in farewell. On the breath of a winter wind, the red birds departed in patterned flight, soaring away to the hidden nests that lay tucked in the recesses of another forest realm. The rabbits and squirrels were gone without notice. With quick movements, they slipped silently into the black holes of a protective earth. When all was said and done and the subtle winds covered the footprints left behind, no one would know the animals had been there at all. No one needed to know. But the animals knew, and they'd never forget!

Morning broke in such a way that even the animals awoke with a sense of appreciation. The sky started off a dove gray and then blossomed into a crisp, clean blue. Random clouds fringed the edges of the horizon as if creating a lacy frame, and the chill in the dawning air nipped at the sleepy noses of those who stepped out into the morning air.

Maggie was tackling her daily chores with a spring in her step and a tune on her lips. The hens were out in the yard, and Abner and Daisy milled about too. As she approached the pasture, Wildfire greeted her as well! "Oh, good morning, everyone," she announced with gleeful warmth. "How lovely to see you all looking so fit and healthy!" Any person listening would have thought she was talking to people, but her heart was so overjoyed that she spoke to her animals as though they would appreciate her praise. The sound of crunching gravel caught her attention, and she turned to see her nephew driving onto the farm. She waved wholeheartedly, tossed the last of her scratch and apples, and then headed over to greet him. "Good morning, Bobby!" Her cheeks were flushed and plump. The corners of her eyes were turned up in a tight, cheerful grin, and her white hair was loose and tumbling about her shoulders. Bobby jumped out of the truck and met her halfway across the backyard.

"My, my, you are looking well, Auntie. I must say you are looking quite young, very fetching!" His words were true, and she blushed as she humbly accepted them along with a hug and a kiss. "I am here to remind you that you are always welcome to our home for Thanksgiving, but my spies tell me that you have a very special evening planned with the Fitzwilliam's and the Colliers. Am I right?"

Maggie let the cat out of the bag and told him all about the plans she and Samuel had in place for giving the Model T to the Fitzwilliam's. He listened to her as she passionately spoke. Her hands as well as her tongue were flying. He caught himself chortling a few times at her sheer delight in expressing herself. He'd never seen her act like this before, and being in her genuinely happy company was worthy of Thanksgiving itself!

"And so you see, Bobby," she said, wrapped her arm through his, and turned to walk toward the house, "Samuel and I got the old thing assembled, and I had a colorful advertisement painted on each door." She looked up at him with a sparkle in each eye. "They can use it to deliver their produce. Folks 'round here will hear 'em coming, and that in itself will make 'em irresistible." She was acting more like a kid with every word. "Oh, we can't wait! Samuel and Janie are just as excited as I am!"

"You're doing a grand thing here, Auntie." He stopped a moment and then gently added, "Johnny would want you to do this too." She knew he was right. He took her into both arms and gave her a great big hug. "Now you'll have to keep me in the loop. I wanna hear all about what happens." He walked her to the front porch. "I need to get going now, but I am looking forward to having a piece of pie tomorrow. May I stop by for leftovers?" His eyebrows arched with expectation. "You know how I feel about pie." He smiled from his full heart and waved goodbye. "I'll stop by at nine, Auntie." He fired up the truck and put it into gear. "How about a cup of that good tea, too?"

They waved goodbye, smiling and thankful. Maggie nodded yes to all of his suggestions and made a mental note for their date in the morning.

She tidied around the inside of her living room, making sure everything was just so. The clock ticked loudly, and when it struck the top of the hour, Maggie was sure it must be time to get ready to go. However, eight o'clock in the morning was bit too early to leave for Thanksgiving dinner.

The clock kept its hands on the pulse of the day. Every time Maggie checked the time, it seemed to have stalled. Five minutes felt as if it took five hours to pass, and she was running out of chores to keep herself busy.

As morning passed to afternoon, Molly stopped by to visit. Samuel saw both ladies out in the pasture playing with Wildfire. He rolled down the window, blew a shrill whistle from the cab of his truck, and waved his hat hello.

"We are heading over a little earlier than planned," he hollered. "Janie and I can't wait any longer!"

"What a splendid idea," replied Maggie as the horse crunched down on the last apple. "We are ready to go too!" Molly trotted around as if she was a horse herself. "We'll see ya soon!"

Samuel smiled and waved. "See ya soon!" and then he stepped on the gas.

With the good news in mind, the two gals decided to get a move on and head over to Molly's house for Thanksgiving. As they began to walk back toward the house, they noticed an old truck driving up the Fitzwilliam's drive. It was a familiar truck too. It was the McGregor's!

"Well, Molly dear, it looks like the McGregor's are here. What a surprise! I hope they are joining the party." She bent down to Molly and whispered, "I dare say we have enough food to feed the whole town!" The two laughed in agreement, Molly remembering that the turkey was already roasting in her momma's oven.

Maggie had her pies and breads ready to go, so she stoked the fire with one solid chunk of oak, filled Snow-Snow's food and water dishes, and handed the bread basket to Molly. "Well, my darlin', shall we go?" Molly was already at the front door and turning the knob.

"After you, Mrs. Green," replied Molly with a silly English accent.

"Capital idea, Molly dear. Simply capital!"

The two walked out the door, down the steps, and into a joyful world of Thanksgiving travelers. As they walked down the road, many cars and trucks passed them. It seemed everyone had somewhere special to go today, and they chose the best time to walk. They must have passed every member of the community church. Toots on the horn triggered waves and holiday greetings from kids piled in the back of wagons, shouting and hollering hello and waving as if they were in the parade again. This holiday was like none other before, and the party hadn't even begun.

By the time Maggie and Molly were halfway up the drive, Samuel and Janie were too. They'd hitched Fiona to the buckboard, and in the bed of the old wagon lay their Thanksgiving contribution. "Fancy meeting you two ladies here," announced Janie as they caught up to them. "When Samuel said we could come over earlier, I said okay!" She was smiling from ear to ear. "It's going to be a marvelous day, ya know. Just look at this weather!" She was rambling. "I don't recall seeing a day prettier than this particular one." She laced her arm through her husband's and looked forward with a contented grin. Samuel looked at Maggie and winked, his own smile keeping his lips quiet as his wife stole the show.

"We'll follow behind ya," said Maggie, walking along with a youthful stride. "I can't wait to see what ya got tucked under that tarp."

Samuel clicked his tongue and continued on. By the time he'd brought the wagon around and in front of the house, William and Mary were standing on the front porch. "Howdy, neighbors. How are you two on this beautiful day?"

Janie and Samuel were off the wagon and on the porch with hugs all around.

"It is a beautiful day," said Janie with excitement. As the freshness of the hellos wore off, the McGregor's came out of the house and ignited the happy greetings all over again. When Maggie and Molly finally joined the festivities, the hugs and kisses resumed one more time, and even Fiona and Wildfire got in on the action, each one stomping and neighing as if to say, "Let me in on a hug too!" William and Mary soon joined the bustle on the porch. William suggested that they unhitch Fiona and lead her into the pasture to frolic with Wildfire. Janie, hardly catching her breath, walked to her wagon and began to unload all of the things they'd brought for the day. She handed out pies and jars of jam, freshly baked breads and muffins, casseroles filled with sweet potatoes, and of course, one large box that was wrapped up tight. The ladies carried all of the goodies into the house and headed straight for the kitchen.

"This seals the deal, Mrs. McGregor," announced Mary as she and the parade of ladies began walking past them. "As you can see, we have plenty of food for Thanksgiving. You must stay and join us!" Mary stopped and flashed Mrs. McGregor those pleading eyes, and they couldn't resist.

"It's a deal!" said the elderly couple with a smile in their eyes, laughing.

"Well, then at least let me carry something," said Mrs. McGregor, taking a pumpkin pie from Mary. "Oh, this does look delicious! Knowing me, it may not make it until dessert!" Everyone laughed at her honest admission.

"Yes, Henrietta, we all know how you love your pie," announced Mr. McGregor as he wiped the tears of laughter from his eyes. "But we must wait till after supper. We will, I tell ya!"

The men attended to the outside chores while the womenfolk puttered in the kitchen. The turkey had about thirty minutes to go in the oven, so Mary and Janie assigned setting the table to Henrietta and Molly. "Bruce and I are very pleased with the wonderful work you and your family have done on the place, Molly. We heard about the tumble you took, and we were very worried! We are so glad that you are okay." She spoke her words from the heart, and Molly felt her genuine concern.

"Thank you, Mrs. McGregor."

"Oh, call me Henrietta, dear," she said, her grandmotherly nature softening her face.

"Thank you, Henrietta. Well, I'll tell ya it sure did hurt a bunch, but the doc fixed me right up." Molly leaned in as if telling Henrietta a secret, "And besides, I did enjoy talking with God. He is one nice fella."

Molly kept setting the table as Henrietta stood there and digested exactly what Molly had just said. "You mean to tell me that you had a conversation with God, Molly?" Her tone was rather disbelieving.

"Yes, ma'am, I do." She stopped placing the napkins at each seat and looked directly into the eyes of the stunned old woman. "And I talked with Johnny, too! He has the bluest eyes." Molly stopped and looked up at the corner of the room. "He's with us

177

all the time, Henrietta. He's our guardian angel." The matter-of-fact tone in her voice was convincing.

"Well," replied Henrietta as she cleared her throat and took a seat, "that is good news." She sounded a bit flustered. "One can never have too many guardian angels."

The house smelled amazing. With the horses fed, brushed, and blanketed, the men were soon lured into the cozy living room by the aroma of the dinner that awaited them. As laughter began to fill the old farm house, the ladies brought in some farm fresh snacks. Carrots, celery, pickles, and olives arranged on a fancy crystal dish appeared on the polished coffee table, while pitchers of icy apple cider graced the sideboard. Mary was at her best that day. Her attention to detail made this Thanksgiving day the finest it could be. Soon, she took the turkey from the oven and allowed it to rest. Maggie Mae was placed in charge of *guarding* the turkey just to keep the men from slicing off a nibble! When the many side dishes were set out and the prize turkey ready to carve, everyone took their place at the table and held hands. Never had there been a finer group in the heart of this happy home. Never had there been more love than there was at this moment.

William cleared his throat and took a deep breath. "I'd like to thank everyone for being here today." His eyes looked at each guest with sincerity. "Mary and I are quite humbled by our good fortune in this town, and I can't begin to tell you how nice it feels to finally come to a place we can call home." His voice caught in his throat.

Mary stepped in and said, "Heavenly Father, we thank you for your wisdom and your guidance. We thank you for the abundant harvest and for all of our wonderful friends."

Now her voice began to crack with emotion, and Maggie stepped in and said, "And Father, I'd like to thank you for protecting our precious Molly dear. Without her, I wouldn't be at this beautiful table today!"

Since she and Molly were already holding hands, Maggie gave Molly's a good squeeze. "And since we're all speaking from the heart," said Janie, following suit, "Thank you, Father, for blessing Samuel and I with our new friendships and ..." She stopped and began tear up. "I ... I am ... I am going to have a baby!" The whole room gasped!

Everyone hugged. "Oh, Janie!" said Mary with abundant tears of joy running down her cheeks. "How wonderful! I don't know what to say except ..." She looked at William, and he gave her a nod. "We're expecting too!" And now the house roared! Anyone looking in the window would have had to smile at the sheer joy of the scene. Dinner? What dinner? These friends were sitting on cloud nine, and Johnny was sitting with them too. When the commotion calmed, William began to carve the turkey. As the dishes were passed and the cranberry relish praised, Maggie Mae took a precious moment to commit this dinner to memory. She noted the buzz in the conversation and the compliments on every bite of food. She loved the laughter, the manners, the attention to detail, and the soft crackle of the fire in the corner of the room. She caught the faintest murmur of farm animals out in the yard, and then she saw the cardinals—all seven sitting on the railing of the front porch and looking in on the Thanksgiving dinner. Maggie stopped and acknowledged the group with a subtle tip of her head. After the past few weeks, she'd become accustomed to miracles, and the cardinals were welcome guests at their table.

They took their own sweet time with the meal. They passed around rolls and butter without a second thought. Mashed potatoes and gravy seemed to magically reappear whenever the dish was emptied. Stuffing? Yes! Sausage and chestnut stuffing was scooped out from the cavity of the roast turkey and devoured with gusto! Buttered carrots were like candy, each bite followed by a savory chunk of sweet potato. This meal and memory would be hard to top, and why would anyone want to?

Outside in the driveway, a car horn tooted! Maggie looked at Samuel. In the excitement of the meal, they forgot about the special delivery.

"Are we expecting more company?" asked William as he pushed himself away from the dinner table. "Let me take a look and see who it is." He stood up and walked toward the front door. Before he could grasp the doorknob, Samuel cut him off and blocked his view. Quickly, Maggie Mae was standing by Mary's chair, suggesting that they go together and see who it was.

"You are acting funny, Maggie." Mary's face looked skeptical. "Here, dear," offered Maggie, "let me get your chair for you." Without missing a beat, Maggie pulled Mary's chair out and walked her to the door. The horned tooted again, and Maggie said, "Years ago before my Johnny died, my parents knew about the great plans he and I had for this farm." She looked at the McGregor's and nodded. "As you all know, Johnny passed, and our dreams didn't come to life. A little while ago, I found a bill of sale for …" She stopped and looked into their waiting faces. "Well, Samuel and I thought it should be yours, the Fitzwilliam's family. So, Happy Thanksgiving. I am so proud of y'all." She stopped but then continued, "Our farm is simply wonderful. This is for you!"

With her sentimental words still piquing their curiosity, Samuel opened the front door and ushered the party out onto the front porch. Molly ran down into the yard. William and Mary stood holding hands, and with shocked expressions, they looked at their new Model T. It was parked out front, its motor humming perfectly. The flat black paint as clean as the day it rolled off the line in 1908. Maggie walked up beside them and shared the story of how her parents had planned for her and Johnny to run the farm, and when he was suddenly lost, her parents didn't have the heart to tell her about the wedding present. Mary and William stood quietly and listened.

"So you see, it really should be yours to use on this glorious farm. This is what my parents would have wanted, and I believe it is what Johnny wants too." Maggie walked down to the car and pointed to the picture painted onto the door. "I took the liberty of creating an advertisement for the door. I hope you don't mind." The Fitzwilliam's didn't know what to say. "I prayed on the idea and came up with this. *Johnny Angel—Apple Orchard and Vegetable Farm. A little heaven in every bite.*"

The bold black words were painted over the background scene of the farm and orchard. The rendering was depicted so well that you could actually see the house next to the barn and the apple trees off in the distance. In addition to a cow, there were three hens pecking at the dirt, and in the pasture stood Wildfire. The colors were primary and bright. The picture was perfect! The gentleman who delivered the Model T was the artist as well. When everyone made it down to the old car, he was standing by the side of his masterpiece and enjoying the words of praise and amazement.

"Well, look there. It's Wildfire and Bessy! Isn't that somethin'!" said William as he squatted down to get a closer look at the picture. "I had no idea," he added as he scratched his head, "that you were havin' this done for us, Maggie Mae. I don't know what to say other than thank you." Mary was now standing by his side, and her warm hand slipped into his.

"Thank you is just the beginning, Maggie Mae," added Mary, her eyes brimming with grateful tears. "We'll make ya proud of us!"

"Oh, my dear friends," said Maggie with the strength of knowing in her voice, "you already do."

"Well, now. If I didn't know better, I'd swear that the whole forest has turned out to see the old car," observed Mr. McGregor, looking about and seeing cardinals and horses and chickens in the yard. "And since we are all together on this point, the missus and I have another announcement to make." He cleared his throat as he looped his weather-beaten thumbs through the button holes of his leather vest. "We are gettin' up in years, ya know, and seeing that you and your family have taken this old ranch to heart and done a fine, fine job of fixin' her up, Henrietta and I have decided to give the place to you and your family." He paused and looked around the assembly. No one could speak. "The sale of the apples will more than pay the taxes, and we believe you'll have a good life in Pine Valley, and now that there's gonna be another youngin' ..." His voice trailed off as he and his wife began to smile at each other.

"Oh, what an amazing day," said Maggie Mae as she walked over to Mr. McGregor. She grabbed him by the hand and shook it wholeheartedly! Next, she took Mrs. McGregor's hand and kissed the back of it, letting her tears of joy flow freely.

Samuel and Janie were quiet too.

"Well then," announced Molly, breaking the silence, "let's go for a ride! Papa, you drive, and Momma and I will sit next to you. Is that all right with you, Maggie Mae?"

"Of course it is, Molly dear. It's your car now!" The mechanic gave William a quick lesson, and away they went. The Model T sputtered and popped and rattled down the gravel driveway like it was humming a long overdue song of freedom. When they turned the car around and came back toward the house, the Fitzwilliam's all waved out the windows as if on parade again. William pulled up, parked the newest member of the family, and went straight for Maggie Mae. He picked her up off the ground and twirled her around in a circle.

"Thank you so much, Maggie. I don't think that's enough, but thank you. Johnny Angel is a wonderful name for the orchard advertising. We couldn't be more proud to honor his memory by using his name." He only stopped a moment. "*A little heaven in every bite*. Clever, Maggie Mae. Clever as can be!" He couldn't stop grinning. "I pray that he's with us right now, Maggie. Ya know, smiling down on us." And with the last word William said, "the great snow owl landed on the weather vane atop the barn." All eyes turned up to see it. His mere presence was a sign that Johnny was indeed there and enjoying the celebration. The horses began to whinny and prance, bringing smiles to all of their faces. Altogether, the farm family was making quite a lot of noise, and the love and joy that everyone felt was very real.

By the time the sun was setting, they had clears the table from dinner and reset everything for dessert. Piping hot tea and coffee was poured out and served with warm slices of pumpkin and apple pie. The conversation never lagged for a moment, and when all was said and done, it was a unanimous decision that this had been the finest Thanksgiving ever! As care packages filled with leftovers were being assembled, the McGregor's handed the signed deed to the Fitzwilliam's and made them promise to keep them in the loop. Of course, William and Mary promised to do so since Bruce and Henrietta had become more like grandparents instead of landlords, and with the baby due in the coming year, they wanted to be sure that they knew they could rely on them for advice and favors.

"Thank you again for having us over for Thanksgiving dinner, my sweet," said Mrs. McGregor as she patted the happy but exhausted Mary on her flushed cheek.

"Oh, Henrietta … Grandmother." She blushed as she spoke the tender and treasured name. "We are truly honored by your kindness and generosity. Please stop by whenever you and Grandfather wish to visit." She looked down as she smiled. We wouldn't be here if it wasn't for your love and kindness. This will always be your home too." With those honest and genuine words, Mary hugged Henrietta and then Bruce; the warmth of her appreciation felt by the entire group.

"Yes, I dare say," began a choked-up grandfather, "we have a good thing going here. A very good thing, indeed." Mr. McGregor clapped William on the back and then shook hands with Samuel and Janie.

Before he could finish thanking them, Molly had tackled his leg and was hugging him tightly. "Don't forget me, Grandpapa," announced Molly in a way that only Molly could. "Thank you for a re-make-able house! I love my room and my trees and … everything!" Her face was lit up with a toothless smile.

"Oh yes, my little poppet," he said, patting her on the head with a gentle hand. "I could never forget you, but you mean remarkable." His correction may have been right, but it was not quite right in the way Molly understood. "No, Grandpapa. I mean re-make-able. Ya see, because of you, our lives are re-make-able. The farm is re-make-able. Even Maggie Mae is re-make-able. We are all re-make-able when can see the purpose in living." She scampered off, her enlightenment putting Grandpapa on the spot.

"Well," he began but stumbled, "I dare say that is some girl ya got there, Mary. Some girl, indeed."

As the evening wound down, plenty of promises were made and many goals were set for the coming year. The men helped load the care packages into the wagons and trucks, and Maggie Mae made sure to thank the McGregor's once again for their generous gift to the Fitzwilliam's.

"We are doing a good thing here," opened Maggie with her heart on her sleeve. "This is a good family we've got here. I've no doubt they'll make wonderful contributions to our community." She paused and then added, "They've already done so much for me."

Maggie hugged the McGregor's one last time, and as she was doing so, she whispered to Bruce, "I know that you'd a mind to give the farm to Johnny and me, but I didn't realize that fact until a short while ago. I am sorry I never said thank you. It was just so hard …" Her voice faltered, and Bruce knew why.

"You never mind that, Maggie Mae." He took her hand in his and added, "Look what we have here and now, and look at you!" He stood back and waved his hand as if he were showing her off. "I am learning we are all—how'd she put it?—re-make-able. We are right where we should be, and the missus and I couldn't be prouder."He looked her square in the eye. "And we're proud of you too!" He hugged her one last time and said, "Happy Thanksgiving, lass. Happy Thanksgiving, everyone. I am stuffed like … well, a turkey!" And he started laughing as he and Henrietta got into their truck and began driving down the gravel road.

Samuel and William put the Model T in the barn for the night as Maggie and Janie tidied the dining room. The conversation between the ladies was one of happiness and blessings. Janie had wanted a baby for so long, and she was finally pregnant along with Mary. The two agreed that it must have been a bit of magic from their guardian angel.

"So much has happened this year, Janie," said Mary as she sipped on her tepid cup of tea. "I am really overwhelmed!"

"Can't say that I don't agree with ya there, Mary. Who knew we'd tie at the pie contest and then both be carrying babies at the same time." She stepped behind her and placed a comforting hand on her shoulder." I may need your help through this whole havin' a baby thing though." She bit her lip as she sat down with a tiny look of fear in her eyes. "I never thought we'd be havin' a youngin', to be sure."Her voice was softer than usual. "We just thought it would never happen."She had a puzzled look on her face.

"Don't fret now, Janie. You've got me, and I've got you. And I know we can get through this together." By now they'd scooted their chairs closer together. "You see Molly there?" Mary nodded toward the living room where Molly was contently playing with Tiger. "We've got this, Jane. Let nature take its course, and we will be just fine. You'll see."

The two just smiled at each other until a hug took over. A moment later the men walked in.

"What are you two lovelies talking about?" asked William as he and Samuel took their usual seats.

"Something splendid," replied Molly as she entered the room and butted into the ladies' conversation.

"Don't ya mean re-make-able, Molly?" asked her papa, surprised by her entrance.

"No, Papa. I mean splendid. Having babies is a splendid thing. I am going to be a big sister, ya know. And that's marvelous!"

The Fitzwilliam's' and Colliers' good news spread through town. The farm also had its glory day when Mr. McGregor formally announced the transfer of title in the local paper and included a letter to the community asking everyone to support and accept the Fitzwilliam's as one of their own. Needless to say, the town of Pine Valley had already accepted the family with open arms, especially the well-known and adored Molly.

The winter was creeping in slowly. All of the local farm animals had their usual winter coats growing in nicely, but it seemed as if the harshness that was common during the beginning of winter simply hadn't reared its frosty head yet. Blue skies were present almost every day, making the month leading up to Christmas crisp and lovely.

Maggie Mae had her nephew along with Samuel and William up ladders and on roofs, winterizing her home for the upcoming snows. Though there weren't any signs of change yet, Maggie didn't want to get caught off guard.

"Since you are up there, Bobby, would you mind hanging these boughs I made for the holidays?" She smiled at him with an irresistible grin, and in thirty minutes, the three men had Maggie's boughs securely in place and ready for the whole town to see and enjoy.

"Oh, well done, gentlemen!" She was standing back in front of her house, her hands up by the sides of her face and her eyes alight because of the way her home sparkled. "Wait until Molly sees!"

"I do see, Maggie Mae, and it looks marvelous!" said Molly, coming up from behind. "Momma sent me to find Papa, but I see you found him first." The two gals laughed as the men gathered their tools and stowed the ladders away.

"I think Momma has the same idea, Papa," shared Molly as she took her papa's hand. "She has homemade boughs too, and since you said she shouldn't be climbin' ladders these days, she sent me to find you." Molly's new front teeth were beginning to show every time she smiled. "Is it okay if I stay and visit a little while with Maggie Mae, Papa?" She was helping him load his tools into his toolbox. "She and I have some Christmas plans to work on," she continued. "I'll be home by five, and I'll be sure to button my coat." Molly was practically telling him what she'd do, but he understood how these two gals worked, and who was he to say no? They may be working on *his* Christmas surprise.

Maggie's work crew said their goodbyes, reminding her to find them if anything else needed to be hung for decorating. Like Mary and Janie, she promised not to climb any ladders.

"Thanks again for everything!" she hollered as each man went on their way.

"I'll tell Momma you are working with Maggie Mae, Molly. See ya at five sharp!" William waved goodbye as he began to cross the white field that lay between their homes.

They walked inside the old cozy house and stayed in the living room.

"Let me stoke the fire, Molly dear. You open that box on the table." Maggie pointed to a stained box and then walked to the fireplace. She poked and prodded the coals, giving rise to the sleeping dragon of warmth and color. One chunk of oak, and the fire was set for the time being.

"Now, mind you, I haven't opened this box for forty years." She was wringing her hands a bit nervously as she walked over to the table, her hair tucked behind her ears. "So you must be patient with me. I am sure I will rediscover many happy memories and shed a tear or two."

"Oh, Maggie," said Molly with her head tipped to the side, "I am glad to share this with you. It will be great fun."

Maggie hugged her with one arm, and with the other, she pulled open the bent flap of the old ornament box. A floating layer of dust scattered upon the table, snowing down from a forgotten place in time. Maggie took a deep breath and peered inside.

Her mother's tablecloth laid neatly folded on top of the contents. In an instant she could hear her mother's sweet voice coming from the kitchen. The musty smell from the forgotten item was replaced by the cinnamon sweet memories of many Christmas mornings.

"I'd forgotten all about this tablecloth, Molly. It was my momma's favorite one." She pulled it out from the box and held it up to admire. "'There's not a hole in it,' my momma would say." Maggie's eyes looked as if see was seeing an old friend. She snapped the cloth open, trying to smooth out wrinkles. All of the sleeping dust was awakened in an instant!

"Would ya look at this?" Something in the box brought her attention away from the tablecloth, and she laid it to the side. "Candlesticks! Oh, these were her favorite too!" Maggie took one candlestick in each hand and lifted them up and out of the box as if they, too, were an old, forgotten acquaintance. "It was my job to polish them every holiday season. I'd forgotten. Oh, Molly dear. Look at this!"

Molly just sat back and enjoyed Maggie's enthusiasm. She sounded as if she herself was a young lady again. By the time the box was empty, the two gals had a treasure trove of precious items to clean and sort. One table was used just for ornaments. Another table was used for the silver candlesticks and candy dishes. The largest table was used for all of the linens in addition to all of the holiday knickknacks. It only took ten minutes to empty the box, but when they were done, they beheld a lifetime of holiday traditions.

When Maggie went to take the empty box out of the room, she noticed she'd missed something. Folded and tucked under the bottom flap was an envelope. She took it into her hand, and at once she knew what she had. She stopped, put the dingy box down, and walked over to where Molly was sitting. She sat by her side and then opened the envelope. The papers inside were clean but slightly yellowed by time. Maggie took another breath and then opened what looked like a letter. She put her hand to her mouth in surprise and then looked up at Molly.

"What is it, Maggie Mae?" she asked in a hushed tone. "You look a little sad."

"Oh, Molly dear, I am not sad." She looked back down, her expression a bit tearful. "I'd forgotten about this. It was a Christmas present for Johnny. Only he had passed before I had the chance to give it to him. It was my gift to him on our first Christmas as husband and wife. He never read it, Molly. He passed in October."

Molly stood up and walked around to Maggie's left side and placed a warm hand on her shoulder.

"What is it, Maggie Mae?" asked Molly with sincere respect.

"It's a poem, Molly dear. You see, Johnny didn't really understand all the *folderol* about Christmas. You know, Santa Claus and such. What he understood was the celebration of the birth of Jesus Christ. So with Moore's poem being printed in all the magazines, I thought I could show him my take on the whole Santa Claus tradition by writing him a poem to complement Moore's timeless classic." She paused a moment and handed the poem to Molly.

"Surely, you've heard Moore's poem. It starts, 'Twas the night before Christmas, and all through the house, not a creature was stirring, not even a mouse." Maggie paused and waited to see the light of recognition in Molly's eyes.

"Yes, I have heard that poem, Maggie. It's old, isn't it?" Molly stopped and waited for the librarian in Maggie to step into the conversation.

"Yes, Molly dear, it's very old. It was first published in a newspaper on December 23, 1823," Molly sat back down and rested her chin on her hands. She knew Maggie Mae wouldn't spare any details in tellin' this tidbit of history.

"Moore was a minister. He and his wife were very poor, and on one particular Christmas, Moore didn't have very much money for gifts. He'd written the poem as a gift to his children and a friend of his thought the poem so good that he surprised Moore by having it published in the New York paper called the

Troy. Reading it aloud every year has been a family tradition ever since." Maggie stopped and then added, "So I thought Johnny would like a poem written just for him on our first Christmas together." She stopped and looked up at his portrait, only this time she didn't seem sad. "I know just what to do with this poem, Molly." She stood up and walked over to the fireplace with the papers in her hand. "Let's start a new tradition in my house. You and I will read the poems aloud to our families every Christmas eve. You read Moore's poem, and I'll read mine. What do you think, Molly dear?"

Molly didn't have to think. She raced over to where Maggie stood and hugged her tightly. "Oh yes, Maggie Mae," declared the excited little girl, "that would be splendid!"

"Let's keep it a secret, my darlin'." suggested Maggie, squatting down to Molly's eye level. "I've already asked everyone to join me for Christmas Eve, and they've all accepted, so this will make it a very special evening, indeed!"

"Oh, it will, indeed!"

The month of December flew by. School was productive and busy, and with the news that the snow would be falling soon, everyone had an eye to the sky. Whatever snow had fallen during the month of November had all melted away; however, the faith in town was a determined faith, and they knew it would snow by Christmas morning.

The town of Pine Valley jumped on the decoration wagon and fancied every lamp and hitching post on Main Street. Boughs of pine intertwined with foot-long pinecones hung gracefully from every available nook. The firehouse put up a thirty-foot-tall Douglas fir and adorned its dark green branches with ornaments that the elementary students had made. They also use decorations that the elderly citizens from the senior home had made with their own hands. All in all, you could see that the town and its citizens lived for the spirit of Christmas.

Before they knew it, Christmas Eve had arrived, though without snow, and Maggie Mae's house was filled with people—her nephew and his family, the Collier's, the Fitzwilliam's, and the McGregor's. Everyone was clamoring around inside the warm home as they nibbled goodies and visited about the tremendous prospects of the upcoming year.

"Oh, yes," announced William with a tone of Santa Claus himself, "we have many plans for the new year, Samuel. The potatoes are coming along nicely, and Mary is sure that a field of squash will do well." He looked over to where the blooming women sat deeply engrossed in a motherly conversation. Molly is going to plant a plot of sunflowers in the hopes of starting a flower stand down on the road." He leaned in toward Samuel and snuck him a fatherly wink. "Our little one has become quite a farmer these days." He leaned back into his chair and took a long pull from his cup of cider. "Yep," he added with a genuine sound of contentment, patting his stuffed belly, " it's gonna be a wonderful new year!"

Samuel and he continued their jovial assessment of the days to come, while the ladies tittered and talked, each one have nothing but joyful blessings on the tips of their tongues. "Yes, my dears," observed Maggie Mae with motherly tenderness. "I do believe you two are beginning to show." She walked by them and patted them affectionately on their shoulders. "We are going to have a busy new year. That is one fact you can count on."

"I couldn't agree more, Maggie," added Henrietta as she took another cookie from the table. "Looks like we will be very busy grandmothers."

The ladies blushed and giggled.

"Well, ladies," said Janie as she reached for the pot of tea, "we are going to need all the help we can get." She smiled over at Mary and looked back over at Maggie and Henrietta. "Your hands are going to be busy, busy, busy! As far as I can see, you two are the best grandmothers our children could hope for." Janie could see them beaming from within! "Why, I wouldn't be surprised if our kids are reading before they even start school!" added Mary.

"Well, you're right there," stated Molly as she jumped into the chat. "Maggie Mae and I have big plans for the lil' ones." She paused and looked up into Maggie's face. "Right, Maggie Mae?"

"Why yes, Molly dear. Big plans, indeed!"

"Auntie," said her nephew Bobby, "your Christmas tree is beautiful this year. When was the last time you had a tree in the house?" He stood patiently in the arch of the doorway, his eyes looking kindly as he waited for a reply to his question, though he already knew the answer. Maggie walked over to where he stood and looped her arm through his. As they turned and walked into the living room together, the rest of the gals followed and patiently waited for Maggie Mae to answer his question. She took her seat to the right of the fragrant fir tree, first stopping to admire the trove of ornaments she'd hung upon its sturdy branches the night before. As she turned to face her family, she noted how the blessings of their presence had trimmed her life beautifully just as she had done to the limbs of her first Christmas tree in forty years!

The room quieted down. The chatter was replaced by the soft sounds of the crackling fireplace and cheerful melodies of Christmas songs from the Victrola. Molly curled up with the two kitties purring contentedly on her lap at the foot of Maggie's chair, her hands laced together as if she was sitting at her desk in school. Maggie took her time with collecting her thoughts and then said, "It's been a long time since this old house saw any holiday decorations, let alone a Christmas tree. After Johnny passed, my parents and I didn't feel much like celebrating, and after they passed, I pulled away from the community altogether." She only caught her breath for a moment and then returned to her story. "Today is a new day, and a new year is ahead of us all." She looked about the room. "The blessings we are all enjoying are because of my Molly dear." They looked at each other and simply smiled. Molly was humble and unaware of the true difference she'd made in the community. "Anyhow, here we are." She looked at each person in the room and silently acknowledged each one with the twinkle in her eye. "Molly and I have a surprise for everyone!" she announced, clasping her hands together. "So without further ado," she said as if she was directing a play, "may I present the timeless classic 'A Visit from Saint Nicholas' read by none other than our own Molly Fitzwilliam's!" With that announcement, Molly stood up and took the tattered book from Maggie's hand and walked over to the warm fireplace. The group applauded enthusiastically as she opened the book that had been secretly stowed under Maggie's chair. She cleared her throat and made sure everyone's eyes were on her and began to read.

'Twas the night before Christmas when all through the house, not a creature was stirring, not even a mouse! The stockings we're hung by the chimney with care, in hopes that St. Nicholas soon would be there. The children were nestled all snug in their beds, while visions of sugar plums danced in their heads. And Mama in her kerchief and I in my cap had just settled down for a long winters nap!

Molly had the room's full attention. Of course, everyone had heard the poem before, and they recited along under their breath; however, Molly's rendition was precious in its own telling! She took her time in dramatically expressing the text where she thought Moore would want her to, her voice going higher and lower with every discovery the papa made when he found that Santa Claus was outside of his family's home. When she reached the part where Santa was calling out the names of the reindeer, she cupped her hand to her mouth and hollered the names as if she were calling them into action herself! "Now, Dasher! Now, Dancer! Now, Prancer and Vixen! On, Comet! On, Cupid! On, Donder and Blitzen!"

She lifted her hands up into the air, the words on the tip of her tongue, ripe with the air of storytelling at its very best! She circled her arms as if welcoming the reindeer to land before her on the living room floor, and when she got to the end of the page, she ran to the frosted window and pointed her finger to the star-filled sky. With a priceless look of wonder in her dancing eyes, she looked back at her audience and said, "So up to the housetop the courses they flew, with sleigh full of toys ... and St. Nicholas too!"

When the poem announced that Santa was coming down the chimney, she walked over to the fireplace, bent down, and looked up into the smoke-filled darkness like the man himself might be there! As she described his clothes and his sack of toys, she picked up an old oil cloth sack Maggie had stuffed with paper and flung it over her shoulder. Then when Molly got to the part of describing Santa's round belly, she walked over to where her papa sat and patted him on his! Everyone started to laugh as William sat up in his chair and pulled his sweater down in front. Then she turned and faced the group with a wink of her eye and a twist of her head, she continued to read. "He spoke not a word, but went straight to his work. And filled all the stockings, then turned with a jerk. And laying his finger aside of his nose and giving a nod, up the chimney he rose!"

Molly had them in the palm of her hand. Even Maggie Mae was on the edge of her seat. "He sprang to his sleigh, to his team gave a whistle, and away they all flew like the down of a thistle. But I heard him exclaim as he drove out of sight, 'Merry Christmas to all and to all a good night!'"

Molly finished her reading with a long, exaggerated bow before the assembly. In a hop, skip, and a jump, she was in her momma's arms, receiving kisses of appreciation. Then Maggie Mae stood up and took her place beside the tree. Molly knew her cue, stood as well, and gave to Maggie the same glorious introduction.

"Ladies and Gentlemen," Molly declared with a flourish that only she could muster. "May I present ... Maggie Mae Green and her tellin' of a new Christmas poem. A poem she wrote herself a very long time ago!"

Maggie stood a moment and then spoke with thoughtful clarity, each word delivered with complete care and intention.

"You see," she began in the middle of her train of thought, "Johnny hadn't been around a world of literature. His understanding of Christmas was founded in the church and Jesus' birthday. When I first read Moore's poem to him, he thought it was wonderful, but he didn't understand how Santa had anything to do with the birth of Jesus." She paused and looked over her shoulder at Johnny's portrait. She began smiling as she turned back around to resume her talk. "Frankly, it was difficult to explain it myself. So I came up with the idea of another poem that I hoped would shed light on what I thought Moore was trying to convey in his holiday poem. I wrote this for Johnny as a Christmas gift. It was my first gift as his wife, but he passed before our first Christmas together as a married couple." She teared up a bit; however, her smile overtook her sadness, and she continued, "Molly and I decided that I should read it aloud tonight for the first time." She looked at Johnny again and then back to the group. She cleared her throat, swallowed back the butterflies, and began,

'Twas Christmas Day morning and all through the house, the children were waking ... yes, even a mouse!

The stockings we'd hung by the fire last night were brimming with goodies of Santa's delight. The children were stirring, all warm in their beds, while dreams they had pondered were fresh in their heads. I arose with a chuckle and awakened my wife, "Christmas is here! What a wonderful

195

life!"When all of a sudden, the quiet was gone. Our children were singing their jolliest song! Away to the door of the bedroom I flew to open it wide and sing along too! The snow that had fallen now caught my eyes' view and christened the morning as magic and new. The rumble and scamper of feet filled the air as everyone ran down the living room stairs. To all of our wonder, the tree was aglow. The fireplace blazing! The presents! The bows! Jolly Saint Nick had come in the night, fulfilling our wishes, then slipping from sight! I'd listened in earnest for noise on the roof, not prancing or dancing from one reindeer hoof! Inspired by legends of Ole Saint Nick's lore, the elfin man tricked us on Christmas once more. A bountiful table was all trimmed in red, with puddings and apples and cinnamon bread.

Hot spicy cider was swirling with steam on crackling hot embers that looked like a dream.

I felt my face flushing as I looked to see. All of my family was staring at me.

A tug on my night shirt and squeal at my side caught my attention and filled me with pride, for standing before me in Santa Claus style was my youngest daughter and her brightest smile!

She leapt up to hug me, her arms held me tight. Together, we welcomed the glorious sight!

Gossamer ribbons of angel-white snow draped upon branches with holiday glow. Shiny glass teardrops, all hung with such care, a star on the treetop for heavenly flair.

Brightly wrapped boxes of bursting surprise, baskets and stockings in gigantic size! Teddy bears looking for kisses and hugs, choo-choo trains chugging around on the rugs.

A flurry of paper and ribbons now flew, gifts being opened in earnest thank-yous.

Hand-to-hand sharing of goodies to eat, smiling bright faces with kisses so sweet! The clinking of glasses and sharing of times. The memories flooding, the rhythm and rhyme.

All joys are timeless when goodness is clear. Centuries brimming with holiday cheer!

"Oh, sweet, dear heart," I whispered with care. "Santa has blessed us with more than our share. This morning's as grand as any could be. Thank you for sharing this Christmas with me!"

Maggie Mae finished, refolded the poem, and slipped it into her pocket. The group was quiet. Even Molly didn't know what to say. Then suddenly, Molly jumped up. The kittens ran for cover. "Maggie!" shouted Molly, her finger pointing to the frosted window, "look!"

Together, the room let out a loud gasp of astonishment! Maggie turned to see. She lifted her hand to cover her mouth, her eyes crinkling up with joy! "Maggie Mae," Molly shouted again, "Johnny heard your poem! Look!" Molly now stood at the window, her breath frosting the glass as she excitedly said, "and it's snowing! Maggie, Maggie, Maggie! Johnny's making it snow! Oh, look everyone! It's snowing!"

Without a care, Maggie threw open the front door of her house and raced out onto the porch. In two shakes of a reindeer's tail, everyone followed. William surprised Maggie and wrapped her shawl around her shoulders as he stood by her side. Molly took Maggie by the hand and stood closely by her other side, the warmth of the woolen shawl drawing her into Maggie's tender embrace. They could hear a group of carolers singing off in the distance, concealed by the snowfall. As they moved closer, Maggie joined in the singing, and so did everyone else."Silent night ... holy night. All is calm. All is bright. Round young virgin, mother and child. Holy infant so tender and mild. Sleep in heavenly peace. Sleep in heavenly peace."

As they continued to sing, the carolers rounded the bend and became louder. The closer they came to the joy-filled party on the porch, the sweeter their harmonies became. Within a minute they were standing in the snowy field in full holiday song. They sang the same verse over and over, the glorious music filling the air with the magical melodies inspired by the timeless words of Christian hymns. And as the snow continued to fall, somewhere behind the veil of heaven and earth, Johnny smiled.

"*Yes, Father,*" he said to the One and Only, "*you are right. There is always hope, and it can be found in the most unlikely places.*" Johnny continued his praise. "*Yes, Father?*" Johnny's spirit paused and waited for the Word of God. "*That would be lovely. Thank you.*" And with that accepted suggestion, one red cardinal appeared as if summoned by magic, and it landed at the top of the snow-tufted pine tree in Maggie's yard. Everyone saw the red bird and simply knew. In an instant, the one was joined by the other six, each one landing on the tip of the branch as if they were poised like ornaments on a Christmas tree.

"Merry Christmas, Johnny!" they all said together. "Merry Christmas!"

The light of day was beginning to fade, and as a result, the carolers decided to venture home. Everyone filed back into the warmth of the cozy home, all talking of the Christmas miracle. It was decided that Johnny was responsible for the appearance of the birds, and of course, the snowfall was his way of thanking Maggie for the lovely poem.

"That was nothing short of a miracle, Maggie," observed Samuel as he handed her a cup of hot tea. "I've never seen anything like it before. The snow and the birds." He scratched his head as he has been known to do when he was thinking deeply. "We will be able to hitch Fiona to the sleigh tomorrow, Maggie." He stopped to see if she'd heard him.

"Yes, we should, shouldn't we!" Her expression was that of a child on Christmas morning. "I swear you're reading my mind, Samuel." She stopped and looked at him with the tenderness of a mother's gaze. "In fact, if I'd had a son, he'd be just like you." She swallowed hard.

Samuel stood up straight. He flashed his most handsome smile and replied with the words of a poet. "Maggie Mae," he began with the slightest baritone of his voice. "Any man would be proud to call you Momma." Maggie beamed, and the two hugged as a son and a mother.

The evening continued, and they made great memories. Maggie Mae made sure everyone had a basket of goodies to take home, and the night became a memory no one would ever forget. They also announced that the sleigh would be out tomorrow and that everyone should expect a ride through their winter wonderland after church service. Of course, no one complained.

"It was a fine evening, Auntie." said Bobby. He and his wife dressed for the cold and headed out of the door, "It's a real blessin' to see you happy again. A real blessin', indeed." She hugged them tightly and made sure they promised to visit again soon. And as the room began to clear out of Christmas partygoers, Maggie realized the true meaning behind the birth of Jesus Christ.

Her heart warmed and filled with the memory of all the misguided years of anger, bitterness, and regret. None of the misery mattered anymore. The lesson of the pain was enough to last her the rest of her life. Now it was her time to live! She wanted to nurture and to shine and to share and to teach.

Maggie stood at her picture window and waved goodbye as each of her Christmas travelers waved back. Molly's tiny face was alight with joy. She blew kisses from the back seat of the truck as her father slowly pulled out of the driveway and headed home. By the time Molly and her parents were going up the driveway, Maggie was at the kitchen window with a match in her hand and her momma's lantern in the other. Maggie waited patiently for the Fitzwilliam's to get into the farmhouse and for Molly to get into place for their traditional goodnight. The snow was still falling, but the flakes were small and light.

One flash, two flash, three flashes from Molly's lantern. Maggie struck her match, lit her candle, and followed along. One flash, two flash and three flashes signaled "I love you," and in Maggie Mae's mind, she wished Molly a merry Christmas too! Somehow, each gal knew the other was smiling and happy. Somehow each gal knew that the New Year to come was going to be one like never before. Somehow each gal knew that Johnny was a guardian angel to them both, and they knew in their heart of hearts that their lives would always be blessed with the very special gift of friendship.

Postscript

I n the two years that followed, these dear friends flourished. Wildfire became a mare of exceptional talent, and Molly Fitzwilliam's became a skilled and knowledgeable horsewoman. The babies were born without concern, and the grandparents had more fun helping the new mothers than any grandparents ever could. Johnny Angel Orchard and Farm thrived! The winter snow melted earlier than usual, resulting in a longer growing season for our entrepreneurs, and the Model T became Pine Valley's pride and joy. Its sputtering and popping became a signature of sorts that the townsfolk came to know and love. Maggie Mae continued to work as the librarian at the school, and she was rewarded by the community with an award ceremony for all her efforts. All in all, you could say Pine Valley was never the same again. The legend of Johnny rescuing Molly became an inspirational story for those looking to find hope and faith, and the meadow where Wildfire protected Molly from the cold is named Rescue Ridge. Soon after that, a plaque was dedicated so that no one would ever forget the miracle on Winter Mountain.

But what about Maggie Mae Green? Well, that afternoon in August was a scorcher! The fair was over, and one could see the dusty line of tired farmers driving home from the fairgrounds, their animals stowed in trailers with colorful ribbons hanging from their rearview mirrors. Maggie was out in her garden. The basket she carried was filled with a bounty of ripe red tomatoes, and with her free hand, she waved with congratulations to all those traveling down the country road and heading toward their homes. A moment later none other than Samuel Collier stopped by. He pulled into Maggie's drive and honked the horn.

"Hey, Mrs. Green!" he shouted. "Can I use your barn? My mare's about to give birth, and that crusty old, fallin' down stack of timber looks good to me!"

Of course, they were both laughing by now. Maggie walked over to meet him as he put the truck in park and opened the truck door.

"My goodness, it's been a while since that day!" noted Maggie as she greeted Samuel with a hug. "How are those twins of yours comin' along?" she said as she set her basket of tomatoes down.

"Why, they're comin' up on two now.

"My, how time flies. Here, darlin', take some of my prize-winning tomatoes home with ya." Maggie had just won first place at the county fair for those very tomatoes in her basket. "I have more than I can eat!"

"Yes, ma'am!" replied Samuel, already eyeing the biggest, reddest one in the lot. "And yes, they are comin' up on two. Janie says they're busier than a three-legged chicken in a field full of bugs!" He laughed as he ran his fingers through his sweaty head of thick hair. He leaned in closer and shared, "Says she wouldn't have it any other way."

The sudden sound of tires on gravel caught their attention and turned them around. A truck they didn't recognize pulled into the drive and turned off the engine. A gentleman rolled down the window and began to talk.

"I beg your pardon," he said kindly as he removed his hat and nodded hello. "I am lost and was hoping you two could help me." Maggie and Samuel walked over to the man's truck with neighborly smiles and continued to listen. "I inherited a ranch in these parts and am not sure where I am or how to get there." He looked bewildered. "My map is so old and dirty that I'm all turned around. Have you ever heard of Sterling Acres?"

Maggie looked at Samuel, and her eyes opened wide.

"Yes, sir, I have." Maggie seemed a little bewildered herself as she turned back to face the man and answer his questions. "When my father was a young man, he learned about proper horsemanship from Mr. Sterling." She continued speaking as she moved closer to the truck. "Daddy always said Sterling was the man to go to when ya had any questions about rearing a horse the right way. He was a legend in these parts." Maggie sounded well informed, and Samuel just stood back and listened. "It's been a real pity to watch the old property sit cold and buttoned up. Are ya thinking about selling the property?" As she asked the question, you could hear her fishing for the man's name.

"Please excuse me," the man said. "Where are my manners? Allow me to introduce myself." He opened the truck door, jumped down onto the gravel, and walked over to where they stood. "Please forgive me. I am Sterling … Richard Sterling." He held out his hand. "My granddad left the ranch to me years ago. It was always my intention to reopen the estate, but my wife wasn't into country living." He took a deep breath and exhaled. "But now that she's passed, there's no reason to keep me away. Our kids are all grown with lives of their own, so I said, 'Buddy.' My momma always called me Buddy. 'It's time for your dream now. Find the ranch, see what kind-a shape it's in, and move on with your life.' So here I am." He stopped his ramblings when he realized he was indeed rambling, and he looked into the compassionate eyes of his new friends. "Listen to me go on." He stopped and suddenly looked like an embarrassed child. "I didn't mean to tell you my troubles."

"No trouble at all," said Samuel, noticing that Maggie was speechless. "Maggie's was born in Pine Valley. If anyone knows where Sterling Acres is situated, it would be her."

"Well," said Richard, "I'd be most grateful if you could point me in the right direction."

"Yes, of course, Richard," Maggie said as she collected her thoughts. "Get back on the same road in front of my house and turn right." She pointed to the dingy line on the map and followed it to the fork on the map. "Turn left here. You'll see a large pine tree on the corner and a row of mailboxes. Drive about a half of a mile, and you'll see the equestrian pens on the right." She smiled as she looked up into the eyes of a man who wasn't looking at the map but rather at her! She blushed a bit, realizing that he was standing so close that she could feel his breath on the loose wisps of her hair. He smelled like spearmint and Old Spice. She continued, "Go a lil' farther, and you'll see the main gate on the right. As I recall, there are two Roman-style horse heads on either side of the gate. In their day they were somethin' else! Daddy said the whole town knew when they were delivered 'cause they weighed so much that the delivery guy squawked all the way from Little Rivers!" The three laughed at Maggie's bit of trivia. "Ya can't miss the house. It'll be right in front of ya. Though it could use a coat of paint and a lil' yard work, I think you'll find it in pretty good shape. Daddy said it was built of solid redwood and that they didn't build 'em like that anymore." Now Maggie was rambling.

"Well, I appreciate your help." Richard was now fishing for their names.

"Samuel Collier and Maggie Mae Green," offered Samuel. "Widow Green is a local legend in her own right. The family's house was the first built in Pine Valley when her great-grand folks homesteaded the land a century ago." Samuel didn't pause for long. "So you stopped at the right house, Buddy! Widow Green is our local historian and equestrian legend in her own right!" He was laying it on thick now. Samuel reached out and shook him by the hand. "So ... welcome home! I think you'll find that Pine Valley is the finest place on earth. Isn't that right, Maggie Mae?" He looked over at her and caught her smiling at him like a mother who catches a son who's full of the Dickens.

"Yes, I guess you could say that, Samuel." She stood there, slowly shaking her head and figuring out his angle.

"Welcome to Pine Valley, Richard," Maggie kindly said as she looked away from Samuel and held out her hand to the gentleman.

"Thank you, Maggie, and it is Buddy." He winked at her, and she blushed. Only this time it was bright enough for all to see!

"Thanks again for your help." He tapped his forehead as if he was tipping his hat, and then he got back into his truck. "You'll be seeing me around. That I can promise ya!"

He waved goodbye, left the property, and followed Maggie's directions.

"Well now, Maggie Mae," teased Samuel as he, too, got into his truck. "Looks to me like there's more than a lil' blush on the tomatoes 'round here." He beamed a glorious smile. "You best keep your eyes open from here on out! If I didn't know better, I swear you've met a good man there." He looked at her with honest eyes. "A good man, Maggie Mae!" She smiled and brushed off what he said with the wave of her hand. "I am too old, Samuel!"

"Maggie Mae," Samuel said, "you are never too old for love!"

About the Author

Inspired by her Scottish story telling roots, Lockhart has spent decades raising a family and working in a Northern California fishing resort. Inspired by the variety of friends made over the years, Lockhart brings to life the possibilities we all need to believe in.

CPSIA information can be obtained
at www.ICGtesting.com
Printed in the USA
BVHW080001180222
629242BV00001B/27